the Boy with the Jade

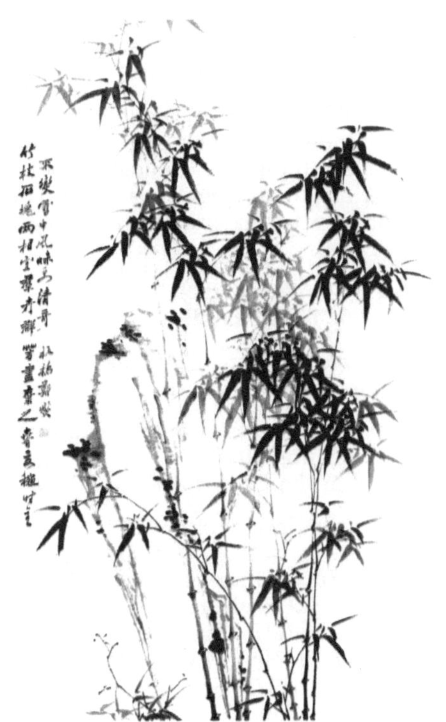

A Novel

Charles Bush

ISBNs: 978-1-963452-21-1 (pb);
978-1-963452-22-8 (hc);
978-1-963452-23-5 (eBook)

Book Cover Design: The Book Cover Whisperer, OpenBookDesign.biz
Interior Book Design: Inanna Arthen, inannaarthen.com

Library of Congress Control Number: 2025903472
First Printing: 2025
Printed in the United States of America

Publisher's Cataloging-in-Publication
(Provided by Cassidy Cataloguing Services, Inc.)
Names: Bush, Charles (Charles Roland), 1942- author.
Title: The boy with the jade : a novel / by Charles Bush.
Description: [Minneapolis, Minnesota] : [HTF Publishing], [2025]
Identifiers: ISBN: 978-1-963452-21-1 (paperback) | 978-1-963452-22-8
(hardcover) | 978-1-
963452-23-5 (ebook)
Subjects: LCSH: Aristocracy (Social class)--China--History--18th century--Fiction. | Pilgrims and
pilgrimages--Fiction. | Social pressure--Fiction. | Self-realization--Fiction.
| Identity
(Psychology)--Fiction. | Love--Fiction. | Grief--Fiction. | China--Religion--
18th century--
Fiction. | LCGFT: Historical fiction. | BISAC: FICTION / Historical / General. | FICTION /
Asian American & Pacific Islander. | FICTION / Buddhist.
Classification: LCC: PS3602.U8378 B69 2025 | DDC: 813/.6--dc23

To Calvin Lau

Beijing

The Eighteenth Century

PROLOGUE

I WAS BORN with a jade pendant in my mouth. In my mouth. At birth.

So claimed the Jia family legend.

The upholder of this legend was my grandmother, matriarch of the Jia family, the sun around whom the rest of us revolved. There were, in my opinion, reasons to doubt Grandmother's veracity. Only three eyewitnesses vouched for the supposed miracle: my grandmother and two nurses, both old family retainers. My mother, I noticed, never said she had seen anything. The two nurses were, of course, going to corroborate anything my grandmother said: they were her bondservants, she owned them. In the end, the legend rested solely on Grandmother's word.

Also, the jade already had a hole in it for a cord. Apparently, the heavenly powers that had placed it in my mouth had foreseen the practicalities of wearing a pendant.

I had no solid proof Grandmother was fabricating. On the other hand, I could easily imagine her lifting the mother-of-pearl lid to one of her many jewel boxes, plucking out an old jade piece that everyone else had forgotten about, and using it to conjure up a family legend that she, in her shrewdness, knew would dazzle for generations. As a result, I could never be sure whether my jade was a message from a higher realm or simply another example of Jia family self-aggrandizement.

While I harbored doubts about the legend, the rest of the world did not. Throughout my childhood and youth, I was known as the boy with the jade in his mouth. Scores of people who did not even know my name, who would not recognize me if I bowed before them, knew about the boy with the jade. Even the Emperor, I had been reliably informed, knew about the boy with the jade.

As a physical object, my jade was unremarkable: a rectangular flat pendant, two fingers wide, carved of pale green jade, covered on one side with an eight-character inscription. Grandmother's telling, however, had endowed it with magical properties. My jade was, according to her, the guarantor of my health, my happiness, my success. She insisted I wear it all the time, which I did, hung about my neck on a woven silk cord of five colors. As long as I did that, she swore, I was protected from all harm.

For most of my childhood, the legend seemed to hold true: my jade did have magical properties. I was extraordinarily healthy. I grew up tall and was deemed handsome. I was always happy. I experienced love in all its manifestations—familial, romantic, sensual. Even I came to believe in the legend of the jade.

As my childhood neared its end and adulthood approached, though, my jade seemed to lose its magic, and Grandmother's claims began to ring hollow. My happiness turned to misery, my health failed, I sank into a profound melancholy.

Then, when I least expected it, the magic of my jade reappeared and showed me the way to a new life.

1

MY CHILDHOOD was unusual in many respects. Not only was I supposedly born with a jade pendant in my mouth, my family, the Jia family, was enormously wealthy, one of the "Eight Noble Families of China." In another deviation from the typical, I did not live with my parents. Instead, I lived with my grandmother in another courtyard of our mansion.

I had lived with Grandmother since birth. The official story was that upon first seeing me Grandmother was so enamored she insisted I grow up, not minutes away in my parents' courtyard, but in her own. Behind my back, but sometimes within my overhearing, people said Grandmother simply wanted a child to spoil rotten. In either case, if Grandmother wanted me, I was hers, for in our household, whatever Grandmother wanted, she got.

I do not mean to imply I lived far away from my parents: Grandmother's courtyard was only a short walk from theirs. Indeed, all my immediate relatives—not only my grandmother and parents but also my older sister, younger half-brother, younger half-sister, sister-in-law (widow of an older brother of mine who had died when I was very young), her son, my first uncle, first aunt, and their three children—lived somewhere or another within our sprawling family compound of four hundred mu in the center of Beijing.

For me, living in Grandmother's courtyard was ideal. While I loved my grandmother and mother, I feared my father.

My problem with my father was that he seemed to detest

me. I could never understand why. I was an excellent student at Jia Clan School, something Father, with his devotion to Confucian values, should have appreciated. I never said anything in his presence except an occasional "yes," certainly never anything to offend. Yet every time he saw me, he berated and belittled me.

Fortunately, living as I did in Grandmother's courtyard, Father's antipathy toward me mattered little. I could luxuriate Grandmother's doting attention, see my mother as much as I pleased, and at the same time avoid my father almost to the point of never seeing him at all.

I have said that as a child I was always happy. Yet my eleventh year saw my happiness increase even more. That year, I met my soulmate.

Two months after my eleventh birthday, I learned that a girl I had never met would soon be coming to our mansion to live with us. Her name was Daiyu, she was a first cousin on my father's side, and she was a year younger than I.

Daiyu lived far to the south of us, in the Grand Canal city of Yangzhou, where her father was imperial salt commissioner. The position of Yangzhou salt commissioner was notoriously lucrative, but in this case wealth did not bring happiness, for Daiyu's mother, my father's sister, died when her child was only ten.

The father was at a loss. Daiyu had no brothers or sisters to keep her company (a rarity in an aristocratic family, but so it was); her father's duties as salt commissioner kept him occupied day and night; and he did not wish to entrust the upbringing of his only child to servants. Meanwhile, Grandmother, who loved nothing more than to be surrounded by happy, carefree children, was entreating him to send Daiyu north so she could live with us. After months of hesitation, Daiyu's father consented.

Grandmother sent a ship and crew of servants to Yangzhou. Since the journey down and back up the Grand Canal would take at least three months, we could not predict the day Daiyu would arrive. As it happened, I was away from our family mansion that day.

I had spent the day making offerings on behalf of the Jia family at a Buddhist temple we supported in the Western Hills. I arrived back after dusk, hastily washed my face and changed from my dirty riding jacket and robe into a clean robe, then headed to Grandmother's sitting room to say goodnight.

Grandmother was reclining on her couch, with two maids massaging her shoulders. I entered and in the dim candlelight saw only her ample figure clothed in a shimmering, gold-threaded robe. "Baoyu," she said. "Come in. Look who's here."

I turned my eyes to the right and saw next to Grandmother a thin waif of a young girl clad in a modest white dress and light mauve vest. "It's your cousin, Daiyu." Grandmother gave the thin waif a push. "Daiyu, meet your cousin Bao."

Daiyu got up from the couch, approached me, and we bowed to each other. When we rose and I finally saw her candle-lit face at close distance, I felt a shiver at the back of my neck, down to the roots of my hair.

We had met before. There was no doubt about it. I recognized the thin but elegantly sculpted face. The knitted eyebrows that almost touched above the nose. The liquid eyes, in which candles reflected like stars. The aristocratic nose. The small mouth. The delectable scent, like osmanthus. Somewhere, somehow, we had already met.

But where? Hadn't Grandmother said Daiyu had never been to Beijing? Was I dreaming?

I turned to Grandmother. "I've met this person before."

"No, no, don't be silly. This is your cousin, Daiyu, the one we've been expecting." Grandmother extended a golden arm toward me. "Show her your jade, Baoyu. We were just talking about it."

I gritted my teeth. I was used to meeting people who were more interested in my jade than in me as a person. But not now, not now! I was poised at a mysterious, possibly life-changing moment. Standing before me was a beautiful girl with whom I felt a special bond. I desperately wanted to be seen as more than a receptacle for a stone.

Daiyu stared at me, awaiting the presentation of the

legendary jade. My grandmother leaned back on her couch, smiling, ready to take delight in yet another awe-struck reaction. I sulked, once again upstaged by my jade.

I had no choice, I had to obey Grandmother. I quickly yanked the silk cord over my head and handed the jade to Daiyu. Or *thought* I handed it to her, for in truth my action was so swift, and her reaction so unsure, the jade dropped between us and clattered across the slate floor.

Eight maids leapt from the dark periphery of the room to corner the precious stone. Grandmother lurched forward, supported by the two maids who had been massaging her. "Baoyu, what are you doing? Your life depends on your jade, yet you toss it around like an old chicken bone!"

Fortunately, the jade was unharmed.

I turned to Daiyu and saw tears in her eyes. Grandmother too must have noticed, for she said, "Now, now, don't feel bad. Come, both of you, sit here with me on the couch."

Daiyu sat down demurely to Grandmother's left. I, as was my custom, plopped onto Grandmother's lap. Daiyu's arresting knitted eyebrows rose in astonishment when she saw me sitting on our mutual grandmother's gold-threaded lap.

"How old are you?" I asked Daiyu.

She needed to clear her throat; crying had clouded her voice. "Ten."

"Have you done much reading?"

"No. I've only studied two years and know just a few characters."

At least she had received *some* instruction in reading; we would have something to talk about. Many aristocratic families followed the maxim that the only things a girl should be taught are the needle and the thread.

"What books are you studying?"

"The *Four Books*."

At this point, the majestic grandfather clock my grandmother had imported from Germany began its sonorous musical announcement of the hour. Daiyu had obviously neither heard nor seen a grandfather clock before: her face went through successive stages of alarm, bewilderment, and finally amazement, the last after I sprang up and guided her to the front of the enormous and mysterious contraption.

The clock had struck nine. "It's late. We should all go to bed," Grandmother said. "Daiyu, you're my granddaughter, you're ten years old, and I've never had a chance to get to know you. I want to make up for all that lost time. You sleep here in my courtyard, with Baoyu and me."

I felt as if I were soaring in air, like a kite in full wind. To be sharing quarters with a ravishing newcomer was more than I'd dared hope for. I wrapped my arms around Grandmother's wrinkled neck. "What a wonderful idea!"

As Grandmother melted into my embrace, I stole a look at Daiyu. Once again, her knitted eyebrows were raised, but this time not as much.

Before Daiyu arrived, my thoughts about her had teetered between eagerness and wariness. Having a friend my own age and social class would be a rare treat. Even at the tender age of eleven, however, I knew aristocratic families liked to marry first cousins to each other, and I couldn't help wondering whether Daiyu's coming to live in our mansion was an audition.

Once she arrived, all worries vanished, joy reigned supreme. For three years, Daiyu and I lived together in Grandmother's courtyard. For three years, we played like kittens.

Added to my joy during those years was the fact my father was rarely around. Shortly after Daiyu's arrival, Father was appointed a vice minister in the Ministry of Works. From that time on, I benefited again and again from disasters. Repeated flooding along the Yellow River, a major earthquake in Sichuan Province, a devastating fire in Hangzhou—each new disaster led to Father disappearing for months. He traveled to far-flung places to inspect damage; then, back home, worked day and night at the ministry to bring about repairs. I was forgotten—out of sight, out of mind.

Daiyu and I developed a routine. Mornings, I would head

off to Jia Clan School, where I memorized, character by character, the Confucian classics: the *Analects, Great Learning, Doctrine of the Mean,* and so forth. She stayed in her room, taught herself characters, and learned to write poetry. She knew more characters than she had admitted the night we first met, and so gifted was she that, with only minimal help from me, she soon became my equal in both reading and writing.

After I came home from school, we were inseparable: first, sharing a midday meal; then, throwing ourselves into our enthusiasm of the moment.

Initially, it was Go: the nineteen vertical and nineteen horizontal lines of the Go board became our universe. Not only did we play, we became students of the game, collecting treatises and learning the tactics of Go masters of the past. Kong Rong and Wang Jixin were our heroes, to us as mighty as warriors. We each had our favorite strategies. I preferred "Crab Strangled in Foliage" and "Yellow Hawk Seizes Hare." She favored "Corner Kill in Thirty-Six Moves" and "Ten Galloping Dragons."

Initially, our abilities in Go were equal. As time went on, though, she became better. Finally, on a freezing winter day, things came to a head.

We played that day atop a kang covered with a Persian carpet patterned in pink and white roses. We placed a low zitan wood table between us, set our Go board on top of the table, and between moves lounged back on rabbit fur pillows. Sandalwood incense sweetened the air, while the kang radiated warmth that kept the clammy cold at bay.

Daiyu wore a cloak of cream silk with an embroidered design of blue-green bamboo. In her hair she wore silver butterflies with tiny ruby spots. When she bent over to study the board, her pose—the line of her long, free-flowing hair merging into the line of her arm—reminded me of a painting our family owned, a portrait of a Ming Dynasty beauty by Tang Yin

The game took about two hours. For the most part I held my own, but at one point I responded to a ko threat I should have ignored, and as a result all my stones on one side of the board were caught in a net. After we had both passed our turns and the game was at an end, we tallied up the score. I had lost by seven.

Despite having won, Daiyu looked dissatisfied. "I'd like to suggest something. I hope you don't mind."

"What's that?"

"I think, maybe, when we play, we should ... give you a handicap."

I felt as if someone had clubbed me from behind. A handicap? Against a *girl*?

Then I thought: Daiyu is the smartest girl I've ever met. Though it pains me to admit it, she's at least as smart as I am. At least.

Why not a handicap?

She proposed a handicap of seven, the number by which I had just lost. This seemed to me excessive: I couldn't agree to a handicap of seven against a mere girl. Finally, we agreed on a handicap of two. Once this was in place, she still won more often than I did, but at least our games were closer.

Our next passion was painting. We started by using our regular writing brushes and ink to produce simple monochrome sketches. Then we began experimenting with colors. One day, as we were sketching flowers in Grandmother's courtyard, Daiyu said, "I'm getting tired of doing just sketches. I'd like to do a painting. Maybe we could do a painting together."

"I'd love to do a painting with you. What should we paint?"

Daiyu put down her brush and leaned back on her stool. As she thought, her knitted eyebrows kissed each other. "If we're going to work on it together, it should be a handscroll, so we won't get in each other's way. Since we're just starting out, we should copy another painting; that would be much better than trying to make up something on our own. The painting we copy should be a very fine painting. Do you think we could find something in Grandmother's collection?"

I remembered a magnificent handscroll Grandmother sometimes brought out on special occasions: an old and excellent copy of the famous painting *Qingming Festival Along the River*. A panorama of Kaifeng, the Chinese capital seven hundred years before, this handscroll offered every painting challenge two budding young artists could imagine: country landscapes, a river, boats, bridges, gates, buildings, shops, restaurants, people (eight hundred of them it was said), animals—an entire world recreated in ink and color.

Grandmother located the painting in a treasure chest hidden in a back room of her courtyard. The moment Daiyu and I saw it, we agreed it was perfect.

We commandeered a large room on the north side of the mansion that was normally used to store produce from our country estates. In it we placed a varnished table long enough that we could lay out—full length, one above the other—Grandmother's handscroll and a blank roll of pongee silk cut to the same height and length. We spent almost a month rounding up supplies: more pigments, brushes, glue, mortars, strainers, water jars, saucers, and two portable stoves.

We spent nearly a year on the painting. I began at the right and worked toward the center, she began at the center and worked to the left. Every afternoon we would take up our positions, both of us standing in front of the varnished table, a considerable distance between us, hazy northern light streaming in through lattice windows. Between strokes of my brush, I would sneak glances at Daiyu—at her slender figure, the graceful movements of her arm, her intense concentration as she leaned over Grandmother's painting and pondered the details of an apothecary's shop, a palanquin, a camel.

The fact I was able to paint at all surprised me: I had never painted before. My talents, however, were limited; Daiyu was much the better painter. Whenever she put down her brush and walked over to inspect my half of the painting, I knew my artistic inadequacies were about to be exposed.

She would bend over, place her elegant right index finger on her lower lip, and closely examine detail after detail. At some point, a slight frown would cross her face. The finger would point up, then down, and finally land on a section of my latest handiwork.

I would lean over to get a closer look. Let's say it was an area where I had tried to paint a two-story restaurant. I would quickly see the problem. "Oops. The railing on the second floor is completely out of kilter, isn't it? I can't seem to do good ruler work. Oh well, I'll do it over."

Once again, Daiyu would scrutinize my work. Once again, the finger would pounce. Once again, with trepidation, I would look.

Perhaps this time the finger pointed to an attempt on my part to paint a group of boatmen. "I see what you're talking about. This one seems to have a swollen hand, and that one's leg looks crippled. All right, more overpainting."

Daiyu would offer a collegial smile. "We want our painting to be perfect, don't we?"

I would smile back. "Of course."

Another enthusiasm of ours was kite flying. One windy spring day I said, "Let's take out our kites and get rid of our bad luck." Daiyu immediately agreed.

She rummaged among our collection of kites and chose one that had seven swans flying in a long line. I chose a "pretty lady" kite: a beautiful woman surrounded by lotus blossoms and two kingfishers.

We each brought along three maids to carry our equipment: kite, raising-stick, cross-piece, and winder. Headed by Daiyu and myself, our eight-person procession wound its way through corridors and gates to the vacant land that lay behind our mansion.

Daiyu preferred to supervise: she would stand at a distance and give orders as her three maids fastened the cross-piece to the raising-stick and paid out the string from the winder. I liked to do everything myself, although I also wanted my three young, attractive maids to hover nearby.

After a certain amount of fumbling, both our kites rose into the air. Her seven white swans looked like clouds in the sky. My pretty lady shimmered with color: the red and blue of the lady's dress and the two kingfishers, the pink of the lotus blossoms, and the green of the lotus leaves.

"It's pulling hard," Daiyu's favorite maid, Swallow, said to her. "Shall we send it off? Here are the scissors."

Daiyu's face turned mournful; she shut her eyes and shook her head. "I don't have the heart to let it go."

"That's the main reason for flying kites," Swallow said. "The pleasure of seeing them fly away. Not to mention the fact it's supposed to get rid of your bad luck. Why is our young lady so stingy this year? Every year we send off a few kites. Here, if you won't do it, I will."

Swallow clipped the kite's string, and the seven swans soared into the empyrean.

By now, Daiyu's melancholy had infected me: the disappearance of the seven swans seemed tragic. "I hope they land somewhere nice," I said. "Where there are people. Children, maybe.

"But what if they land someplace terrible? What if they land in the middle of a desert?"

Tears started to form in Daiyu's eyes. I realized I was depressing her when I should have been trying to cheer her up.

"What about this?" I said. "I'll let my pretty lady go, and she can follow your swans and take care of them. If they land in a desert, she can lead them out."

I cut my kite's string, and the brilliant colors of my pretty lady hastened after Daiyu's seven white swans. As we both looked up, Daiyu's tears turned into a resigned smile.

Daiyu and I loved being active, loved being engaged in a pursuit or a challenge. Sometimes, though, we liked to be still. Often when we were still, we slipped into one of what we called our Zen conversations.

One baking day in the middle of summer, Daiyu and I sat on porcelain garden stools inside the covered veranda of Grandmother's courtyard. Rows of birdcages filled with parrots, cockatoos, and canaries surrounded us. The canaries sang.

Daiyu wore a simple blue-and-white dress of lightweight, supple silk. Cloisonné chrysanthemums bloomed in her hair. From my vantage point, the foliage of a crabapple tree in the center of the courtyard framed her face. Even from a distance, I could catch whiffs of her delectable osmanthus scent.

The heat had flattened our energy, neither of us had stirred for minutes. A bucket of ice sat beside each of us, but the mist from the ice dissipated as soon as it met the parched air.

"Can I ask you something?" Daiyu said.

I adored her soft Southern accent: the way she left off *r*'s at the ends of words, turned *sh* into *s*.

"Of course."

"You have four beautiful girls to choose from. One of them is an accomplished musician. The second, an accomplished painter. The third, an accomplished poet. The fourth, an accomplished seamstress. Which of these four beautiful girls do you choose?"

I let out a sigh. Various possible answers floated through my mind. If I wanted to be simple and direct, I could say: I don't want any of those girls, Daiyu, I want only you. But to say something that honest and straight-forward would violate the complexities of our relationship and the joy we found in word play. Daiyu and I reveled in ambiguity, indirection, literary allusion. Thus, instead of giving the simple answer, I said, "Though the river may be immense, one gourdful will suffice me."

Daiyu said nothing. Only the songs of the canaries sounded. After three or four still breaths, she said, "What if the river carries away your gourd?"

"It will not. My gourd cannot be carried away."

"What if the river dries up and your gourd is lost?"

I ransacked my brain for literary inspiration. Finally I said, "My heart is like a willow catkin caught in the mud. How can it fly away like a partridge in the spring wind?"

"The first rule of Zen is not to tell lies."

"I'm telling the truth. I swear it by the Buddha, the Dharma, and the Holy Brotherhood."

An imperious red-and-blue parrot in a cage across from us let out a brazen *"Kee-waak."*

I laughed. "See, doesn't that verify what I was saying?"

Daiyu wrinkled her nose. "Good or bad fortune in the affairs of men does not depend upon the cry of a bird."

I had a theory as to why Daiyu and I were so close, why we seemed to fit into each other's personalities like yin and yang. My theory went back to a feeling we both had on that awkward evening when we first met in Grandmother's sitting room.

We had never met before, never even been in the same city before. Yet the moment I laid eyes on her, I felt to an absolute certainty we *had* previously met. I later learned Daiyu too had had the same reaction: immediately upon seeing me, she knew we had met before.

Throughout my childhood the concept of karmic amnesia fascinated me. All of us have gone through prior lives, and those prior lives determine what happens to us in our present lives: this is our karma. Yet we have no memory of those prior lives.

Isn't that odd? Our lives are governed by events in our own past, yet we have no memory of those events.

What fascinated me about our relationship was that it seemed an exception to the rule of karmic amnesia. She and I hadn't met in our present lives, yet we remembered each other. Therefore, we must have been remembering something from our prior lives. In this one rare instance, a slight rent existed in the curtain separating present and prior lives.

I tried with all my might to remember more of what had transpired between Daiyu and me in our prior lives, but I came up with nothing: karmic amnesia reasserted itself. I knew only that Daiyu's and my relationship was more than a childhood infatuation. It had a significance that transcended different existences.

2

TWO-AND-A-HALF YEARS after Daiyu arrived, another female first cousin of mine came to live at the Jia mansion. Her name was Baochai, she was from my mother's side, and she was the same age as I.

Baochai came not by herself, as Daiyu had, but with her widowed mother and older brother, all moving to our mansion from their previous home in Nanjing. Baochai's family was wealthy: they owned pawn shops scattered across the land. Her father had died, however; her brother had proven irresponsible; and her mother, who was originally from Beijing, wanted to be near relatives. The two sisters, Baochai's mother and mine, were particularly close.

My family invited Baochai's family to reside in Pear Tree Court, a small but complete residence located on our grounds with its own separate entrance to the street. Years before, my great-grandfather had built Pear Tree Court as his retirement retreat. With little hesitation, Baochai's family accepted our offer.

Everyone agreed Baochai was beautiful. She had a face shaped like a goose egg, black reflective eyes like pools of water, and a mouth like a little red cherry. Everyone also agreed Baochai had, to use the language of the older generation, a marvelous disposition. She was quiet except when spoken to, polite when a response was called for, obedient at all times, and as even-tempered as a girl could be. She was, in short, the type of girl of whom every mother of an unmarried son would say: she would make the ideal daughter-in-law.

Baochai and Daiyu made an interesting contrast: both were beautiful, but in opposite ways. Baochai's beauty was classic; Daiyu's, individual. Baochai's rounded features suggested solidity and tranquility; Daiyu's thin face and restless eyes, a type of nervous energy. Their eyebrows epitomized their differences. Baochai's brows were exquisite, almost to the point of cliché: "as thin and finely curved as the sickle of the new moon." Daiyu's knitted brows were unusual, arresting—and to me, irresistible.

From the time she arrived, Baochai was better liked among the members of our household than was Daiyu. Baochai exuded a graciousness that drew little distinction between masters and servants; even the most junior maid knew the warmth of her smile from time to time. She was highly intelligent but cloaked her intelligence in humility.

Daiyu, on the other hand, struck many as arrogant: she was smart, and she knew it. Daiyu inspired fierce loyalty in her favorite maid, Swallow, but ignored most of the other servants in our household.

I differed from the household consensus. Daiyu was my soulmate, our relationship transcended existences, we had met in prior lives. In our present lives, we had for two-and-a-half years lived together in Grandmother's courtyard, sharing our meals, our enthusiasms, our studies, our idle hours. Baochai was a beautiful, intelligent, well-mannered girl. I was, however, already taken.

I wondered how Baochai's arrival affected my marriage prospects, whether this was another audition.

I still regarded Daiyu as the strong favorite to become my bride. For one thing, Daiyu, as a first cousin on my father's side, was a closer relative than Baochai, merely a first cousin on Mother's side. More importantly, Grandmother would have the dominant say, and from the first night Daiyu arrived Grandmother had done everything in her power to bring Daiyu and me together. Grandmother had decided that Daiyu and I should live together in her courtyard. She had watched the two of us become inseparable. She had always taken joy in seeing the two of us live, study, and play together. It was hard to imagine she had in mind any bride for me other than Daiyu.

On the other hand, I couldn't ignore the strange relationship of our three names: Baoyu, Daiyu, Baochai. Each girl shared half my name, but they shared different halves. I saw a triangle, with me at the apex—an image that concerned me.

While Daiyu and I were soulmates, I also felt a pull toward Baochai. One cold winter afternoon I walked over to Pear Tree Court to visit her. I found her seated on the kang in her inner room, sewing. Her hair was in a simple bun, without ornamentation. She wore no cosmetics, and her clothing seemed a bit worn: a dun padded gown, topped by a mulberry fur-lined vest. Lack of adornment only enhanced her beauty; she looked delicious.

Baochai put down the perfume sachet she was embroidering, invited me to sit on the edge of the kang, and ordered her maid to serve us tea. In formal fashion, she asked after the health of my grandmother, mother, father, sister-in-law, half-sister, half-brother, uncle, aunt, and all my various cousins.

All the while she seemed to be staring at my chest. Finally she said, "Cousin Bao, I've heard so much about your jade, but I've never seen it up close. Do you think I could have a good look at it?"

Normally I resisted requests of this sort, but so charmed was I by Baochai that day I immediately said yes. I took off my stone and handed it to her.

She examined it closely. "Why it has an inscription!"
"Yes."
She read the inscription out loud:

"Never lose, never forget,
Fragrant youth, eternal life."

Baochai seemed surprised by the inscription. I wondered why: it didn't seem that remarkable to me. Baochai read the characters out loud again. Odd, I thought.

I looked over and saw Baochai's maid, instead of serving us tea, staring at us, slack jawed. Noticing the same thing,

Baochai said to her, "Why aren't you serving us tea instead of just standing there?"

The maid let out a nervous giggle. "The inscription on Second Master's jade is almost the same as the one on your pendant."

"You have an inscription too?" I said to Baochai.

Baochai looked away, adjusted her hair. "Don't pay any attention to her. She doesn't know what she's talking about."

"Cousin, I think there's an inscription."

"It's of absolutely no importance."

"Cousin, be fair. I showed you my inscription. Now you should show me yours."

Baochai paused, forced a smile, and reached into her mulberry vest. Her hand emerged with a massive rectangular object that shone like the rising sun on a clear morning—solid gold, with a border of pearls, rubies, and sapphires.

She handed me the brilliant ornament. I brought it to my eyes and read out loud the inscription:

"Never leave, never abandon,
Fragrant youth, always lasting.

"Why cousin, it's virtually the same as mine!"

Baochai shrugged, said nothing.

I was baffled. Was the similarity of our inscriptions a message from a higher realm? If so, what was the message?

Maybe, though, the explanation was more mundane: engravers were an unimaginative lot and employed the same themes repeatedly, assuming the wearers would never notice. If this was the case, the similarity of our inscriptions was meaningless.

I looked at Baochai. "You weren't born with this thing in your mouth, were you?"

She looked at her bulky pendant and laughed. "No."

"The words were given to our lady by a scabby-headed Buddhist monk," Baochai's maid said. "He said it should be engraved on—"

"That's enough, Oriole," Baochai interrupted. "Serve the tea." Oriole made haste to obey.

Did this added bit of information, that Baochai's inscription had come from a Buddhist monk, support the theory of a message from a higher realm? Possibly.

I might have pondered myself into a headache had not Baochai's mother come into the room and said, "I have some goose foot preserve and pickled duck tongues. Why don't you join us for something to eat, Baoyu?" I accepted, and after the third or fourth cup of wine, the similarity of our inscriptions took its place as simply another anomaly in my already irregular life.

Secrets did not exist in the Jia mansion.

We owned around three hundred servants. Servants surrounded us every moment of our lives. Wherever we were, whatever we did, whatever we said, servants were watching and listening. On top of that, most of those servants had little to do except stand around all day and gossip.

Two days after my visit with Baochai, I came home from school and hurried in to see Daiyu. She was reclining on her kang, reading a book of poetry.

I sat down on the kang. "Hello."

She ignored me.

"Cousin, hello."

Again, she ignored me.

"Cousin, is something the matter?"

She slammed down her book of poetry. "No, nothing's the matter."

"Would you like to do something together?"

She turned away. "You don't need *me* anymore. You have a new playmate. One who's beautiful and rich and whom everyone likes. I'm sure she's much nicer to be with than I am."

"What are you talking about?"

"I'm talking about what everybody else is talking about." She threw her head back, raised her arms above her head, and began waving them around, as if in celebration. "The marriage of the jade and the gold."

I snorted and shook my head. "Cousin, how could you possibly believe I'd rather spend time with Baochai than with you. Why, compared to you, I barely even know Baochai. Think of all the things we've shared. Our feelings of having met before. Our years of living together—almost three now. Our games. Our painting. Our Zen conversations."

Daiyu continued to glare at me.

"Also, you're much more closely related to me than Baochai is. You're a first cousin on Father's side, she's only on Mother's side. I'm hardly even related to Baochai."

Daiyu's hands flew to her face. Tears came to her eyes.

I scooted across the kang and took hold of her hands.

"Baoyu, you do things that provoke people," she said between sobs. "You're always doing things that provoke me."

"What? What have I done today?"

Daiyu looked around the room, her eyebrows squeezed together in a worried frown. Then she focused on me. "You don't have your fox fur cape on, and today's even colder than yesterday. You're going to make yourself sick, and then we'll all be in trouble." She grabbed my arm, rested her head on it, and continued to cry.

3

THE BEST PRESENT I ever received was the one Grandmother gave me for my fourteenth birthday.

For several years Grandmother had had among her numerous junior maids a girl named Amber. Grandmother thought the world of Amber: Amber was the smartest junior maid Grandmother had ever had, also the best seamstress, a matter of no small importance to Grandmother.

For my fourteenth birthday, Grandmother gifted me with Amber.

From birth I had always been attended to by ten or so junior maids, but these maids belonged to Grandmother and worked under Rosebud, Grandmother's chief maid. Now, Grandmother had decided I would have my own chief maid, and all my junior maids would report to her. That chief maid would be Amber.

I was delighted. Partly because I now had my own independent household—a milestone on the road to adulthood. Mostly because I now had Amber.

Amber, a year older than I, was too short, her body too stocky, to be a classic beauty, but she had a pert ebullience that was just as appealing. She greeted the world with sparkling round eyes, a winsome smile, a ready laugh, and a cheerful word. Gifted with practical intelligence, she could solve any problem, unravel any mystery. Her high cheekbones, turned-up nose, and soft hair hypnotized me.

Amber soon came to play a major role in my life. It all took shape one memorable day in Second Month.

First Uncle and Aunt's courtyard in the Jia mansion backed onto a splendid garden, one never more splendid than in late winter when its many plum trees came into blossom. One morning soon after my fourteenth birthday, my aunt invited the ladies of the family to a plum blossom viewing party in her garden. I too was invited, for at this time in my life, wherever the ladies went, I went. Usually, I was the only male included.

The plum bloom was now at its peak, my aunt informed us with excitement. I had an additional reason to be excited at the prospect of a visit to First Uncle and Aunt's courtyard. Their son, my cousin Rong, had recently married, and his new wife, Crimson, was stunning. She had a slender, supple waist, and she swayed like a branch in the breeze when she walked; seeing her walk made me light-headed. She wore only red clothing—to go with her name, I assumed—and the tight-fitting dresses she favored left little to the imagination.

The plum blossom viewing party lived up to everyone's expectations. All my female relatives were there: my grandmother, mother, Daiyu, Baochai, my other girl cousins, my sister-in-law, my half-sister. The plum trees were indeed magnificent, their butterfly-shaped white blossoms visible not only against the hazy sky but also mirrored in the artificial pond the trees encircled. Magnificent too, at least in my opinion, was Crimson. Dressed in a form-flattering red gown, she spent the morning serving us drinks—weaving between tables, swaying from her slender waist.

We began with tea, progressed to wine as the morning wore on. By midday, my head began to nod, my eyelids drooped. I desperately needed to lie down and take a nap.

Grandmother ordered a group of servants to escort me back to her courtyard, but to my amazed pleasure, Crimson intervened. "He doesn't need to go back. We're not so poor we can't find a place for him to nap here."

Grandmother agreed, and Crimson led me, along with Amber and a group of nurses and junior maids, into her part of the courtyard. She first showed me into a room dominated by a large scroll painting entitled "Scholar Working by Torchlight." The painting depicted an aged, gnarled scholar hunched over a dog-eared book.

The painting repulsed me, a wave of nausea swept through my body. "Please, do you think I could have a different room?"

Crimson looked at the painting, laughed, then placed a red fingernail on her red mouth. "I know what. You can have *my* room. You should be satisfied with that."

"You can't have him sleeping in his cousin's wife's bed," an old nurse accompanying us blurted out. I wanted to strangle her.

"Goodness gracious, he's only a child," Crimson said to the nurse. "He's not going to misbehave. We don't have to worry about that ... yet." She laughed and winked at me. I cursed myself for being too sleepy to wink back.

As Crimson led me toward her bedchamber, the fragrance of a voluptuous incense enveloped me. What was the fragrance? It had the aromatic redolence of sandalwood, the sweetness of roses, but also layers of scent that seemed overripe, decadent. Whatever it was, the incense had an immediate effect on me: I was even sleepier than before, all my joints dissolved into jelly, my eyelids felt leaden.

I staggered into Crimson's bedchamber. It was, predictably, decorated entirely in shades of red. Cinnabar silk covered the walls; a scarlet canopy enclosed the bed. On a table finished in carmine lacquer rested a magenta-hued porcelain platter, in the middle of which stood a ripe apple. On one wall hung a scroll painting—a cardinal.

I slumped onto cerise bed covers. Crimson and Amber straightened me out, spread a ruby-colored gauze coverlet over me, and slipped a rouge pillow under my head. Feminine fingers smoothed the coverlet, tucked the pillow around my head, and stroked my forehead. A hand gently tugged at my shoulder, and the same hand helped me as I struggled to rise out of bed. Fingers brushed gently across my face.

I opened my eyes and saw the fingers. Long, slender, delicate, so pale as to be almost colorless, they looked as if sculpted of white jade.

The hand belonged to a young woman standing across from me, someone I had never seen before. She was astonishingly beautiful. Her face, like her hands, had the smoothness and luster of white jade. Her eyes, preternaturally large, were black as ink, and a silver-toned gown enhanced her elegant figure.

The woman and I were standing amidst a series of terraces and pavilions, like part of a rich prince's pleasure palace, except that everything seemed, like the beautiful woman, to be formed of white jade. The buildings, stairways, and balustrades were all a translucent white, their surfaces sleek, glossy, unblemished by even a speck of dust.

"Who are you? And where am I?"

"My name is Disenchantment."

"That's a strange name."

She laughed softly to herself. "To you, I suppose it is."

"What about my other question? Where am I?"

"You are in my land, the Land of Disenchantment. I'm afraid there's little here that would interest a visitor like you. If you want to follow me, though, I could offer some entertainment."

"Yes, I would like that."

"Then come with me, Baoyu."

"You know my name?"

Her prominent black eyes bored into me. "Yes. None of this is happening by accident."

We walked along more terraces of white jade, bordered by gardens of green jade. After a few minutes, a lapis lazuli ceremonial gate appeared.

We passed through the gate, and immediately everything changed. Frangipani incense perfumed the air. I was inside, but not inside a room; rather, a tent. A tent voluptuously soft and smooth, for every surface in every direction was silk.

The tent itself was a rich golden-hued silk. Layered inside was a silk canopy, lilac in color, that encircled an oversized bed. Tousled on the bed were foamy silk bed covers in shades of aqua and midnight blue. Nestled in the bedcovers, clad in a sheer yellow silk gown, was a beautiful girl.

I stared. At first, I was bewitched: the girl was ravishing. Then a queasy feeling came over me. Something was wrong.

One moment, the girl looked like Daiyu; the next moment, like Baochai. I thought initially the girl looked like Daiyu from the left and Baochai from the right, but then I held my head steady and the girl continued to change back and forth—Baochai, Daiyu, Baochai, Daiyu.

I turned to see if Disenchantment was still there. She was, her large black eyes fixed on me.

I pointed to the girl on the bed. "Who is she?"

"She's my little sister, Two-in-One."

"That's another strange name."

"You seem to find all our names here strange."

"She looks like a girl I know. Actually, two girls."

Disenchantment reached out and, with her long, slender fingers of white jade, playfully tugged at my ear. "That's what I love about you, Baoyu. You are the most lustful man on earth."

"Me? Lustful? The most lustful man on earth? You must have me mixed up with someone else. I'm only a young boy. True, I sometimes neglect my studies, and my father thinks I'm lazy. But I'm not lustful. I'm not at all aggressive with girls. The truth is, I've never ...." I hung my head. "You know what I mean."

"That's exactly what we're here to correct. I'm giving you Two-in-One as your bride, and the two of you shall consummate your marriage tonight, here, in this bed.

"I should explain to you my motive in doing this. I hope that, as a result of your experience here, you will see that love is nothing but an illusion. Once you see that even in this magical land love is an illusion, then you will surely understand the same is true in the dust-stained mortal world you normally inhabit."

Her words drifted past me, like the frangipani incense in the air.

"You must take this knowledge to heart and mend your

ways," she continued. "Devote the remainder of your youth to the study of Confucius and Mencius. Dedicate your life to the service of your family, your country, your Emperor."

I barely heard her. I could think only of the girl, the bed, the promise of consummation.

"All right, let's get started," Disenchantment said. "Since this is your first time, I'll be staying here to help you along, giving you a few little pointers to help you maximize your pleasure. First, why don't you shed that coat of yours and come over to the bed."

Disenchantment proceeded to give Two-in-One and me a private tutorial in sexual pleasure. She taught us the art of undressing. She showed me Two-in-One's seats of pleasure and showed Two-in-One mine. We explored the possibilities of the mouth, the tongue.

Initially, I found the fact Two-in-One looked alternately like Daiyu and like Baochai disconcerting. After a while, I managed to merge the best features of each look and found the alternation positively erotic.

Disenchantment taught us a multiplicity of positions and seemed ready to teach us even more. Finally, however, there came a point at which I had to cry out, "I can't hold out any longer!"

And I couldn't.

After that, I fell into a deep sleep.

Awakening the next morning, I felt Two-in-One's warm, soft body cupped into mine. I looked around. We were still in our silken bed under our silken canopy. Disenchantment, though, had disappeared.

I heard birds singing outside. "Let's go for a walk," I said to Two-in-One. She, looking for the moment like Baochai, agreed.

We walked through the flap of our tent into a luxuriant garden. The air bore the scents of magnolia and gardenia. A bright sun warmed us, a gentle breeze caressed our cheeks. Two-in-One and I held hands as we strolled along a grassy path under a cerulean sky.

After a few steps, however, the garden disappeared. Only a few desiccated, diseased-looking weeds remained. The path we were walking on—barefoot, for some reason—turned to jagged rock. The sky became ashen gray. A hot wind assailed us, my eyes began to sting. In the distance I saw a hyena.

We entered a forest of thorn trees. Blood dripped from the thorns. Smoke filled the sky, an acrid odor penetrated everywhere. Vultures hovered above. I looked around and realized Two-in-One was no longer with me. Instead, a wolf was stalking me. I ran.

Suddenly, I was at the edge of a precipice: before me the ground ended, and beyond loomed an abyss so deep I could not even see the bottom. I trembled with fear, sweat poured off my body.

From behind me came a hissing sound. I turned around and faced an enormous king cobra, rearing onto itself, about to strike. My body collapsed backwards. I lost my footing. I tumbled into the abyss.

I fell and fell and fell. The air scraped my face as it rushed past. Birds flew underneath me. I landed at the bottom with a bone-shattering crash, a crash so violent I bounced off the ground and shot back up into—

"Second Master! Second Master!"

I opened my eyes and looked around. I was in Crimson's red bedchamber. Amber hovered over me.

"Second Master, are you all right? You jumped halfway to the ceiling."

"Yes, I'm all right, but ... did I have a dream!"

"You did? What was it about? Tell me."

As I was formulating an answer to Amber's question, I felt something wet and sticky in my groin. I sat up to inspect.

The slick, milky liquid had infiltrated not only my underwear, but also the elegant pair of lime-green satin trousers I had donned specially for the party.

Amber looked too. Her eyes grew wide as plates, she put her hand over her mouth.

She knew what to do. She shooed the other maids out, commandeered a pot of cold tea someone had left behind, and after a lengthy search located a pink towel. Then she scrubbed away.

The results were an improvement, but not perfection. The stickiness was gone, but my satin pants now had an obvious wet spot. Still, I could not stay away from the party forever; it was long past time to return.

We arranged my jacket to cover as much of the wet spot as possible, and back at the party I sat down at a table and scooted myself as far underneath as possible. Fortunately, due to high alcohol consumption, the party guests' level of alertness had declined considerably in my absence. No one noticed my predicament.

After an hour or so the spot had mostly dried. I took my leave and, with my coterie of maids, headed back to my room. Once there, Amber dismissed the other maids, I changed my underwear and trousers, and she set about giving the be-smirched set a proper washing.

Once she had the garments soaking, she said, "Tell me about this dream of yours, Second Master."

I started telling her an edited version of my dream. I mentioned the white jade terraces and meeting Disenchantment. When I got to the silken tent portion, I said simply that the person lying in the bed was a beautiful girl, not mentioning that she had looked alternately like Daiyu and like Baochai. I slurred over Disenchantment's lecture to me as "a bunch of Confucian nonsense." Then, without giving it much thought, I mentioned that Disenchantment had given the beautiful girl and me "sort of a private sex lesson."

Amber gasped. "She did what? She gave you a private sex lesson? Too great! What did you do? What did she show you?"

"Amber, I don't think it's appropriate—"

"Please, Second Master, I'm *so* curious. I've never heard of anything like this before. I'll *die* if you don't tell me."

"Well, she started off by teaching me how to undress the beautiful girl."

I paused, stymied by the difficulty of trying to recreate in words a scene in which words had played little role.

"What did she have you do?"

"She .... The first thing we did was ...." I lowered my head and sighed. "You know, Amber, it's hard for me to talk about what happened in my dream. Because we didn't talk, we just did things."

Amber's expression turned from pleading to sly. She flashed an impish grin, leaned over to my ear, cupped her hands around her mouth, and whispered, "You could show me."

I drew her toward me. "So I could."

Once we started, there was no logical stopping point. We covered all the topics of Disenchantment's sex tutorial, from beginning to end. For the second time that day, I experienced the ecstasy of sexual release.

Amber, as my chief maid, had previously slept in my room, but always outside my bed, on the other side of the purple canopy. That night, she slept in bed with me.

The following night, as we were getting ready to go to bed, Amber said, "Sometime we should go over your dream again."

I said, "Why not now?"

Once again, we brought Disenchantment's sex tutorial to life, once again Amber spent the night in bed with me.

The next morning, fear seized us. What if Amber became pregnant? We wanted to continue revisiting the dream, but we needed to take precautions.

I consulted my best sources in matters of this sort—my four young male pages. They agreed what I needed was musk deer scent. I sent my resourceful chief page, Tealeaf, off to acquire some. He returned with an ample, albeit expensive, supply, and I gave the pungent-smelling substance to Amber. She made a patch out of it and pasted the patch over her navel.

Now adventure could safely become habit. Amber began spending every night in my bed, and most of those nights we "went over the dream again." Her soft hair, high cheekbones, and turned-up nose were mine, all mine. Other young men might experience the agony of sexual frustration. I did not.

I felt no need to hide my relationship with Amber. No rule prohibited Jia masters from consorting sexually with their servants. Indeed, it seemed expected of them: witness my cousin Rong, who, at least according to rumor, had seduced half the maids in the mansion.

Nor did I worry about what Daiyu would think. I knew word would soon filter back to her that Amber and I were sleeping together. If anything was reliable in the Jia mansion, it was our servants' gossip network. Daiyu, however, was a full-blooded daughter of the high aristocracy; she knew the rules. She might be my soulmate, she might be the love of my life, she might become my bride, but she would never be my only sexual partner. As long as my other partners were mere servants, it didn't matter.

I didn't even worry about my father. He had two concubines; was he going to criticize me for having one? After all, I was fourteen.

4

Two months later, a figure from my early childhood reappeared in my life—my older sister, Spring.

We were once close. She was my first teacher, we started when I was only three. We would arrange ourselves on a couch, or if it was winter, on a kang, its heated brick surface covered with silk carpets. Servants would place a low table between us and serve us tea. Spring would then teach me characters.

We began with the numbers, moved on to words. For each character, Spring would draw the first stroke, I would copy it, she would then draw the second, I would again copy, and so forth. Finally, I would write the entire character on my own.

I still remember the first twenty-five characters I learned, which, recited in proper order, formed an invocation:

> Honorable Father,
> Confucius himself taught three thousand, seventy
> gentlemen.
> You young sons, eight or nine,
> Excellence leads to virtue,
> And gentle manners too.

I worshiped Spring and adored our writing lessons. I assumed they would go on forever. They ended when I was eight, and ended abruptly.

We were celebrating my father's thirty-eighth birthday in the main courtyard of our mansion. On one side a hired troop of actors was performing scenes from popular operas. On the opposite side we Jia family members sat at tables on the veranda, gorging ourselves on steamed crabs, baked sturgeon, Siamese pig smoked in cedar, salted goose slices, and hot wine.

With no warning our head gatekeeper burst in. "The chief eunuch of the Forbidden City is on his way here with a decree from the Emperor!"

A wave of fear ran through all of us. The Emperor was singling out our family. Was it for good or for ill?

Father ordered all evidence of the party cleared. We family members arranged ourselves according to rank and gender and got down on our knees, facing our front triple gate. The gatemen opened the central door.

A minute or two later, the chief eunuch arrived on horseback, followed by forty additional mounted eunuchs. The chief eunuch's empty hands told us he bore no imperial decree. Instead, he dismounted, walked a few paces inside our gate, and said, in a high, effeminate, yet penetrating voice, "By special order of the Emperor, Lord Jia Zheng is to present himself at once for an audience in the Forbidden City."

We offered the chief eunuch the customary cup of tea. He declined our offer, remounted his horse, and, trailed by his entourage, rode away.

At first Father was speechless. Then he began conferring with Grandmother. "What is going on? Why am I being summoned?"

"I don't know," said Grandmother.

"He was so peremptory," Father said. "And he refused our offer of tea. Do you think those were bad portents?"

"I don't know."

Father left to change to formal court dress. He emerged resplendent in his dragon-patterned robe, one hundred eight-bead court necklace, and round Manchu hat topped by a coral finial.

After Father left, the rest of us remained in the courtyard. My grandmother, mother, and first aunt huddled together. They tried to reassure each other, but from time to time broke into tears. Spring and I attempted to work on characters, but we couldn't concentrate.

We stewed for four hours, until one of our managers rushed in. "It's good news! First Master's daughter is to be an imperial concubine!"

Grandmother threw herself on her knees to thank heaven for the show of imperial favor. First Aunt enthusiastically joined her. First Uncle and his son, Rong, embraced each other. "We're going to be imperial kinsmen!"

My mother, on the other hand, hesitated. She and Spring were devoted to each other. This meant she would rarely, if ever, see her daughter again. That was the fate of daughters: to be married into other households, which might be located near or far, open to visiting or not. In the end, Mother joined Grandmother in kneeling to give thanks.

I was standing next to Spring. She was stunned; for several minutes she didn't even move. No hint of either a smile or a tear appeared on her face.

Those few words had revealed to her the course of her life. She would have the honor and glory of being a concubine of the Emperor. In recompense, she would lead a life of near-total isolation—immured in the Forbidden City, unable to leave even for an afternoon, surrounded by eunuchs, separated from her family. Whether or not this was the life she wanted, it was the one she now faced. It had been decided. She was sixteen.

I was the only one totally unhappy. My older sister, my reading teacher, my closest friend, my protector was leaving our household. I would likely never see her again. The rank of an imperial kinsman was little comfort to an eight-year-old boy.

A frenzy of activity consumed the next two weeks. Grandmother, Father, Mother, First Uncle, and First Aunt made multiple trips to the Forbidden City to offer thanks. Relatives and friends filled our mansion with congratulatory visits. Eunuchs circulated between our mansion and the Forbidden City to instruct Spring in her new role. Seamstresses demanded hours of her time for fittings to create her new imperial wardrobe. Meanwhile, our lessons ended without so much as a word.

On the appointed day, I stood with the rest of my family in our main courtyard to see Spring off. She offered a personal farewell to each of us. My father beamed with pride as he embraced her. My grandmother, mother, and aunt all cried. When Spring came to me, she said, "Baoyu, I'm expecting my star pupil someday to become first scholar." First scholar was the title given to the highest-ranked of all five thousand two hundred candidates in the Imperial Examination, the test I would be expected to take when I was seventeen or eighteen. I had planned on remaining the stoic little man, but as she embraced me, I too cried.

The Forbidden City had sent a palanquin to transport Spring to her new life. Its imperial-yellow lacquered surface glistened in the sun, its silk tassels swung in the breeze. Spring stepped in, and two eunuchs closed the door. I will never see her again, I thought.

I was wrong.

Every day our family received a copy of the *Court Gazette,* the newspaper that published the edicts of the Emperor and the various government ministries. Normally this publication was of interest only to my father if he was around. One day, however, six years after Spring had left our mansion for the Forbidden City and a few months after my aunt's party and my dream, our daily copy of the *Gazette* set the entire family abuzz.

The Emperor had issued a new edict. The highest duty of mankind is filial piety, he had stated; everyone, regardless of rank, has strong family feelings. The Emperor realized that the secondary consorts and ladies-in-waiting in the Forbidden City who had been away from their families for many years must long to see those families again, for it is only natural that children should miss their parents. Therefore, it was decreed that all those court ladies with adequate accommodation at home for the reception of an imperial retinue might leave the Forbidden City for a single day to visit their families.

Our family was ecstatic: Spring would be coming home, if only for a day. My grandmother, mother, and aunt once again shed tears into their weeping towels, this time for joy, not sorrow.

They read the edict again. One phrase stuck out: "with adequate accommodation at home for the reception of an imperial retinue." We wondered what that meant, whether our mansion qualified.

Over the next few weeks more news arrived. The Zhou family, parents of another imperial concubine, had already started building a separate courtyard for their daughter's visit. The Wu family, similarly situated, was buying a site outside the city. We realized we had to do more than just give the old family mansion a dusting.

My father and uncle conferred with surveyors, architects, and garden designers. To my delighted surprise, they came up with a plan that was sheer genius. They would combine the garden behind First Uncle and Aunt's courtyard with the vacant land behind our mansion, wall in the entire area, and create within those walls a larger and entirely new garden.

For the next five months our mansion was a day-and-night construction site. First came demolition: workmen took down the old walls, removed most of the features of First Uncle's garden, and stored those features for later use in the new garden. Next, cartful after cartful of materials arrived: earth, rocks, timber, bricks, tiles, trees, shrubs, plants. A counter-movement also took place: chests full of spindle-shaped silver ingots emerged from our basement vaults and disappeared into the hands of contractors, suppliers, and laborers.

Directing the creation of the garden was a man known as Gardener Ye, said to be the best garden designer in Beijing. Gardener Ye was imperious to a fault, but he worked miracles on our property. A stream had always existed at the north-west corner of First Uncle's garden. Gardener Ye transformed this stream into a wide river, bounded by artificial mountains and wild-looking rockeries. Elsewhere, an abundance of trees, bamboos, and flowering plants softened the landscape. Most imaginatively, at seven selected beauty spots within the garden, Gardener Ye located seven picturesque cottages, each of a different design.

Gardner Ye forbade Daiyu and me from visiting the new garden during the construction period, but a few days before the anticipated date of my sister's visit he allowed us in for a look. Gardeners were still planting roses, peonies, plantains; decorators were putting up silk curtains, blinds, wall hangings. The garden smelled of newly applied lacquer and recently upturned earth.

The beauty of the new garden staggered us. Everywhere we turned a new wonder appeared: an arbor of apricot trees, a trio of snowy egrets standing motionless in a small pond, a pergola topped by a cluster of pink roses, a pathway of black-and-white pebble mosaic depicting the animals of the zodiac, a bank of lilies in full bloom, a moon bridge over a stream teeming with carp.

Daiyu and I adored the seven cottages. A dense grove of bright-green bamboo surrounded one of them. A zigzag cobblestone walkway led through the bamboo to the cottage itself, while behind the cottage a murmuring brook meandered through a small garden of wisteria and hibiscus.

Nearby, but still separated by a waterfall covered with ferns and flowering vines, another cottage enchanted us. Here a moon gate opened onto a large courtyard enclosed on all sides by a covered veranda. On one side of the courtyard grew green plantains; on the other, a solitary crabapple tree. The tree's branches were trained in the shape of an umbrella, and beneath the umbrella hung clusters of blossoms red as cinnabar.

The cottage itself, located at the back of the courtyard, resembled more an art gallery than a conventional residence. Instead of interior walls, it had partitions in the form of open shelves filled with books, bronze tripods, flower vases, miniature dish gardens, scholar's rocks, and other treasures.

As Daiyu and I were leaving this cottage, I heard a sound that made me cringe—the nasal voice of my father. He was talking to a group of other men, and they were about to enter the courtyard.

This was typical of my rare encounters with my father. I never saw him alone, he was always with a group of other men. My father never introduced me to any of them. To the best of my knowledge, most of them were young men who had passed the Imperial Examination but not yet secured an official position. My father called them his secretaries and used them to write letters and the like. Mainly the young men spent their time angling for a government position and hoping my father would be the connection that led to one. I called them his cronies.

I looked around for a way to escape, but the courtyard was a dead end. The only opening was the moon gate through which my father was now entering.

The maids, nurses, and pages who had accompanied Daiyu and me through the garden melted into the background. Daiyu stepped back and dissolved into their midst. I faced my father alone.

His eyes alighted on me. "I see you're neglecting your studies again, you worthless cur."

"I was talking the other day to his instructor," one of my father's cronies said. "He said your second master is quite the good student."

My father snorted in disgust. "Don't flatter him. He's big-headed enough." Father bathed me in an acid gaze.

Father turned from me to examine the front of the cottage. He pointed to an empty plaque above the cottage door, obviously intended to bear an inscription, and said to his cronies, "Who has a good idea for the inscription there?"

"Plantains and Storks," one of the cronies suggested. His colleagues nodded and murmured, "Very good, very good."

"Towering Radiance, Shimmering Splendor," another crony said, to a similar wave of approval.

"Flaming Tree in Winter," a third suggested, again to unanimous assent.

Father glared at me. "What about *you*? You're supposed to be such a good student. What do you think would make an appropriate inscription?"

I thought for a while. Finally I said, "It seems to me the designer of this garden intended a contrast between the red of the crabapple blossoms and the green of the plantains. Therefore, the ideal inscription would refer to both colors. Something like: 'Red Fragrance, Green Jade.'"

Father stared at me, his eyes narrow, his lips tight. The acrid smell of raw lacquer hung between us. His cronies remained silent.

"That's pathetic," Father said. "The reports of your being a good student are obviously false."

I looked down. Father continued to glare at me. The cronies turned their heads.

"What are you standing around for?" Father said. "Go back to your grandmother's and return to your studies."

No words could have made me happier. Daiyu and all the maids, nurses, and pages emerged from the shadows. We passed by my father and his cronies and exited through the moon gate.

The last few days before my sister's anticipated visit were even busier than the previous five months. Animal handlers brought in white peacocks, spotted deer, quail, partridges, ducks, and geese. Our family purchased twelve young actresses; they arrived and began rehearsing opera excerpts they would perform. A parade of eunuch officials from the Forbidden City, representing the protocol and security divisions, passed through the new garden, making sure our preparations were adequate, planning the imperial concubine's movements to the last step, showing us which doors and passageways would have to be blocked off, and instructing us on how to behave.

The police closed the street in front of our mansion and sent the usual loiterers and beggars packing. Government workers leveled the ruts in the street with shovels and brooms, then tamped down the dust and ashes by sprinkling water.

The day appointed for Spring's visit turned out warm and clear. All of us arose before dawn, and by the sun's first rays every family member was in full ceremonial dress, down on his or her knees, arranged in order of rank and gender inside our triple gate. Incense burned in bronze tripods, fresh flowers filled innumerable vases, banners of dancing dragons and flying phoenixes fluttered in the breeze, and pyrotechnicians hovered over an arsenal of fireworks.

We waited. And waited and waited. Not a soul passed by on the cordoned-off street. After several hours, a single eunuch, clad in red satin and riding a white horse, appeared. Grandmother invited him in for tea and asked when the imperial concubine could be expected.

"Oh, it will be a long time yet," the eunuch said in a womanish voice. "Her Highness is to dine at one, pray to Buddha at half past two, and go to evening feast at five. She can hardly ask the Emperor for leave to go until all that's happened. I imagine it will be at least seven in the evening before she can possibly set out."

Deflated, everyone in the family retired to his or her quarters to wait out the long delay. Fortunately, we had purchased hundreds of colored lanterns and were well equipped for a nocturnal visit.

Toward sunset we sent out scores of servants to light the lanterns, and we ourselves assembled once again inside our triple gate for yet another wait. This time we were not disappointed.

Ten eunuchs on foot ran through the gate, panting and clapping their hands in rounds of three. Then, twenty eunuchs on horseback formed a double row along the street. Finally, to the sound of an orchestra (plucked strings, flutes, and percussion), Spring's procession appeared. Surrounded by a battalion of eunuchs hoisting dragon banners, pheasant plumes, and censers, Spring's palanquin—lacquered in imperial yellow, topped with gold, embellished with phoenixes, and born by eight eunuchs—moved slowly forward.

The eunuchs carried the palanquin through the center door of our triple gate into our main courtyard. A eunuch carrying a whisk opened the palanquin's door, and Spring emerged. At a signal from my father, fireworks began exploding overhead, lighting up the now completely dark sky. Spring's eyes took in the banners, the curling drifts of incense smoke, the flowers, the fireworks, the scores of colored lanterns. Her first words were: "This is *too* extravagant."

The next hour brought a torrent of sensations, all competing for attention. Our new garden, haloed in the soft light of hundreds of candle-lit lanterns. The opulent variety of lanterns—silk, goat horn, glass, gauze. The rich, fatty smell of the imperial incense the eunuchs burned. The pure voices of our twelve child actresses singing opera snippets. My sister stepping onto a magnificently caparisoned barge for a boat trip along our garden's river. The river's shimmering reflection of the clouds of lanterns overhead. The hundreds of eunuch servants who infiltrated our mansion over the evening, adding to our own three hundred or so servants. The heaviness of the ceremonial brocade robe I wore, the stiffness of my formal leather boots.

Once the boat trip ended, Spring traveled by horse-drawn carriage to Grandmother's reception hall to pay her respects as a granddaughter of the house. Along with all the other male relatives, I stood outside, staring at the glass-beaded curtain. Only women and eunuchs could enter. While we menfolk stood outside, the sounds of crying emerged from within.

A eunuch came out and whispered in my father's ear. Father stepped forward to the outer side of the beaded curtain and began addressing Spring from there. After a brief conversation, he stepped back.

I had been told that, as a young man without an official position, I could not approach my sister; in other words, I could see her only if she summoned me. I wondered whether this would happen, and if it did, whether my contact with Spring would be any more intimate than my father's shouted greetings through the glass beads.

Also, even if I were so fortunate as to be summoned to Spring's presence, how would we relate to each other? I remembered Spring as my big sister and myself as her little brother. Now she was a member of the imperial clan, and I was her subject. What did one say across a gap that wide?

A rosy-cheeked eunuch about my own age emerged from the reception hall and asked, "Is there a Baoyu here?" After my relatives pointed me out, the eunuch said, "Her Majesty wants to see you."

The eunuch guided me to the outside of the beaded curtain. I made my kowtow, assuming this was as close to Spring as I would get. As I was raising my head, however, Spring said, "Come in, Baoyu. I want you in here." The rosy-cheeked eunuch took my hand, parted the glass beads, and ushered me through.

The scene inside startled me. Spring's entry into our mansion had been spectacular and joyous. Here, all was somber and subdued. Grandmother and Mother had obviously been crying; they seemed drained, almost in a daze. Only four or five eunuchs were present, all but one very young. I later learned that during this phase of Spring's visit most of the eunuchs were attending a banquet my family had arranged for them in another part of our mansion.

Spring, clad in a golden gown embroidered with dragons, was seated on Grandmother's couch. She said nothing but held out her arms toward me. Guessing at her meaning, I sat down beside her, opened my arms, and we embraced. Only then did I understand why she had been silent. She was crying—softly and in a suppressed manner, but still crying, crying too much to talk. She seemed at that moment not like a member of the imperial clan, nor like the sister of my childhood, but like a sad and lonely young woman.

I had forgotten how much I had grown in the six years since Spring had left our household. When she was my reading teacher, I was smaller than she; now, I was much bigger. As we embraced, the only words she managed to eke out between sobs were: "You're so big!" Everyone in the room let out a nervous laugh.

Two maids came in to announce the banquet was ready. Spring rose and recovered her composure enough to say, "Baoyu, you must have dinner with us. You can lead the way." I was overjoyed. Spring's words meant I could eat with her and the other women. I would not have to sit through the banquet with my father and the men.

Spring, the female relatives, and I walked from Grandmother's reception hall into the garden, and once there to a banqueting hall built specially for the occasion. Our walk took us past many of the new garden's finest features: mountains, streams, groves of trees, banks of flowers, cottages. Seen at night, softly lit by hundreds of colored lanterns, the garden seemed a fantasy—a vision of the Western Paradise.

I was so happy I wondered if I was dreaming. I pinched myself to find out. I was not.

The banquet itself was sumptuous. Our Jia family cooks ably reproduced the classics of imperial cuisine: shark's fin, bird's nest, deer tendon, camel paw, boar tongue, turtle. My only regret was that, feeling somewhat constrained in the presence of a member of the imperial clan, we did not drink as much as we usually did at a Jia family party.

By the end of the banquet Spring had regained her regal bearing. She stood up, her golden gown radiant in the candlelight, and gave a short speech, thanking the family for its hospitality and saying how good it was to see everyone again. Then she summoned seven of us: myself; Daiyu; Baochai; my sister-in-law, Silk; my half-sister, Tingting; and First Uncle's two daughters, Lotus and Peony.

"One of the things that has delighted me during this visit," Spring said to the seven of us, "is seeing all of you, a new, younger generation of our esteemed Jia family. I tried to teach Baoyu a few characters while I was here, but I understand by now he has gone far beyond my feeble attempts and become an accomplished scholar. I'd like to see that myself, so I'm going to set him to work. And the rest of you"—she pointed to the other six—"can join him.

"Baoyu, I want you, here in my presence, to write four wu-lü poems. The rest of you can write one each. The subject of each of your poems shall be this magnificent new garden, or any part of it you choose."

All the food in my stomach congealed. The wine turned to vinegar. Disaster had struck.

A wu-lü poem had to be constructed in accordance with numerous precise and demanding rules; writing one was like solving a mathematical puzzle. The basic form was simple enough: eight lines, five characters each. But everywhere, pitfalls lurked. For example, the first character of the first line and the first character of the second line could not have the same tone. The rhyme had to make its initial appearance in the tenth character and could not appear in any of the previous nine. All told, the creator of a wu-lü poem had to avoid what were called the "eight don'ts."

Writing a wu-lü poem, to say nothing of writing *four* wu-lü poems, was difficult even at the best of times. Now was the worst of times. By the time Spring spoke, it was well past midnight. I had been up since before dawn. I had been at our mansion's triple gate at dawn. I had then waited twelve hours—anxious, nervous hours, made even more stressful by my worries about how Spring and I would interact. The excitement of Spring's long-awaited arrival and the tension of meeting her in Grandmother's reception hall had further drained my energy. During the past three hours, I had eaten a multicourse banquet, most of the courses consisting of some dense, fatty animal part, and had drunk as much wine as I thought I could handle without seeming obviously drunk. In addition, all night I had been inhaling the ripe, cloying incense the eunuchs kept burning.

I was not a bad poet. On a good day, I could put together a wu-lü poem as well as anyone my age.

This, however, was not the time.

Maids scrambled to bring in desks, paper, inkstones, and ink. I noticed mixed reactions on the part of the other six members of what Spring had called "the younger generation." Daiyu looked positively eager for the writing to begin. Baochai looked calm and composed. The other four—my uncle's two girls, my half-sister, and my sister-in-law, none of whom claimed poetic excellence—looked as apprehensive as I felt.

Once we were all seated at our desks with plenty of paper and ink at hand, my worst fears became reality: I couldn't write a thing. I stared at the lined paper in front of me. I wrote a few tentative characters. Despite my best efforts to concentrate, all the myriad rules involved in writing a wu-lü poem went fuzzy, and every time I wrote a character I had the vague feeling, but never the positive certainty, I was violating one of the "eight don'ts."

I looked around at my fellow poets. Daiyu had already

finished; she looked bored and ready for another challenge. Baochai looked like she was still working on her poem, but I sensed she too had finished and was simply being polite to the rest of us. The other four were all grimly hunched over their writing desks, strain evident. Catching Daiyu's eye, and hoping Spring wouldn't notice, I pressed my hands to the sides of my head and grimaced. Daiyu laughed.

Again, I bent over my poem—the first of *four* I needed to write, a voice inside my head kept reminding me. Gradually, by lowering my standards and ceasing to worry about the rules so much, I managed to fill eight columns with five characters each. The result was not a good poem, perhaps not even a wu-lü poem, but at least it was a poem, enough to count as my number one.

Just as I was starting to write out the clean copy of my poem, a wadded-up piece of paper landed on my desk. I opened it, and inside was ... a beautifully constructed wu-lü poem on the subject of our garden. In Daiyu's calligraphy.

I felt immense gratitude. I wanted to thank Daiyu, but first I needed to see if Spring had noticed. Fortunately, she had not; some of the servants who had attended her when she lived in our mansion were paying obeisance to her. I turned to Daiyu and, with prayer hands and a bow, signaled my indebtedness. Then, putting on a pleading face, I cupped my hands, palms up, and wagged them toward me. Daiyu smiled and nodded yes. Again, I gave her prayer hands and a bow.

I wrote out clean copies of the two poems now in my possession, mine and Daiyu's, then set to work on another. This time I was able to work faster, perhaps because my standards were even lower than before. Shortly before I finished my own poem, another wadded-up paper ball arrived. Once again, Daiyu had gifted me with a fine wu-lü poem.

After we had all finished, Spring made a show of having each of us read our efforts out loud. When my turn came, I first read the two poems Daiyu had written, then my own two. Spring's face glowed with satisfaction as I read Daiyu's poems, dimmed noticeably as I read my own.

Even more embarrassing was what happened next. Spring

declared that she was going to pick the best poem of the evening, and she chose—what else?—one of the poems Daiyu had written and I had passed off as my own.

Once the poetry competition was over, a eunuch presented Spring with a list of the presents to be distributed. Spring approved the list, and the eunuchs began bringing out red boxes. Meanwhile, I scurried over to Daiyu and, on my knees, thanked her for her help.

The gifts from the Forbidden City were lavish. I received a gold necklace, silver necklace, two gold medallions, two silver medallions, and some junket and mince that were specialties of the Forbidden City kitchens. Everyone else in the family received numerous valuable gifts, and the imperial largess was not limited to masters: strings of newly minted copper coins— six hundred in all—went to our servants, the entertainers, and all those who had worked on the construction of the garden.

It was three in the morning before the chief eunuch announced that all the presents had been distributed and it was time for Her Highness to return home. The family gathered in our main courtyard to see Spring off. Grandmother and Mother cried uncontrollably. Spring maintained a tight demeanor but was obviously fighting tears. I felt totally exhausted.

The eunuchs closed ranks, and Spring disappeared into the gold-topped imperial palanquin. The dragon banners, pheasant plumes, and censors that had accompanied her journey to our mansion rose again; the eunuch orchestra resumed its swaying melody; and Spring's palanquin, born by its eight eunuchs and followed by twenty more on horseback, exited our triple gate and disappeared up the street. Our servants began extinguishing, one by one, the lanterns still lit, and all of us in the family headed off to bed. The magical night was over.

The next day, my father locked up the garden. Gardeners could come in to tend the trees and plants, but otherwise the wonderland my family had spent so much treasure creating would be off-limits to everyone. We hoped Spring would return some day for another visit. If so, the garden, still in pristine condition, would be waiting for her.

Two weeks after Spring's visit, a message arrived at our mansion. I was in my room, memorizing a passage from *Doctrine of the Mean*, when one of Grandmother's maids rushed in. "Second Master, go quickly to Her Old Ladyship's reception hall. There's good news."

When I arrived, Grandmother and Daiyu were looking at an official-looking document. "Read this," Grandmother said, handing it to me. Signed by Spring and bearing the red imperial seal, the document read:

> Daiyu, Baochai, Silk, Tingting, Lotus, and Peony should move into the garden. The garden should not be closed. Baoyu should accompany the young ladies into the garden and continue his studies there.

I started jumping up and down. "That's wonderful! When can we move in? How do we decide who lives in which cottage?"

Suddenly one of my father's pages appeared and stood directly in front of me. "First Master wants to see you."

I stopped my jumping up and down, my chattering. Damn, is Father going to try to stop me from moving into the garden?

"Has Father seen this message?" I asked Grandmother.

"Of course. It went to him first, then he sent it here."

I let out a deep sigh, my body slumped.

"Now, now, my treasure." Grandmother wrapped her arms around me. "Go to your father. I won't let him be harsh on you. It's because you wrote such good poems that Spring thinks you deserve to move into the garden. I'm sure your father just wants to tell you to behave yourself there. Say 'yes' to whatever he says, and all will be well."

I dragged my feet from Grandmother's quarters to my parents'. On the way, I thought more about the possibility Father would try to prevent me from moving into the garden. If that was his goal, he had grounds.

Once past the point of puberty, a boy was not supposed to share living quarters with any unmarried girl except a sister. My relationship with Amber constituted convincing evidence

I was past the point of puberty. If all of us listed in Spring's message were living together in the garden, wouldn't we be "sharing living quarters"? And weren't four on the list—Daiyu, Baochai, and First Uncle's two daughters—unmarried girls who were not my sisters?

On the other hand, I was already living with Daiyu in Grandmother's courtyard, and Father, afraid of challenging Grandmother, had never made an issue of that.

I entered my parents' courtyard. Father was not in his study; rather, he and Mother were in their sitting room, facing each other on the kang. Mother smiled at me lovingly. Father scowled.

"Your sister, Her Imperial Highness," Father said, "has come to realize that living where you are now you are wasting far too much time and neglecting your studies. Therefore, she has decided you should move into the garden, so you can concentrate and give up your frivolities.

"This is an opportunity for you to mend your ways. You are far behind where you ought to be in terms of your preparation for the Imperial Examination, and that must change. I'm warning you: if you do not give up all your tomfoolery and devote yourself exclusively to your studies, you will face the most serious consequences."

"Yes sir."

I waited for Father to say more, but he didn't. After a decent interval, I went over to kiss Mother. She held onto me longer than usual, while Father glared. Finally she said, "Run along now. Your grandmother is probably waiting for you to have lunch."

Outside my parents' courtyard, Amber and three other maids waited, their faces weighed down with worry.

I jumped up and thrust my arms to the sky. "Everything's fine, we're moving into the garden!" They too started jumping up and down, and soon we were all kissing and hugging.

I raced back to Grandmother's to talk to Daiyu. "Which cottage would you like? We should decide which ones we want as soon as possible. That way we can get to Grandmother before anybody else does."

Daiyu decided she wanted the cottage nestled in the dense

grove of bamboo, the one with the zigzag cobblestone walkway in front and meandering brook behind. I chose the cottage entered through a moon gate and large courtyard, with plantains on one side and a crabapple tree in spectacular red bloom on the other.

By now all the cottages had names: at the family's request, Spring had named them during her visit. Daiyu's chosen cottage was "Bamboo Lodge." Mine was "Happy Red Court."

Daiyu and I were the first to register our choices with Grandmother, and of course she immediately granted our wishes. Grandmother also assigned each of us four maids and two older nurses, in addition to the servants we already had. The family hired an astrologer, who picked the twenty-second day of Tenth Month as an auspicious date, and on that day Daiyu, Baochai, Silk, Tingting, Lotus, Peony, and I, along with roughly seventy female servants, moved into the garden.

As I pranced in, I thought: This is paradise. I am living in a garden of astonishing beauty, in a cottage of rare architectural distinction. I am head of my own household, with my own staff of servants. I live far enough from my father that I will rarely see him, but close enough to my grandmother and mother that I can visit them every day. I am the only male in a garden filled with girls. Daiyu is my next-door neighbor, Baochai's cottage is only a short walk beyond. In my own household, I have Amber and the nightly delights of her warm, yielding body. In addition, most of the other seventy or so maids living in the garden are young, nubile, and beautiful.

Happiness is mine, guaranteed. My future life will be painted entirely in pastels, never any grays or blacks. Sorrow will never cross my path, I will never know gloom.

I patted my jade as I headed to Happy Red Court. Grandmother was right. My jade *was* a gift from heaven. It *did* ensure me a life of bliss.

I was pathetically naïve.

5

I IMMEDIATELY SET OUT to make Happy Red Court my own. The cottage had no interior walls, only open shelves and display niches that served as partitions. The designers who had created the garden had filled these shelves and niches with a wide variety of decorative objects, which were not bad, but I wanted my own stamp on everything. I moved out all the designers' choices and replaced them with things that had special meaning for me: antique porcelains I had received as presents, Buddhist and Taoist statues I had collected over the years, favorite books, inlaid boxes, scholar's rocks, bronzes.

The courtyard was a different story. I dared not alter the landscaping scheme: on one side the crabapple tree with its stunning red blossoms, on the other the bright-green plantains. My only change was to imitate Grandmother and fill the surrounding covered veranda with cages filled with exotic birds: parrots, macaws, cockatoos, canaries.

My living quarters were thus ideal. Nevertheless, no sooner had the seven of us moved into the garden than troubles began.

Three weeks after the move, messengers arrived from the south. Daiyu's father had died.

The news devastated her. She had lost her mother at ten. Now, at fourteen, her father was gone. She was—no other word for it—an orphan, without protection. She also needed to pack up immediately and leave for Yangzhou to attend her father's funeral. The long, difficult journey would take place in the dead of winter.

Daiyu was gone five months. For me, those months were a time of intense loneliness. She had become so much a part of me that her being away was like having an arm or a leg ripped off. She was the first thing I thought of when I woke up in the morning, the last thing in my mind as I drifted off to sleep.

I believed at the time that every man had implanted in his brain at birth an ideal of feminine perfection. For me, that ideal was Daiyu. She was perfection in her beauty, perfection in her intelligence, perfection in her grace and elegance. To have so many perfections embodied in a single human being was beyond my comprehension.

Not that in Daiyu's absence I lacked female companionship; never in my young life did I lack that. I had Amber, with her sensuality, her willingness, the joy and vivacity with which she approached life. There were parts of me, however, that Amber could not satisfy. Though intelligent, Amber was illiterate. I could not write poetry with her, I could not have Zen conversations with her. Nor was Amber the type of slender, striking beauty who, seen from afar, took one's breath away. Daiyu was. To me, Daiyu was indispensable.

When, after five months, Daiyu returned from her long journey, she seemed different. Diminished.

I had assumed I would be notified as soon as she arrived. As it turned out, I didn't hear about her return until a day later. Immediately I rushed to Bamboo Lodge.

When I first saw Daiyu, my breath caught, my throat tightened. She had lost a startling amount of weight. Before her journey, she had been thin. Now she was ethereal.

Trunks and packing crates filled Bamboo Lodge. It seemed she had left a good deal behind in Yangzhou when she first came to live with us. When I arrived, she had a book in her hands. She barely looked at me.

"How was your trip?"

She inspected the title of the book she was holding, then placed it on a nearby shelf. Her movements were slow and laborious. "Difficult."

"How was the weather?"

She went to an open crate and reached in. "Cold."

"How was your father's funeral?"

She picked up another book. "Sad."

"I didn't realize you had left so many things back in Yangzhou."

After examining the book, she took it to the other side of the room and placed it on a table. "I did."

"You seem tired today."

She again reached into the crate. "I am."

"Maybe I should go and let you get some rest. I can come back tomorrow."

"You don't have to do that."

The tone of her voice made clear she was simply being polite. I excused myself and went back to Happy Red Court.

I returned to Bamboo Lodge the next day. Daiyu still seemed tired and subdued, but at least she was willing to converse. Several more days followed a similar pattern. Then, a troubling incident occurred.

The day was warm and sunny; spring had finally arrived in Beijing. I went looking for a secluded spot in the garden to read. Tealeaf, my ever-resourceful chief page, had procured for me the complete libretto of *The Romance of the Western Chamber*, an opera full of love and longing, and I was eager to immerse myself in its libidinous pleasures. I had seen a few scenes from this opera performed at family gatherings, but never any of the scenes I was most eager to experience—the risqué ones.

I found a spot where a peach tree had been in bloom for several weeks. Its pink blossoms were now falling to earth, and the sweet scent of the blossoms complemented the earthy smell of the garden. Spreading myself out on a grassy slope that descended from the peach tree to a small stream, I began to read. Peach blossoms kept falling on me, but I was too absorbed in the secret love affair of Zhang Sheng and Cui Yingying to notice. I raced from page to page, drinking in the beauty of the poetry and eagerly anticipating the notorious scenes of out-of-wedlock sex between the young scholar and his highborn girlfriend.

Over the normal background sounds of the garden—the

buzzing of insects, the twittering of sparrows, the squawking of magpies—I heard something discordant. Someone crying.

I got up, shook pink blossoms off my robe, and listened. The crying seemed to come from the other side of the ridge on which the peach tree stood.

I climbed the ridge and looked over to the other side. Daiyu was there. She had a small shovel in her hands and was pushing dirt into a hole in the ground. She was also crying.

I rushed to her. "What's going on?"

Her face was flushed, her eyes red. Her knitted eyebrows ended in deep worry lines above her nose. I was still unaccustomed to her new thinness.

She seemed surprised, and not particularly happy, to see me, shaking her head as if to say: I don't want to talk about it.

"Please, Daiyu, tell me what's on your mind." I suspected she was still mourning her father, but I wasn't sure.

Daiyu continued to cry, wiping her eyes with a handkerchief. When she had regained enough control of her emotions to speak, she said. "I was burying some of the blossoms that had fallen to the ground."

I looked askance. "You were ... burying fallen blossoms?"

She nodded and bit her lip. I noticed that to one side of the hole in the ground rested a gauze bag with blossoms inside.

"Why? What's the matter with just letting them lie on the ground?"

She leaned on her shovel and turned her head away from me. "It's so sad to see them lying on the ground, turning brown and getting dirty. This way is much cleaner. Eventually, they'll all turn back into soil."

This didn't make sense to me. Wouldn't they turn back into soil even if they were just left lying on the ground? I didn't want to challenge Daiyu, however, given the state she was in. Instead I said, "Why are you crying? It doesn't seem to me that fallen blossoms are worth crying over."

Still looking away from me, she shook her head. "It isn't the blossoms. I was thinking"—she wiped her eyes with her handkerchief—"I was thinking of some lines from *The Peony Pavilion*."

What a coincidence! *The Peony Pavilion* was a romantic opera about two young lovers, similar to *The Romance of the Western Chamber*, the work I had been reading.

"Why should *The Peony Pavilion* make you cry? What lines were you thinking of?"

She bit her lip again. "I was thinking of:

"For you who are as fair as a flower,
Youth flows away like water."

These words hit me with the force of a fist. For the first time, I realized a gap had opened between Daiyu and me. To me, operas like *The Romance of the Western Chamber* and *The Peony Pavilion* were about awakening youth—yearning, passion, florescence. She drew from them only images of decay and decline. I believed the best years of my life lay ahead of me. She thought the best years of her life were already behind her. She was only fourteen.

I tried to embrace her, but she slipped out of my grasp and drew back a couple of steps, dropping her shovel in the process. "Please, Baoyu, don't do that."

"I was just trying to cheer you up. You shouldn't be out here in the garden crying and making yourself miserable."

A coughing fit overtook her. I stood immobile, not knowing what to do. When her coughing finally subsided, she said, "I think I'd rather be alone."

I pleaded for her to let me stay, but my pleas only confirmed her resolve to see me go. I walked back up the ridge. When I reached the top, I turned to take a last look. Her head was bowed, she was holding the handkerchief to her eyes, and the fallen shovel lay at her feet. She was thin as a stalk of bamboo.

The next day she seemed to have recovered from her extreme melancholy but was still muted and distant compared to the previous fall. Neither of us brought up the previous day's incident. Nor did we ever discuss her weight loss. I was afraid to broach the topic; she didn't speak of it.

We continued to see each other on a regular basis. Occasionally she would come to Happy Red Court. More often, I would walk to Bamboo Lodge. Since we no longer lived in the same courtyard, though, we inevitably saw less of each other than before.

One afternoon I walked over to Bamboo Lodge and found Swallow, Daiyu's chief maid, sitting by herself on the veranda, sewing. "My mistress is napping. Better not go inside."

I sat down next to Swallow. "How is she? Is she in good spirits?"

"Yes, but today she's a little tired."

A cold wind blew that day, spring had turned back to winter. I noticed Swallow had on only a cotton dress and an unpadded sleeveless jacket. I took hold of her jacket and felt its thinness. "On a cold day like this you should be wearing warmer clothes."

She slapped my hand back. "Do you mind keeping your hands to yourself?"

Her reaction stung. She had completely misinterpreted my gesture. I was not trying to touch her; I was genuinely concerned her clothes were not warm enough.

I needed to get along with Swallow. Swallow was fiercely loyal to Daiyu, and Daiyu was fiercely loyal to her. If Daiyu was mine for life, so too was Swallow.

I got up, bowed my head, and clasped my hands in prayer. "Please, Swallow, forgive me. I didn't mean to offend you. I was just worried about how thin your clothes are."

She sniffed in disdain. "This sort of thing keeps happening all the time. My mistress knows about it too. She's warned all the servants to keep away from you."

I found this hard to believe. But I didn't have long to think about it, for Swallow next shrugged and said:

"I guess it doesn't matter now. By the end of the year, my mistress and I will both be gone, and we won't have to deal with you anymore."

I jolted back. What had Swallow just said? I must have misheard.

"What did you say?"

"Why, surely you must know. Your cousin is moving back to her home in Suzhou this year."

My mind went blank.

After a long, agonized pause, I said, "You must be joking. What you're saying doesn't make sense at all. Both of Daiyu's parents are dead; she doesn't have any home to go back to. By the way, she came from Yangzhou, not Suzhou."

"My, my," Swallow said, drawing out the words and giving them a snooty tone. "We certainly have a low opinion of other people's families, don't we?"

"What do you mean?"

"Everybody agrees you Jias are a rich and powerful family. But does that mean other families have only a mother and father and no other relatives? Your cousin's relatives on her father's side, the Lins, have been a family of scholars and officials for generations. Don't you think there might be some uncles and aunts and cousins who take pride in the family name? Also, the Lin family *is* originally from Suzhou. Your cousin's father was in Yangzhou only because he held an official position there."

"She came here because nobody down there wanted her."

"You can think that if you wish, but the truth is she came up here because your grandmother made such a fuss about it, about how your cousin needed companions her own age and all that. Anyway, now that she's coming into marriageable age, the Lins definitely want her back. Even if they were desperately poor, which they certainly are not, they still would never abandon responsibility for one of their own to in-laws. So, this summer, or fall at the latest, my mistress and I will be going back to Suzhou."

I thought about Daiyu's recent trip back south to attend her father's funeral. Had all this been discussed and arranged then? Did Daiyu's knowledge she would soon be going back to Suzhou explain the incident by the peach tree? It seemed possible.

"Another thing," Swallow said. "My mistress has asked me to gather up all the presents and things you've given her over the years, so she can return them to you. Do you think you could do the same for her—gather up all her presents to you and return them?"

I stared at Swallow, speechless. I had never heard of returning presents. Was this some strange southern custom Daiyu was raised with?

A jelly-like weakness came over me. My knees trembled. My legs gave way under the weight of my body. I toppled over.

The next thing I knew, Amber was standing over me, her face panic-stricken. "Second Master, what happened?"

I was too dazed to answer.

I struggled to get up but couldn't. Amber began assisting me, and eventually I was able to raise myself to a crouch. I noticed Swallow was nowhere in sight.

With Amber's assistance, I managed to thread my way back out Bamboo Lodge's cobblestone path, then across to Happy Red Court. Once home, I lay in my bed, numb and enervated.

The love of my life is leaving me, I mourned. Daiyu and I will not be spending the rest of our lives together. I will probably never see her again. Soon she will be married to someone else.

At some point, Amber slipped out, leaving four junior maids to watch over me. While Amber was gone, Grandmother's chief maid, Rosebud, appeared to ask why I hadn't shown up at Grandmother's, as requested. I then remembered Amber telling me she had come to Bamboo Lodge to notify me of Grandmother's request.

Soon after Rosebud's arrival, Amber returned, tugging Swallow by the arm. Amber's face was tense with anger. Swallow cowered when she saw Rosebud. As Grandmother's chief maid, Rosebud was one of the most powerful individuals in our household. One word from her could get a maid fired.

Amber yanked Swallow's arm. "All right, tell them what you just told me."

Swallow fell to her knees before Rosebud and began crying. "Please don't tell Her Old Ladyship!"

"Why don't we find out what it is," Rosebud said, "and then we'll decide whether or not to tell Her Old Ladyship."

Swallow suddenly noticed me; up until that point she had been so concerned about Rosebud she hadn't even looked in my direction. I was lying in my bed, dazed and vacant. Still kneeling, Swallow shifted to face me. "Please, Second Master, forgive me. For the death of me, I never intended for things to end up like this."

"Forgive you for *what*?" Rosebud answered on my behalf.

"It was supposed to be a joke," Swallow said, before unleashing a new torrent of tears.

"Swallow, what did you do?" Rosebud said.

"I told Second Master my mistress and I were moving away and going back to Suzhou and that we'd never see him again. It was all untrue; I made everything up. Please, Rosebud, don't tell Her Old Ladyship. I'll do anything you want, just don't tell Her Old Ladyship."

Swallow, Rosebud, and Amber went round and round on the issue of whether to tell Grandmother. Amber would have preferred to see Swallow's head chopped off, but in the end, Rosebud decided, as she generally did in these types of situations, that Her Old Ladyship would not be told. Rosebud tempered her mercy to Swallow by giving her a stern lecture. Oddly, neither Rosebud nor Amber showed any interest in *why* Swallow had told me she and Daiyu were moving away.

By the next day I had recovered and was able to return to Bamboo Lodge. Swallow came out to greet me as I was walking up the cobblestone path. I sensed she'd been waiting for me.

She began by kneeling and begging forgiveness. I told her to stop, that I had gotten over it. "Just to confirm, there aren't any Lin family members who want Daiyu back?" I asked.

"No. The Lins aren't a big family to begin with, and the few there are don't seem to give a fig about Miss Daiyu. I hate to say it, but except for this family, my mistress is all alone in the world."

As I was mulling this over, Swallow said, "Can I please ask you a favor, Second Master?"

"What?"

"When you see my mistress, can you please not tell her about what happened yesterday? You see, she never heard about what I told you or how you reacted. The only thing she heard was that you were sick. I'm afraid if she knew the truth, she'd get angry and upset. Her health isn't good right now, so I don't want to make her upset."

"I see. Very well, I won't tell her anything. Since you've asked me a favor, though, I'd like one in return."

"What?" Swallow's face reflected grim worry. While she might be willing to do business with me, she didn't trust or even like me. In this respect, she was a challenging contrast to the dozens of young maids in our household who schemed to get closer to me.

"*Why* did you tell me the story about you and Daiyu moving to Suzhou?"

Swallow blushed. Taking a deep breath, she said, almost inaudibly, "It was a test."

"A test? What were you testing?"

"Your feelings about my mistress."

"You doubt my feelings about Daiyu? I don't see why. I think my feelings are obvious."

"But you're engaged to this Miss Liu."

"What?"

"You're engaged. To some woman named Liu."

For a moment, I was completely lost. Then I remembered a conversation I had been part of a few days earlier.

"Swallow, people talk about my being gullible. You're even more gullible. Do you want to know about this Miss Liu? All right, here's the true story.

"Miss Liu is a distant relative—a grandniece or something—of Baochai's mother. Personally, I've never met Miss Liu. Recently, she became engaged to a man named Wei. A couple of weeks ago, a group of us were in Grandmother's sitting room, and Baochai's mother was telling us about the engagement and about Miss Liu. Baochai's mother talked about how beautiful Miss Liu was, how intelligent she was, how well-mannered, how she could paint and write poetry, how she was also a good seamstress—on and on. After Baochai's mother had been singing Miss Liu's praises for a while, my grandmother said, as a joke, 'If this Miss Liu is as marvelous as all that, I should marry her to Baoyu.' Everybody laughed.

That's the end of the story. I'm not engaged to Miss Liu. The only engagement is between Miss Liu and Mr. Wei."

Swallow flinched and looked down. "You're right. I was gullible, and I'm sorry. But when it comes to my mistress' future, sometimes I can't control myself. I know my mistress. I know her better than anybody in the world. Second Master, if you were to marry somebody else, it would destroy her. Just destroy her. That's why, when I heard this talk about you marrying Miss Liu, I got so upset and felt I had to do something."

"If it was a test, did I pass?"

Swallow grimaced. "Yes. Maybe too well."

"Swallow, listen to me. I want to marry Daiyu. I've never thought about marrying anybody else. I'm sure that someday we *will* be married. We have to wait for Grandmother, though. I can't bring it up with Grandmother, Daiyu can't bring it up with Grandmother. We have to wait for Grandmother to bring it up herself."

Swallow looked away, disconsolate.

"I'm sure someday Grandmother *will* bring it up," I continued. "She knows how much we love each other, she sees us together all the time. She's treated us like a couple ever since Daiyu first arrived. Remember how Grandmother had us live together in her own courtyard. Then, when everyone moved into the garden, she put us in cottages that are side by side. I'm sure when it comes time to arrange our marriages, Grandmother will put us together again."

Swallow said nothing. Dense bamboo grew along both sides of the cobblestone path on which we were standing, lending our conversation the luxuries, rare in the Jia household, of privacy and quiet.

After a period of silence, I said, "I'd like to ask you another question, if you don't mind."

Swallow nodded yes.

"Have you ever discussed this business of marriage prospects with Daiyu? What does she say?"

Swallow shook her head slowly. "I've tried, again and again, but she won't talk about it, even with me. Every time I mention anything having to do with marriage, she gets angry and tells me to go away."

We both stood silent, surrounded by the tall, dense bamboo. At last I said, "Maybe I should try to talk to her. I know it would be improper: young people are not supposed to talk or even think about who they're eventually going to marry. Young people certainly aren't supposed to scheme about getting married to each other. But if it's just Daiyu and me—Bamboo Lodge is empty, no one else around—who would know? Daiyu's and my relationship has always been unusual, we've always been closer to each other than young people normally are. I don't think the rules of filial piety apply to us."

"I hope she's willing to talk to you," Swallow said. "She needs to talk to somebody."

I decided not to go to Daiyu immediately. Instead, I returned to Happy Red Court to devise a strategy.

To broach the taboo subject of marriage with Daiyu, I needed something to break the ice. A gift, maybe. But what?

I wandered around Happy Red Court, seeking inspiration. Eventually my eyes landed on a small object displayed on one of my open shelves. It was a jade carving, small enough to fit into the palm of my hand, of mandarin ducks nestled side by side and jointly holding a stalk of flowering lotus in their beaks. It was perfect. Mandarin ducks, particularly when combined with lotus, were a traditional and universally recognized symbol of marriage, and the beauty of the translucent light-green jade made the carving an ideal present.

I packed the carving into an appropriately sized box, then headed off to Bamboo Lodge. Swallow greeted me at the door curtain. She told me two junior maids were inside, cleaning, but she would send them away. Daiyu and I would have complete privacy.

Inside, I found, to my surprise, Daiyu playing a lute. She was massaging the strings and moving the plectrum with her long expressive fingers. She looked thin, but in this pose, exceptionally beautiful. The fineness of her features complemented the spare perfection of her bones.

"I didn't know you played the lute," I said.

"I brought this back from Yangzhou after my father's funeral. I played when I was little, but when I came here, I didn't bring my lute with me. Now, after having not played for so many years, I can't play at all."

Daiyu and I exchanged small talk for a while. We talked about the lute; my recent illness and recovery; her health, which she claimed was fine; and some items she had added to the interior decoration of Bamboo Lodge.

When I felt the moment ripe, I brought out my box and handed it to her. "I brought you a present."

She held the box at arm's length and looked at it suspiciously. "What is it?"

"Open it."

Daiyu pulled out the luscious jade and stared at it. As she held it longer and thought about it more, her face changed from wariness to concern to alarm. She knit her sulky brows, hooded her eyes. Her face reddened to the tips of her ears.

"You're hateful! Giving me this licentious sculpture, just to taunt me." She slammed the two mandarin ducks back in their box and threw the box at my feet. "Take this ... *thing* and please leave."

I apologized, apologized every way I knew how, but Daiyu's anger was unyielding. In the end, I retreated from Bamboo Lodge, carrying my connubial ducks back with me. On my way out, I passed Swallow. I shook my head no. She sighed and lowered her head.

From that time on, I could never think about Daiyu without feeling an ache in my heart. She was so anxious, so unhappy.

Her worries about her marriage prospects were understandable. She probably feared that if she did not gain my hand in marriage, she would be cast out from the Jia family, an orphan with nowhere to go. She could also be worried about her health. Her weight loss might be a sign of serious illness.

I lamented that Daiyu was in such pain. I lamented even more that she was determined to bear her pain alone.

6

I HAD A YOUNGER HALF-BROTHER, Huan, son of my father by one of his concubines. If Huan has thus far been missing from this narrative, it is because I, along with almost everyone else in our household, wanted it that way.

Huan blamed his near-universal unpopularity on his illegitimacy. "You wouldn't treat me this way if I weren't a concubine's son," he whined incessantly.

Our family's warm acceptance of his sister, Tingting, belied his claim. Tingting and Huan shared the same concubine mother; they were full brother and sister. Yet Tingting was liked by everyone and always included whenever invitations were extended for some special treat. When Spring summoned seven of us to write poetry, Tingting was included, Huan was not. When the same seven of us were given permission to live in the garden, each in his or her own cottage, once again Tingting was part of the group, Huan was not. Illegitimacy was not what held Huan back.

Huan's life revolved in a vicious circle. His constant complaining about being treated badly resulted in people avoiding him and excluding him from social gatherings *precisely because of* his constant complaining.

Huan's jealousy only increased when the seven of us moved into the garden, while he continued to live with his mother in modest quarters near the communal kitchen. He couldn't understand his exclusion. It couldn't be because he was a male: I was living there. It couldn't be because he was a concubine's child: his full sister was living there, as was Peony, First Uncle's daughter by a concubine. In fact, Huan was the only young master in our far-flung household who was *not* living in the garden. It gnawed at him day and night.

While Huan resented almost everyone in the family, he bore a special animus toward me. He was obsessed with the contrast between our physical appearances.

Huan was, to put it tactfully, not good-looking. He was short and scrawny, his coarse hair stuck out in all directions, and he had a bad case of acne. He also had some sort of sinus problem that caused his nose to run constantly, a condition he dealt with by using his fingers or the back of his hand to wipe away the drip.

I, on the other hand, was tall and generally deemed handsome. Personally, I disagreed with this assessment: I thought I had a baby face—too round, too much fat, too little structure. I was often complimented on my looks, however, and if Huan was present, I could see the rage inside of him build.

One evening, I returned home from a birthday party for one of my aunts. My mother, feeling out of sorts that day, had decided to skip the party, and I stopped by her courtyard on my way back to Happy Red Court.

Mother was in her sitting room; with her was Huan. Mother had assigned him the task of copying out some Buddhist incantations. Huan sat on my mother's kang, with a low table in front of him. On the table were the originals of the incantations, sheets of paper, writing tools, and a large candle. Mother sat on another part of the kang.

I was a bit drunk. After shedding my headband and boots, I flung myself onto the kang.

"You've had too much to drink, child," Mother said. "Your face is red. You'd better rest or you may get sick. Why don't you lie down quietly over there?" She pointed to an area in front of Huan's table. I lay down as instructed.

Huan had only one maid; her name was Dawn. Rumor had it Huan and Dawn were intimate. Resting on the kang, I saw Dawn out of the corner of my eye and asked her to come over and massage me. She refused. My judgment impaired by alcohol, I lurched up and began pawing at her. She, however, slipped out of my grasp. Feeling tired and realizing my desire for Dawn was not to be satisfied, at least that evening, I lay back and soon drifted off.

Suddenly I felt a searing pain on the left side of my face. The pain drilled through my skin, clawed into my flesh, and headed toward my left eye, now flooded with tears. "Huan, you fool!" my mother screamed. I jerked my hand to my face. My fingers reported a scalding, greasy liquid.

Four of Mother's maids rushed to my side. "The wax is over half his face!" one of them said.

By now I understood what had happened. My dear half-brother, Huan, had knocked over his candle in just such a way that the hot wax had splashed onto my face.

The next few minutes were excruciating. The maids peeled and scraped the wax, along with large chunks of skin, off my face, then covered the exposed flesh with almond oil. Fortunately, the flow of wax had stopped short of my eye, and my vision was unimpaired.

My mother said nothing to Huan after her initial outburst. Instead, she sent a maid to summon Huan's mother. When the latter arrived, my mother exploded at her. "What a worthless son you've given us! Have you ever, ever, tried to teach him any manners? It's impossible to be with him, he's so uncouth. You should be ashamed of yourself."

My mother ordered both Huan and his mother to leave, which they did, their heads bowed. Then she came over and, with tears in her eyes, daubed my face with an ointment.

After spending the night in Mother's courtyard, I was able to return to Happy Red Court the next morning. Unfortunately, the blistering all over the left side of my face took two months to heal.

During my convalescence, my social life continued to evolve. I saw little of Daiyu. I did not visit her—I was not supposed to go out, and in any event I wasn't eager for her to see me with my face scarred—and she rarely visited me. I wondered if she was still angry over my thwarted gift of the two connubial ducks. I knew she was squeamish, however, and most likely she simply did not like looking at a scarred face.

I saw more of Cousin Baochai; she was better at comforting the sick.

Most of all, I saw much more of Amber. I was excused from school during this period, almost never left the cottage, and as a result Amber and I were together at Happy Red Court almost all day, every day.

All the servants in our household who had relatives in Beijing were entitled to take one day off every month for a family visit. Amber qualified and was used to taking her monthly day off. While my face was healing, Amber offered to forego her usual monthly visit to her family, but I insisted she go, and in the end, she did.

When Amber returned that evening, she was uncharacteristically pensive. The same was true the next morning: she was not her usual ebullient self. She sent all the other maids outside to clean up the courtyard; then, ignoring me, busied herself with some sewing.

Grandmother had given me a basket of dragon eyes, one of my favorite fruits, and to encourage Amber to open up, I proposed we eat them together. She agreed. We sat down across from each other at my small table and began squeezing off the shells and eating the sweet, translucent flesh.

"Second Master," Amber said, after downing a couple of dragon eyes, "there's something we need to discuss."

I positioned a dragon eye between my thumb and knuckle. "Oh?"

She took a deep breath. "My family wants to buy me out of servitude."

I put the dragon eye down without cracking it. "What?"

"They were talking about it yesterday. They want me to stay here one more year. Then they think they'll have enough money to buy me back."

A queasy feeling crept over me. "Why would they want to do that?"

"That's a silly question. Maybe you're used to servants who were born in this household and don't have any family outside. But in my family, everybody's free except for me. That's why all my relatives feel so bad about me still being in servitude. What if you had a relative in servitude? Wouldn't you want to buy her out?"

My queasiness remained, but now shared space with doubt. I tapped my dragon eye on the table a couple of times. "Amber, is this another test, like Swallow telling me she and Daiyu were moving back to Suzhou?"

Amber reared back. "Second Master, how could you think that? You were a little gullible to believe Swallow's tale. Miss Daiyu has no family at all—no mother, no father, nobody. You know *I* have family, they live right here in Beijing. You can go visit them if you want. I'll take you."

"I thought both your mother and father were dead."

"That's true, but I have cousins, and I'm very close to my cousins. Seems to me you of all people should know how close cousins can be."

She had a point: Daiyu, Baochai, my uncle's two girls—if any of them were in servitude, I'd certainly try to redeem them. The queasiness gripped me again.

My thoughts turned darker. "What if I won't let you go?"

"Second Master, I can't believe you'd do that. You know it would be against the law. Sure, you're a noble family, but you remember the contract you signed with my family. Why, even in the Forbidden City they give the serving maids their freedom if their families come to redeem them. What about all those claims your family makes about being so fair and generous to your servants? Is that all just a big lie?"

She scowled at me.

"Let's be honest about it. Why are you against this? Because it doesn't suit your convenience, that's why. But is that any reason to keep me a slave?"

I got up from the table, wandered to one of my open shelves, picked up a bronze tripod, and began revolving it in my hands. "What if my grandmother offered your family a lot of money to have you stay here?"

72

"Look, my relatives are humble people, and to be honest, they're scared of your family. If your family made a big fuss about my leaving, my family would get down on their knees, kowtow, and back off, whether they were offered a lot of money or not.

"But is that what you want: to keep me here even if I don't want to be here? Is your grandmother going to go along with that? Is she going to be willing to break the law just so you don't have to change chief maids?"

I put down the bronze tripod and walked back to Amber, who was still seated at the table. "What about you? We've talked about what your family wants, but is this what you want too?"

She shook her head. "I have to be realistic. There's no future for me here."

"What do you mean?"

"Exactly what I said. There's no future for me here."

"I'm the heir to Lord Jia Zheng, and you're my concubine. That's not a future? I'll tell you one thing: a hundred serving girls just in this household alone would *love* to be in that position."

Amber arched her back and lifted her eyebrows. "I'm your concubine?"

"Why yes. Isn't that obvious? Do you think you're *not* my concubine?"

She shrugged. "All I know is, I'm paid like a chief maid, not like a concubine."

"What are you talking about?"

"In this household, a concubine gets two taels a month, a chief maid gets one. I get one."

"Is that what this is all about—money?"

Amber looked shaken. "No, no. You asked a question, I answered it. That's all."

I went back to my bronze tripod. The truth was, Amber and I had never gone through the formal ceremonies needed to make her an official concubine, nor was this likely to happen anytime soon. As an unmarried man, I could not take on an official concubine without my father's consent. I didn't want to ask my father. Not only would he refuse, he would take the occasion to administer a tongue-lashing about my being lascivious and frivolous.

This wasn't what I wanted to say to Amber, however. Instead, I turned to her and said, "What about this? I get more allowance every month than I can spend. I'll give you an extra tael every month out of my allowance."

"Let's not talk about it anymore. I don't want it to be all about money, as you put it."

"All right, if it's not all about money, what is it about?"

Amber pulled a dragon eye out of the basket, removed the shell, popped the translucent fruit into her mouth, and discarded the seed.

"There's something I probably shouldn't bring up," she said at last, "but I'm going to anyway. It's about Miss Daiyu. Are you going to marry her?"

I needed a moment to think.

"It's ... not up to me. My grandmother, along with my parents, will decide who I marry. But my choice would be to marry Daiyu, and I'm sure my grandmother and parents will take that into account. I've always assumed that someday Daiyu and I will be married, since Grandmother has always favored us and liked seeing us together. So, I guess the answer to your question is: yes."

Amber nodded slowly, pursing her lips. "That means, as your concubine, I'll be under Miss Daiyu's thumb."

I didn't like where this was going. I recalled the dressing down I had recently seen my mother administer to Huan's mother, a concubine. I sat back down at the table and pulled another dragon eye out of the basket. Finally the right response came to me. "Let's say, both of you will be under *my* thumb."

Amber laughed, then got up to bring us some more tea. While filling our cups, she said, "Sometimes I don't think Miss Daiyu even knows who I am."

I took a sip of my tea. "I've heard this before. I'm aware she's not—how to put it?—good at relating to servants."

Amber remained silent, staring at her cup of tea.

Since Amber didn't seem satisfied, I tried again. "If you're worrying about how Daiyu will treat you if she's my wife and you're my concubine, I think your worries are overblown. Daiyu may have her faults, but she's not unkind, and she doesn't like to boss people around. The worst that can be said about her is that she's aloof, off in her own world. How does that affect you? It doesn't."

As I was saying this, I again thought about my mother, normally the most mild-mannered of women, berating Huan's mother.

"I hope you're right," Amber said. "I also hope that if you're not right, you'll protect me."

"Of course I will. But it's not going to come to that. Believe me, there's not going to be a problem."

Amber continued to stare at her tea.

"By the way," I said, "that story about your family wanting to buy you out of servitude, that was a test, wasn't it? Like Swallow's story. It wasn't true."

Amber hunched her shoulders, lowered her head, and looked up at me with big child-like eyes, what I called her don't-be-angry-at-me pose. "It was, maybe, a little exaggerated."

"Maybe a *lot* exaggerated?"

She nodded. "Yes."

I reached over, pulled her toward me, and kissed her. "If it was a test, did I pass?"

She cocked her head. "I suppose." She kissed me back.

I buried my face in her soft hair, kissed each of her provocative high cheekbones, poked my finger at her impish turned-up nose, then smelled her musky navel. We took off our clothes and retired to my canopy bed.

Amber and I made love a lot while I was convalescing. We had little else to fill up the time.

7

ONCE MY FACE HEALED, I resumed my normal life. One hot summer afternoon, when the only movement in our mansion seemed to be the buzzing of flies, I went to visit my mother. I found her in her sitting room, fast asleep on a couch, with a single maid listlessly massaging her legs.

The maid, one of Mother's junior maids, was someone I had had my eye on for a while. Her name was Goldie, and not only was she beautiful, with the most entrancing almond-shaped eyes I'd ever seen, she was sensual and alluring in a way most of our maids were not.

It may sound odd, and I certainly wouldn't defend it now, but when I was young the taste of lipstick infatuated me. Its odd sticky-sweet taste was to me like a love potion. Goldie also loved lipstick, wore generous amounts, and knew I shared the attraction. On more than one occasion, she had allowed me to sample her delectable lips.

I had discussed with Goldie the possibility of her coming to work for me. I already had around fourteen maids, but given the right candidate, I could always use another. Goldie had agreed, and by now I was only awaiting the appropriate moment to bring up the subject with my mother.

When I entered Mother's sitting room, Goldie was nine-tenths asleep, her head drooped over Mother's legs. With my finger, I flicked Goldie's earring. She awoke and started to say something, but I hushed her. We looked in unison at my sleeping mother, then exchanged knowing glances. Goldie's lips were, as usual, glazed with cerise lipstick.

I sat down beside Goldie and drew from my pouch a small peppermint candy. I held out my tongue and placed the candy on its tip. She laughed silently and held out her tongue. Pressing our lips and mouths together, we transferred the candy from my tongue to hers. The taste of her thickly applied lipstick filled my mouth with voluptuous joy.

Just as we began parting our faces, Mother stirred. I ducked behind Goldie, who was closer to Mother.

"What are you doing?" Mother said.

I crouched down on the floor on all fours, too low for Mother to see me.

"You little whore. You think you can get away with that in this household?"

As quickly and quietly as I could, I scooted toward the door, parted the beaded curtain, and snuck out.

"In this household, we don't put up with maids who lead masters astray."

I tiptoed away.

Why did I sneak out and leave Goldie to face Mother's wrath alone? Perhaps at first I thought Mother had not clearly seen our kiss, and that if I slipped out unnoticed Goldie could convince her she had only imagined things. After hearing my mother's subsequent words, however, surely I could no longer cling to that illusion. Why *even then* did I abscond and leave Goldie to her fate?

I had a feeble excuse: everything took place rapidly, there was little time to think. That was not the real reason. The real reason, which I did not understand at the time, was that I was a selfish, spoiled child, concerned only with the satisfaction of my lust, caring little for the fate of a mere serving girl.

That evening, Amber, having gone out for a walk, returned to Happy Red Court looking somber. "I just heard some sad news. Your mother fired Goldie today. She summoned Goldie's mother and told her to take Goldie away."

Goldie's mother, father, and sister all worked for our household. As far as I knew, she had no relatives outside, no one to take her in now that she couldn't live in our mansion.

I felt nauseous and couldn't eat dinner. Later, I tossed and turned in bed, unable to sleep. Again and again I went over in my mind the rapid succession of events that had led to Goldie's firing. Poor Goldie. What would happen to her if she had no place to go? Would my mother be so cruel as to force her out, even under those circumstances?

The next morning, I dragged myself to Jia Clan School. When I returned midday—a heavy, hot summer day, with gritty yellow dust hanging in the air—I had the feeling people were avoiding me. Maids would see me from a distance, but rather than making sure our paths crossed, as usually happened, they turned and headed the opposite direction.

Back at Happy Red Court, Amber seemed distant. She served me my lunch, but said nothing, showed none of her usual signs of affection.

"Amber, what's the matter?" I finally asked. "Everybody seems to be avoiding me, like I'm some kind of leper. Does it have to do with Goldie?"

Amber hung her head. "Second Master, there's something you need to know, and I guess I'm the one who has to tell you." She paused, tears came to her eyes.

"What? Tell me now."

"This morning they found Goldie's body at the bottom of the well near the entrance to the garden. She was dead."

I felt as if a stone wall had collapsed on top of me.

Goldie had killed herself. Because of me. My lasciviousness, combined with my cowardice in failing to shield her from my mother's anger, had caused Goldie—beautiful, alluring Goldie—to throw herself into a well. Goldie's death would haunt me for the rest of my life.

I staggered around Happy Red Court, gasping for air. Amber said nothing. I sensed she knew the whole story and was as disgusted with me as I was myself. I needed to go outside and be alone.

I slowly shuffled around the garden, trembling all over. I didn't cry; I was barely able to breathe. I covered my face with my hands.

I heard footsteps and looked through my fingers. Standing

barely an arm's length in front of me was ... my father.

"What are you doing, you moron? You look pathetic."

Father stared at me with unremitting hostility. "What I don't understand is this: You have nothing to do, other than amuse yourself. You don't study, you don't work, you devote yourself entirely to your own pleasure. Yet you walk around like you're the most miserable person on earth. I simply do not understand."

I said nothing. Speech was beyond me. After a tense silence, my father swept past me on the path. Two cronies followed.

I returned to Happy Red Court; the outside world was too frightening. Once back in the cocoon of my cottage, I took to bed, not to sleep, but to go over in my mind the tragic sequence of events that had led to Goldie's death. Amber kept to another part of the cottage.

Two hours later, we heard a knock at the door. When we opened it, two of my father's pages stood there. They demanded I come to Father's study.

I shriveled with fear.

The pages led me to the closed door of the study and knocked. "Bring him in," my father shouted. The air inside was stale, hot, and dusty; the lighting, dim. Father always had dabs of a poisonous paste planted around his study to kill rats and preserve his precious books. The heat was now causing this paste to exude a putrid smell.

Father stood in front of his rosewood scholar's desk, sweating, breathing heavily. His fists were clenched, his knuckles stuck out like knots on a branch. The two cronies who'd been with him in the garden were also there. They kept looking at each other, their eyes and faces tense.

"Come here," Father shouted at me. I stepped forward, passing rows of open shelves filled with Confucian books, all bound in dusty black silk.

"Get some heavy bamboo rods and some rope," Father said to the two pages.

For a few breaths, the pages cast worried looks at each other. Then they obediently left the room. The two cronies cringed backwards, their eyes wide with disbelief. I prepared myself for a beating.

The pages were gone about five minutes. Father's study seemed as hot as the inside of a pottery kiln. He said nothing to me, instead he paced back and forth in front of his scholar's desk, muttering to himself and making jerky motions with his head. I looked down and said nothing. The two cronies slowly crept away from my father and tried to make themselves as inconspicuous as possible.

The two pages returned with heavy rope and two thick bamboo rods.

"Close the door and bolt it," Father said. I heard the thud of the door closing and the metallic sound of the bolt.

My father pointed to a long pine bench at the back of his study. "Bring that here." The pages dutifully moved the bench to the center of the room.

"Now strip him and tie him up." The young men, only a few years older than I, looked as frightened as I felt. They had never done anything like this before. They turned to me, their faces apologetic.

I voluntarily began to strip down to my green linen underwear, and as I took off my outer garments, the pages carried them away. Then I lay down on the bench, face down, and the two pages tied me up with the heavy rope. The room felt even hotter than before, sweat was starting to soak my underwear.

"Now gag him." Somehow a gag appeared. I couldn't tell from where; by now I was facing the floor. When the pages brought the gag to the front of my face, I realized it was grotesquely oversized. The pages tried to put the gag into my mouth, but their respectful pushes were not enough. It simply wouldn't fit.

"Get out of the way," Father said. He pushed the pages aside, reached his hand under my face, and, with a single angry blow, stuffed the huge gag into my mouth. My jaw felt as if it had been ripped apart.

Father stepped back. "Now beat him!"

The pages took up the bamboo rods and began striking me on the buttocks. They were obviously playing their roles unwillingly. Their blows landed without force, as if for show.

"You're not beating him, you're trying to protect him, you traitors!" Father shouted. "Get out of here, you useless dogs!" I heard Father shove the pages aside.

My father himself now took up one of the bamboo rods and began hitting me. His blows were a thousand times heavier than those of the pages. Each of my father's blows landed with a loud crack and sent a spasm of pain through my entire body. The blows were not just to my buttocks: Father's wild aim landed on every part of my backside. Soon fire erupted from my neck to my heels.

Craning my neck, I saw Father's red, sweaty face contorted in anger. His eyes bulged and he panted, spewing metallic breath into the hot, dusty air.

The two cronies stepped forward. "Please, Lord Jia, you'll harm your health if you continue like this. It's a hot day. For your own sake, take a rest."

"You don't have a monster for a son, like I do. He's a rapist!—"

A rapist? I couldn't believe my ears. Father had always had a habit of making false accusations against me, but this was a new low. Where had he come up with this? I wanted to shout out a denial of Father's accusation but couldn't; the gag prevented me.

"—His disgusting behavior has gone on long enough. I need to teach him a lesson he'll never forget." Father's voice was becoming hoarse from shouting.

The cronies retreated. From my face-down position, I could see their shoes face each other and hear the two men talk quietly. After a moment, they unbolted the door and left the room.

Father continued to beat me with the thick bamboo rod. Blood oozed out of my lower back, buttocks, and upper legs. I vomited up an acidulous mix of bile and food, but the monstrous gag in my mouth blocked the vomit from getting out, and the vomit ended up soaking the gag. I struggled to breathe. Sweat poured into my eyes and started blinding me. The heavy, dusty air enveloped me like a shroud.

With one of his blows, Father shattered the bamboo rod. I heard and felt it crack into splinters. Father cursed, threw the broken rod down, picked up the other rod, and continued the beating.

Dozens of blows later, I heard the door open and several pairs of footsteps enter. "What is going on?" The voice of my mother.

Father again hammered the bamboo rod onto my prostrate body.

My mother's feet went toward Father's. I heard grunts, a scuffle; my parents' legs swayed back and forth. Suddenly, the bamboo rod dropped onto the slate floor with a loud clatter.

"You're trying to stop me from doing my duty," Father shouted. "I'm an unfilial son for fathering this degenerate. Now that I've gotten this far along, I need to finish the job and put him down like the vermin he is. Bring me some rope so I can strangle him."

Mother's feet drew back from his. "If you want to kill him, kill me too! He's my only surviving son. Without him, I have nothing left. If Baoyu and I die together, at least I'll have someone to take care of me in the next world."

Mother came over, knelt beside me, and cradled my head in her hands. "You poor boy." Father was silent.

Mother directed her maids to remove the vomit-soaked gag from my mouth and untie the ropes from my wrists and ankles. Even then, the taste of vomit and bile remained in my mouth, my jaw muscles throbbed, my backside from my shoulders to my calves screamed with pain, my body was drowning in sweat, and blood was dripping onto the floor.

"Her Old Ladyship is coming," a woman said.

"Oh no," said my father.

Three pairs of feet entered the room: my grandmother, supported on either side by a maid. Grandmother hobbled toward me as fast as her aged legs would carry her. "What has happened? Baoyu, you poor child. I can't believe this." She bent over and stroked my head. "Oh Baoyu."

Grandmother straightened and faced my father. "Are *you* responsible for this?"

Father broke out crying.

"Answer my question."

"Yes," he managed between sobs.

"You pathetic worm. How disgusting can you get? Are you trying to kill your own son? You are sick, completely sick. You can't even act like a human being. You're not my son, you're some sort of savage beast that wandered in from a garbage heap."

My father fell to his knees in front of Grandmother, bobbed up and down in multiple kowtows, trembling like a leaf in the wind. Tears and sweat streamed down his red face. "I was only trying to discipline my son, like a father should. Everything I did was for the honor of our family. Please, Mother, I can't bear your harsh words."

"*You can't bear my harsh words!* What about Baoyu? Don't you think it's a lot harder for him to bear your beating than it is for you to bear my harsh words? Do you ever think about anybody but yourself?"

Father responded with more tears, kowtows, and strangled apologies.

"You claim you did this for the honor of our family. Let me ask you a question: Did your father ever beat *you* like this?"

My father, his forehead and hands on the floor, said nothing, instead he continued to blubber incomprehensibly.

"Well, did he?"

"No."

"I can't live in this household anymore," Grandmother said. She turned to the crowd of servants that by now filled the room. "Pack up my belongings and ready some carriages. Baoyu, his mother, and I are moving out. We'll go back to Nanjing and live with *my* family. At least there they have some human decency."

She turned back to my father. "We'll be gone, so you can indulge yourself as much as you want. You can beat the servants, you can beat the walls for all I care. But you can't beat Baoyu. I won't let you destroy his life."

My father remained on his knees, crying. "You're all against me."

The servants made some perfunctory moves toward obeying Grandmother's orders, but everyone realized her talk about moving back to Nanjing was hyperbole, not a serious plan. Meanwhile, a group of maids had gathered around my bench and were trying to figure out what to do with me. Several maids tried to help me stand up, but that was a mistake: in my weakened condition, I could not rise. Finally, Rosebud, Grandmother's chief maid, called for my pages and ordered that a wicker couch be brought in so that I could be transferred onto it, still face down, then moved out of my father's study.

While we were waiting for the wicker couch to arrive, my father, sobbing and sniffling, started to approach me. "What do you think you're doing?" Grandmother said. "Are you hoping to see him die? Get out of here." My father left the room. Evicted by Grandmother from his own study.

The pages transferred me to the wicker couch and moved me to Grandmother's courtyard. A doctor had been summoned. He concluded that, although I had deep bruises, gashes, and contusions from my upper back down to my calves, I had no broken bones. With this, I asked to be moved back to Happy Red Court, and Grandmother agreed. Six pages carried me, lying prone on the wicker couch, from Father's study to my cottage. I must have looked like the deceased in a funeral procession.

8

Back at Happy Red Court, no longer surrounded by crowds of people and a family crisis, excruciating pain from both my backside and my jaw overwhelmed me. Everything from my shoulders to my calves felt as if it were being roasted over a raging fire. The over-stretched jaw muscles on both sides of my face tortured me.

No matter how many times or how many ways I readjusted myself, no matter whether I lay face down, on my side, or somewhere in between, I could not escape agonizing pain. Baochai, always helpful in an emergency, brought over a salve compounded of corydalis root, frankincense resin, and feverfew. It brought some relief, but still I lay in my bed consumed with what seemed to be fresh waves of beatings every few minutes. I never knew pain could be so intense.

Amber left for a while; she wanted to "hear what people are saying." When she returned, she looked angry. "I learned what set off your father today."

"What?"

"A lot of your beating you owe to your sweet half-brother. Huan told your father you raped Goldie and that's why she threw herself into the well."

I squeezed my eyes shut and pounded my bed with my fists. I started to scream, but remembering the many listening ears and mouths eager to gossip that lurked nearby, I stifled it.

At least I now understood why Father had called me a rapist.

My recovery was lengthy and torturous. For a month I couldn't lie on my back; I had to lie either on my stomach or one of my sides. The muscles of my neck started to hurt from being constantly forced to twist. My shoulders ached from bearing weight so much of the time.

The worst part was that every day the dressings on my wounds had to be changed. Often the silk would stick and have to be peeled off. When that happened, I felt as if I were being flayed alive.

While the dressings were off, my entire backside was exposed to the world: my wounds gaping, pus oozing out, everything raw and red. My maids had always thought of me as their handsome prince. Now, watching the changing of my dressings, they held their hands over their mouths.

Fortunately, several pieces of good news arrived at my sickbed. The first day after my beating, Grandmother visited me at Happy Red Court. This was an occasion: Grandmother, with her bad legs, rarely ventured into the garden. She arrived with my mother and aunt, plus a battalion of maids and nurses. Happy Red Court was jammed by the time everyone was inside.

Grandmother sat down on a chair beside my bed. "Tell me what you'd like to eat."

I didn't feel hungry, I was in too much pain to think about food. Finally, I remembered a comforting, easy-to-digest food out of my childhood. "What about that soup we used to have with the little lotus leaves and lotus pods in it?"

"Have it made! Have it made!" Grandmother said. A maid scurried to relay the message to the communal kitchen.

"I think a lot of the reason for your frail health," Grandmother said, "is all the pressure you have on you from school. I don't want you going to school if it's going to injure your health. If you don't feel like going back to school, don't."

This remark both delighted and mystified me. I was delighted to be excused from school, seemingly for the rest of my life. But my frail health? I thought my health was excellent—as long as my father wasn't beating me half to death or my half-brother wasn't spilling wax onto my face.

Three days later, more good news arrived. My loving half-brother, Huan, and his mother had "decided they preferred to live on their own." They had moved to a small house our family had rented for them on the other side of Beijing. The move had already taken place. Fortunately, Tingting, Huan's sister, whom we all liked, was not part of the move; she remained in the garden, with the rest of us.

This news sent a wave of indulgent pleasure through my otherwise pain-racked body. Karmic retribution, in the form of an order of expulsion from Grandmother and Mother, had finally caught up with Little Brother. I particularly liked the part about Huan and his mother "preferring to live on their own." Grandmother and Mother probably needed a team of twenty mules to drag wormy Huan and his grasping concubine mother out of our mansion.

Still, a part of me regretted Huan's departure. I had been looking forward, once I recovered my health, to pummeling him into the dirt, strangling him to near asphyxiation, and leaving him battered and bruised. I was not a violent person, but for Little Brother I was willing to make an exception.

Four days after I heard about Huan, yet more good news arrived. My father had been appointed chief provincial examiner for Guangxi province. In other words, he would be the head of the group of officials who would administer the upcoming Provincial Examination there. He would be gone from Beijing for approximately a year.

My father had been ordered to leave for Guangxi within five days. Normally, when an official left Beijing to take up a post in one of the Middle Kingdom's far-flung provinces, his sons accompanied him on the first part of his journey, to an inn called the Pavilion of Parting, located on the southern outskirts of Beijing. I was told that, since I was in ill health, I was not expected to perform this ritual. In the end, I did not see my father before he left for Guangxi. I was too ill to visit him, he did not visit me. Even though he was going to be away for a year, he chose not to say goodbye to his only surviving legitimate son.

Was the timing—my father's departure coming so shortly after his savage beating of me—mere coincidence? I preferred to think that, as with Huan, karmic retribution was at work. I knew Father had been under consideration for an examiner's position for months, and that midsummer was the time of year when provincial examiners were appointed. Immediately after my beating, however, Grandmother had declared that she, my mother, and I were moving out of the mansion because we couldn't live in my father's house. How the tables had turned. Now the mansion was *our* house, my father was moving out.

My father's appointment added to the animosity I had long felt toward the examination system. A provincial examination, like the one my father was to administer in Guangxi, was a step below the Imperial Examination, the one he expected me to take in a few years. They were all part of the same Confucian system, though.

The examination system set the standard for what a gentleman was supposed to be. Passing the Imperial Examination was both a prerequisite for holding an official position and the mark of an educated man, a certificate of good character.

Yet at the apex of the examination system, at least in one province, was the very man I least respected in the world. The father who constantly berated me, who had beaten me to within a gnat's wing of death, who had not even cared to ask whether a lurid accusation leveled at me was true.

The system had set up my father as the model toward which we were all striving. I shuddered. This could not possibly be what Confucius had intended

Unfortunately, my convalescence dragged on long after the flow of good news stopped. In all, I was confined to Happy Red Court for three months. They seemed like years, even decades.

I missed the carnal delights that had been so large a part of my recovery from my face burn. For weeks after my beating, any movement in the middle part of my body caused extreme pain. Sex was not a possibility.

I wrote poetry, of course; I always wrote poetry in my youth. But one can write only so many poems a day, and after writing two or three, I still had many unoccupied hours on my hands.

My maids constantly tried to amuse me. Unfortunately, their ideas of amusement extended only to simple games of chance, and since they were going to so much extra trouble for me during my recovery, I couldn't say no to them all the time. I ended up spending endless hours playing dice and—a game as pointless as it sounds—guess-fingers.

Confined as I was, my thoughts turned inward. My reflections focused on some of the people in my life.

I thought about Goldie. To a degree, I was less harsh with myself than I had been immediately upon learning of her death. Factors apart from my lasciviousness and cowardice had contributed to Goldie's death: my mother's harshness, when leniency was an alternative; Goldie's rashness in choosing suicide, when her situation was by no means impossible.

Try as I might, however, I could not ignore my own grievous culpability. I wanted to go back and retrieve the moment in which I snuck out of Mother's room and left Goldie to face Mother's wrath alone. I wanted to substitute for that moment one in which I courageously stood between Goldie and my mother and told Mother the kissing was all my fault. Or failing that, one in which, as soon as I heard Mother had fired Goldie, I rushed to Mother, explained to her I was the one to blame, and begged and pleaded with her to take Goldie back.

Alas, those were only daydreams.

My thoughts turned to Daiyu as well. During my recovery, Daiyu made only a few brief visits to my bedside. I wondered why she remained distant.

One possibility was that she was squeamish. I remembered she had visited me only rarely when I was recovering from my burn. Perhaps comforting the sick was simply not a talent she possessed.

Another possibility was the melancholy I had first noticed when I found her crying and burying peach blossoms. I still didn't entirely understand the reasons for that.

One thing was certain: when I recovered from my beating, I would need to rebuild my relationship with Daiyu.

Always looming in my reflections was my father. To a tiny extent, I was willing to forgive him. If I had done as Huan claimed—raped Goldie—Father would have been justified in punishing me. He might, however, have taken the time to investigate whether Huan's accusation was true. Furthermore, any forgiveness I might have been willing to grant Father was dwarfed by the constant pain I felt and by the memory of his assault: "I need to put him down like the vermin he is. Bring me some rope so I can strangle him."

The more I thought about it, though, the more I decided Father's words didn't matter. I no longer cared if he hated me. What difference did it make if he wanted me dead?

I had absolutely no respect for my father. His pretensions to being a proper Confucian head of household were a joke. Our household was a travesty of a proper Confucian household.

According to Confucian principles of filial piety, the eldest male in a household should rule, and everyone else should be subservient to him. Who ruled our household? Grandmother. Ask anyone.

After my beating, I had seen my father grovel at Grandmother's feet, kowtow, cry, plead for her mercy. He, the eldest male, groveling to a female.

Not only that, in the struggle for physical possession of the bamboo rod that had taken place between my father and my mother, she had emerged the victor. My mother had bested my father in a contest of physical strength!

Within the space of a few minutes, Father had been humiliated by two different female members of his own household. Confucius would have been appalled. I wondered whether my father realized how pathetic he was.

As far as Father wanting to kill me was concerned, I now realized I had been far too servile in allowing my beating to proceed as far as it had. I needed to break free of the bonds of filial piety. If Grandmother and Mother had stood up to my father, I could have too. When he got back from his year-long posting in Guangxi, I would have to be on my guard, but I had seen what a weakling he was. If he came after me again, I would stand my ground.

I kept returning to two questions: Why did Father hate me so much? Why was he so subservient to Grandmother?

Over time, I worked my way to a theory that answered both questions simultaneously. Father had always yearned for Grandmother's love and attention, but never received them. My birth only made things worse. Once I was ensconced in her courtyard, Grandmother doted on me, lavished me with love, kisses, favors, presents, servants. She paid barely any attention at all to my father—her son.

Father regarded me as a rival for Grandmother's affections. Because she favored me, Father was jealous.

Huan, my father—what a sorry, envious lot my male relatives were.

9

AFTER THREE MONTHS of convalescence, I was fully recovered and ready to step out into the world. I decided to celebrate by burning all my Confucian books, the ones I had been studying at Jia Clan School. Now that I was never going back to school, I had no need for them.

My maids and I gathered in the courtyard of Happy Red Court. I placed the pile of books in the center and applied the flame. The sight of Confucian admonitions crackling into flames and dissolving into dust and smoke helped assuage the anger I felt—against my father, against Confucianism, against the examination system. My only regret was that, for weeks afterward, I kept finding half-burnt Confucian pages nestled among my beautiful plantains and caught in the branches of my splendid crabapple tree.

A few days later, Grandmother announced that Spring had commissioned a Taoist purification ceremony to be held at the Temple of the Clear Void, located in the Western Hills. Spring herself would not be there; she could not leave the Forbidden City. Grandmother would represent the family and burn the incense. The entertainment would consist of three scenes from three different operas, the scenes chosen by lot in a noisy Taoist ritual. Grandmother wanted all of us to go with her.

Several of us were leery. It would be a long day: the distance to the temple was considerable, and the opera scenes could go on and on. In addition, the temple had a mixed reputation as a place to visit. No one wanted to say no to Grandmother, though, and in the end we all agreed to go.

Normally, our household maids were forbidden to venture beyond our mansion's triple gate. However, our family would need at least a few maids to accompany us on this journey, and every maid in the mansion envisioned herself as being among the few. My maids—everyone's maids—begged and schemed to be included on the list of servants who would go. Since most of us were soft-hearted, the list grew and grew. In the end, a procession of two hundred people, forty horses, and twenty carts made the trek to the temple.

The trumpeting colors of our procession put to shame the drab gray construction that lined our route. Our carts overflowed with large red boxes of temple donations. Our bearers and grooms wore green uniforms. I wore a turquoise robe and rode a white horse.

Crowds lined the streets as we wove our way through and out of the city. We passed scores of entrances to hutongs, where the poor of Beijing lived. In front of the hutongs, rows of people dressed in patched robes and fraying straw sandals lined up two or three deep to gaze in awe at our extravagant procession.

I was a particular object of admiration, mounted as I was on my white Ferghana steed, seated in a saddle decorated with opals and agates. The adulation embarrassed me and set me to thinking.

Why should I, by accident of birth, be up here? Why should they, by accident of birth, be down there? Should I feel guilty that fate had endowed me with enormous wealth and privilege?

That seemed unfair. I had not *chosen* to be born into the Jia family. Plus, whatever the crowds below might think, being a member of the Jia family was not all parties, fawning servants, and silk sheets. I thought of my recent beating.

Was that the end of the discussion, though?

Granted, I had not chosen to be born into the Jia family, I continued to live as a Jia, continued to wallow in all the luxury and privilege my fortuitous birth afforded me. Was I guilty simply by reason of that?

How could that be? I was only a boy, only fifteen. Was it a crime for a boy of fifteen to live with his family?

That answer was good enough for now. Did it imply, however, that as I grew older, as it became a reasonable possibility I could separate myself from my family and create my own independent existence, I would be guilty if I did not do so?

I had no answer to that question; I had not thought about it before. I realized that in the future, I needed to.

When we reached the temple, the abbot greeted us in the first courtyard. Abbot Li had huge white eyebrows, like pelts of arctic animals; a long wispy beard he kept fingering; and an unctuous, ingratiating manner. Today he wore full Taoist regalia: dark red robe, mantle of crane feathers, nine-story tiara, and scarlet shoes with upturned toes.

Abbot Li was an old favorite of Grandmother's; she insisted all of us in the younger generation address him as "Grandfather Li." One reason Grandmother liked Abbot Li so much was that he was the only person she knew who was older than she: he was said to be well up into his eighties.

Grandmother and the abbot exchanged small talk, while we members of the family stood in a reverent circle. The courtyard smelled like a privy; I was sure priests had been living there until a day or two before. The smoke of innumerable joss sticks dirtied the air.

"How is your grandson?" Abbot Li asked.

"Come here, Baoyu," Grandmother said. "Say hello to Grandfather Li."

"Hello, Grandfather Li." I bowed and tried to smile.

The abbot inspected me closely. "He's grown some more. He looks very healthy."

"He may look all right, but he's delicate, and his father has been ruining his health by making him study day and night."

The abbot let out a noncommittal grunt. I said nothing. I didn't agree that I was delicate, but neither did I want to get into a public argument with Grandmother.

The abbot, fingering his beard, sized me up some more. "You know, he looks to me to be the spitting image of the Old Duke."

Grandmother sighed. "You're right. Of all my sons and grandsons, he's the only one who takes after the Old Duke."

The Old Duke was my great-grandfather, founder of our Jia dynasty. He was one of the prior Emperor's most successful generals, victor at important battles on the northwestern frontier. To him had been awarded the mansion in which we still lived, the annual stipend we still received from the Forbidden City, and the hereditary title of nobility—Duke of Rongguo—that First Uncle, elder brother to my father, now held.

"We're probably the only two still around who remember the Old Duke," the abbot said. "Everybody else is too young."

Again Grandmother sighed. "I'm afraid that's true."

"By the way, the other day I was visiting a certain family, whom you probably know but I won't name. They had a beautiful daughter, age fifteen. I thought of how it was becoming time to arrange a marriage for young master Baoyu here. This young lady would be an excellent choice. She has the looks, the intelligence, and the family. But I didn't know your thinking on the subject and didn't want to do anything rash, so I didn't say anything. If you're interested, I'm on very good terms with this family and can easily go back."

I froze. Nor was I the only one: everyone in the circle around Grandfather Li now exuded tension.

Everyone except Grandmother, that was. She gave out a hearty laugh. "One time we had a monk tell his fortune, and the monk said Baoyu shouldn't marry young. So I think we'll wait a while to settle anything definite. But by all means, keep your eyes open. Good looks and a sweet disposition, that's all we're looking for. We don't care about riches or rank. Just good looks and a sweet disposition."

I stole a look at Daiyu. Her face had turned bright red.

There were many, many ways to sing Daiyu's praises. Saying she had a "sweet disposition" was, unfortunately, not one of them. Baochai, on the other hand, was the very model of a sweet disposition. Grandmother might be signaling a preference for Baochai over Daiyu as my future bride.

A monk approached the abbot, bowed, and said, "The ceremonies are about to begin." Grandmother began hobbling toward the shrine, and our family circle broke up.

I raced to be beside Daiyu. When I caught up with her, she, pointing to the abbot, was asking my half-sister, Tingting, "Who was that old fool?"

"A senile social climber who's probably hoping he can make some money out of the deal," I answered on Tingting's behalf.

Daiyu looked at me. Her wrinkled nose and puckered eyebrows radiated disgust. "Who asked *you*?" She marched off, leaving me behind.

The courtyard where the opera scenes were performed was not as smelly as the first, but close. Daiyu took sick—a persistent cough—during the first scene. I didn't feel well myself.

Meanwhile, Grandmother was upset that some of our relatives had sent offerings to the temple to be included as part of our ceremony. She pointed to a row of carts containing red boxes. "I wanted this just to be a small family outing. Now it's gotten blown up to all this."

Our procession that morning had included two hundred people, forty horses, and twenty carts clattering through the heart of Beijing. Grandmother had been happy to view that as a small family outing.

By the end of the second opera scene everyone had had enough, and we all went home early. Riding my white horse, I looked like a prince but had a headache and felt depressed. I knew Daiyu's ride home would be tense. She was sharing a carriage with Baochai.

Early the next morning, I went to Bamboo Lodge to see Daiyu. She was standing in her dayroom, thin as a candle wick, talking to Swallow. "When you do the room, leave the window open so mama and papa sparrow can get back in. And put the lion doorstop at the bottom of the blind, so it won't flap."

"Good morning, Daiyu."

She ignored me.

"Good morning, Daiyu."

Again she ignored me.

"Daiyu, why are you ignoring me?"

She looked at me. Her knitted eyebrows, once so piquant,

were turning into permanent frown lines. "I saw how angry you got yesterday with that Li character when he tried to interfere with your marriage plans. I don't want to suffer the same fate."

"You're complaining about *my* being angry with Li? You were just as angry."

"I need to remember my place here. I don't have what you and your family are looking for in a potential bride. I don't have anything gold to match your silly jade pendant."

"Cousin, don't be ridiculous." I moved toward her and reached for her hand.

She jerked her arm back. "Don't touch me!"

I apologized, and shortly after that withdrew from Bamboo Lodge.

A week later came Baochai's fifteenth birthday. Grandmother, always eager for a party, decided to celebrate the occasion with an afternoon of drinking, feasting, and opera scenes. Since we still owned the twelve child actresses we had purchased for Spring's visit, putting on opera scenes required no extra expenditure on our part.

Even if we had tried, we could not have staged an event more diabolically calibrated to exalt Baochai and offend Daiyu than Baochai's birthday party turned out to be. Baochai, seated next to Grandmother, was the guest of honor, center of everyone's attention. The selection of the opera scenes to be performed followed a familiar ritual. Grandmother insisted Baochai choose. Baochai refused and insisted Grandmother choose. Grandmother again refused and insisted Baochai choose. Baochai then chose a group of scenes she knew Grandmother would enjoy: noisy, lively ones from operas like *Liu Er Pawns His Clothes* and *The Drunken Monk*. Grandmother was not one for soft music or subtlety.

The opera scenes, which were performed not in our main courtyard but rather on a temporary stage in Grandmother's courtyard, went on until dusk. By that time, Grandmother, who adored young people, had fallen in love with two of the child actresses: the one who played the heroines and the one who took the clown roles.

Grandmother invited the two over to our tables. The player of heroines was eleven, we learned, and the clown only nine. Surprised at how young they were, Grandmother ordered that the two be given delicacies from our feast—lotus root, fried sesame-seed cakes, rolls filled with pine nuts and cream cheese. She also gifted them with strings of copper coins.

After receiving their presents, the two child actresses circulated among our tables to thank each of us individually. Extravagant makeup covered the face of the younger of the two, the player of clown roles. Her eyebrows, painted darkest black against her white-painted face, descended in a tight arc toward the bridge of her nose and once there met in the middle. A feathering of other lines gave her face the look of a perpetual frown.

Making her way among the guests, the little clown-actress came to Peony, the youngest, funniest, and most uninhibited of our band of cousins. Peony broke out giggling.

"What are you laughing about?" her half-sister, Lotus, asked.

Peony pointed to the clown-actress' made-up face. "She looks just like Cousin Daiyu."

Everyone laughed. Caught up in the moment, even I laughed, until I turned my head and saw Daiyu's red face and contorted features. Daiyu left shortly after, not saying goodbye to anyone.

Later that evening, I went to Bamboo Lodge. Daiyu refused to let me in, and I ended up standing outside, trying to talk to her through a window. "Why be angry at me? I wasn't the one who compared you to the clown."

Daiyu's voice came through the parchment. "You laughed, along with the rest of them. I'm just an object of ridicule, lower than an actress. I guess I know where I stand in this household."

"Please, Daiyu. Everyone respects you. It was just a joke."

"Get out of here, and never come back again."

For five minutes, I stared at the parchment window, watching the dim flicker of a single candle inside. I said nothing, she said nothing. Occasionally, she coughed. Finally, I walked away and returned to Happy Red Court.

Daiyu's rejection plunged me into despair. For three years after her arrival at our mansion, we had been so close. Now we seemed to be drifting apart. I wanted to get back to our earlier intimacy, but ever since she had returned from her winter-time journey to attend her father's funeral, a barrier seemed to have grown up between us.

I could understand her feeling of isolation. Both her mother and her father were dead; she was an orphan. Baochai, by contrast, had, if not a father, at least a mother. Not only that, Baochai's mother—my aunt, my mother's sister—lived in another part of our mansion and came over almost every day to have tea or dine with Grandmother and Mother. Baochai had a champion, Daiyu did not.

I had tried to reassure Daiyu of my affections, but she had pushed me away. Unfortunately, I could not give her what she wanted most: a firm assurance we would someday be married. The right to choose my future bride belonged to Grandmother. In a family like ours, even a noble son held limited sway.

What worried me most was that Daiyu was working against herself. She wanted to marry me, but her erratic behavior was reducing the chances of that happening. Grandmother wanted my bride to be someone with a "sweet disposition." Daiyu's recent behavior fell far short of that description. I wished she would bend a little, try to be more ingratiating to Grandmother and the rest of the family, but pretending to be someone she was not was alien to her nature.

To see Daiyu—brilliant, talented, beautiful—growing bitter and full of self-pity broke my heart. I was losing the best part of my life and felt powerless to right the situation.

If I did not spend my entire time worrying about Daiyu, it was only because I now had someone else to worry about—Amber.

Winter came early that year, a sharp cold snap. Immediately, Amber caught a cold. She needed medical attention, but I was hesitant to summon our family physician, Dr. Wang, because I didn't want Grandmother or Mother to hear about her illness. Our family generally preferred that sick servants leave the mansion and return only when recovered. The fact that Amber had family in Beijing would give Grandmother and Mother even more reason to apply the rule in her case.

As Amber's illness lingered, however, I decided I had no choice but to summon Dr. Wang. Soon the doctor arrived, accompanied by four pages. Amber was resting in bed. She had her own bed now; since the onset of her illness, we had stopped sleeping together. The red embroidered curtains in front of her bed were completely closed. The doctor seated himself on a stool in front of the bed and said, "You may present your hand."

Amber's right hand emerged through a slit in the curtains. Dr. Wang bent down, then drew back, a shocked look on his face.

The nail on Amber's little finger was as long as the finger itself and colored red with balsam. Amber prided herself on having two long red nails, one on the little finger of each hand. Unfortunately, the doctor was unwilling to deal with a hand sprouting a nail so lascivious.

While I was pondering what to do, one of the nurses who had accompanied Dr. Wang to my cottage threw a handkerchief over Amber's hand. This seemed to placate the doctor, for he again bent over and began feeling Amber's pulse.

Dr. Wang sat with his fingers on Amber's wrist, nodding his head, his eyes closed. After what seemed an eternity, he let go and said, "You may remove your hand." The hand disappeared behind the curtains.

"She has a cold, and perhaps some indigestion as well," Dr. Wang said, confirming my own thoughts. "I will provide a prescription for a tisane." His pages presented him with a pink form, and he began writing. His prescription called for angelica, orange peel, and white peony root, in small doses.

Soon Happy Red Court was fragrant with the smell of boiling herbs. "Tell them to do it in the tea kitchen," Amber said. "You'll stink up the whole place if you do it in here."

"I want it in here," I said, "I love the smell of boiling herbs."

The next several days brought both good news and bad. Despite my fears that calling in Dr. Wang would lead to a demand that Amber leave the mansion, not a peep was heard from Grandmother or Mother. Sadly, Amber's illness dragged on.

Several days later, I needed to attend a two-day birthday party for one of my cousins. Neither Grandmother nor Mother would be going; I would represent the family.

The morning of the first day of the party, I rose early to check on Amber's condition. She was no better, and her frequent coughing had kept her awake most of the night.

I gulped down some date-and-lotus-seed broth and pickled ginger, then began dressing. The day was freezing cold, and cloudy skies promised snow. I put on a brown velvet vest lined with fox fur and over that a scarlet felt cape embellished with gold thread.

I stopped by Grandmother's on my way out. "Is it snowing?" she asked.

"No, but it looks like it will."

"Rosebud, get that cape we were looking at yesterday."

The cape Rosebud brought back looked like no garment I had ever seen before. Knee-length, fastened at the neck with a gold broach, it shimmered with iridescent greens, blues, and browns, and had a pattern of repeating oval shapes that looked like eyes.

"It's made of peacock feathers," Grandmother said. "It came from Russia. Somehow the Russians manage to weave the feathers into these beautiful capes."

I threw myself next to Grandmother and hugged and kissed her in gratitude.

"You'd better take care of it," she said. "It's one of a kind. You could never replace it."

"Don't worry, I'll take good care of it."

"Don't drink too much and come home early."

"Yes, of course."

At my cousin's birthday party, I drank what I considered to be a reasonable amount and came home at what I considered a reasonable hour. When I dismounted from my horse back in our stable, however, I noticed a burnt spot, a thumb-sized hole, near the lapel on the right-hand side of the peacock cape. A wave of shame coursed through me.

I managed to conceal the hole when I went to say good night to Grandmother. Her room was dark, and I stood in a way that created a crease exactly where the hole was. This could only be a temporary expedient. Grandmother reminded me the next day was my cousin's actual birthday, and I should be sure to wear the peacock cape *that* day.

I needed to have the hole repaired immediately. Still, the first thing I did upon returning to Happy Red Court was to see how Amber was. The news was discouraging: she did not feel any better, she had spent a difficult day coughing and spitting up phlegm—and wondering whether the doctor's diagnosis was correct. I tried to comfort her.

After attending to Amber, I showed the burn hole to Pansy, my senior maid after Amber. "It must have been caused by a spark from your hand warmer," she said. "We've got to get it fixed quickly. Otherwise, Her Old Ladyship will blame us maids, and with Amber sick, things will look even worse."

Pansy admitted that repairing a peacock cape was beyond her capabilities as a seamstress, and my other fourteen or so maids were even less likely candidates for so difficult a sewing job. Despite her two long red fingernails, the expert seamstress at Happy Red Court was Amber. But I could not ask Amber, sick as she was, to undertake a rush sewing job.

We decided to send the cape outside to a professional tailor. Calling in Tealeaf, my chief page, Pansy told him, "Go to the hutong where all the tailor shops are and find a respectable one. Even though it's late, most of them should still be open. Tell the tailor the cape has to be completely mended and back to us by tomorrow morning. We'll pay whatever he wants. Also, make sure not a word of this gets back to Her Old Ladyship."

I spent the next several hours watching over Amber and waiting nervously for Tealeaf's return. When he finally reappeared, he was almost in tears. "I tried every tailor's shop I could find that was open. Every place I went, they took one look at the cape and said, 'I've never worked on anything like that before. I'm afraid I can't help you.' Please, Second Master, forgive me. I did the best I could. Don't tell Her Old Ladyship it was my fault."

Pansy was now beside herself with worry. "Her Old Ladyship is going to be furious. She'll probably fire us all." Even I was beginning to panic. To me she may have been "Grandmother" rather than "Her Old Ladyship," but I too was frightened of her wrath.

"What's going on?" a weak and parched voice asked. It came from the other side of Happy Red Court. From Amber's sickbed.

Pansy explained the situation to Amber. "Let me see the cape," Amber said.

Pansy brought over the shimmering garment. Amber strained to sit up, and once up needed a few breaths to regain her composure. Then she examined the cape, cupping in and out the spot where the hole was.

"We can fix it here," she said at last. "The whole thing is made out of just two things: peacock feathers and gold thread. We've got both of them here."

"Nobody can do the work," I said.

"I'll do it."

"No, you're sick. You'll make yourself worse. I forbid it. *Lie back down*, Amber."

"I'll do it."

Pansy fetched gold thread from our sewing cupboard; I plucked a peacock feather from the collection we kept in a blue-and-white vase; and we brought the two materials to Amber's bedside. She was still sitting up in her bed, her skin ashen, sweat dripping down her face.

Amber picked up the gold thread and a needle. It was almost midnight; there was no light other than candlelight. I cringed as she struggled to thread the needle in the meager light provided by the three-flame candelabra I held next to her.

Amber worked on the cape for four hours, sweating profusely, periodically pausing for long, painful coughing spells, spitting up phlegm. I did what little I could to help her: brought her hot water, urged her to take rest breaks, put a squirrel cape over her shoulders. When she was done sewing, she fluffed up the feathers with a soft brush, handed the cape to me, and sank back into her bed, exhausted.

The result was everything I could have hoped for: you could not tell where the hole had once been. I thanked Amber profusely and watched her fall asleep.

I slept for little more than an hour, then rose for day two of the birthday party. Wearing the peacock cape, I dropped by Grandmother's. Once again, she could not keep her eyes off the spectacular garment. She had no idea of the turmoil it had caused over the previous night. The cape was likewise a cynosure of admiration at my cousin's party. Even if I was sleepy, my clothing was sumptuous.

Tired and slightly drunk, I arrived back at Happy Red Court well after dark. Pansy stood before the doorway, in tears. "Second Master, I'm so glad you're home. Something terrible has happened."

"What?"

She held up a spittoon. "Amber's been coughing and spitting up phlegm all day. A few minutes ago, when she did it again, I looked at it, and ...." Her arms trembling, Pansy handed me the spittoon.

Inside was a large lump of phlegm. Inside the phlegm was a coil of purplish blood, throbbing with a life of its own.

I felt as if a cold knife had severed my spine. This was every young person's nightmare. I had tried not to think about the possibility before, but now I could not avoid it. Amber had consumption.

10

THREE WEEKS PASSED. Amber's condition worsened, stabilized, worsened again. She pushed away most of her meals, her weight dropped precipitously. With increasing frequency, she spat up bloody phlegm.

I dared not call in Dr. Wang again. If I told him about Amber's bloody phlegm, he would be sure to report the fact to Grandmother and Mother, and they would want Amber out of the mansion immediately. A cold was one thing; consumption, another.

Instead, knowing the best medicine for almost any illness is bird's nest soup, I contacted Baochai. Her family's pawn business traded bird's nest, and upon learning of Amber's condition, she gave me a generous amount. As far as I knew, neither Grandmother nor Mother knew anything of Amber's illness.

Then, one night shortly after sunset, a loud knock rattled the door of Happy Red Court. We opened the door, and five older women servants walked in. I recognized my mother's chief maid, three wives of managers of ours, and one woman who was both First Aunt's chief maid and wife of one of our managers.

This last one—the one who was both my aunt's chief maid and wife of one of our managers—seemed to be in charge. I knew her simply as Wang Shan's Wife; if she had a name of her own, no one ever used it. Squat in build, dark in complexion, she had an insincere smile and an oily demeanor.

Wang Shan's Wife had long been an antagonist of the maids living in the garden. She felt they were overindulged, overclothed, and overbejeweled. At bottom, Wang Shan's Wife was jealous. The garden maids were young; she was old.

I vaguely remembered Wang Shan's Wife and Amber had had some sort of altercation in the past. Certainly Amber, with her long red fingernails and love of jewelry, was the type of garden maid Wang Shan's Wife detested. Wang Shan's Wife's presence in Happy Red Court was not a good omen for Amber. At the time, however, Amber was safely tucked away in a bed located in a far corner of the cottage, the curtains in front of her bed drawn. I could reasonably hope Wang Shan's Wife would not notice Amber's presence, let alone her illness.

By now, my three live-in maids other than Amber were lined up behind me. Facing us were Wang Shan's Wife and the four other older women.

Wang Shan's Wife broke the silence. "The reason the five of us are here tonight is because we've had some problems in the garden. Serious problems. We've had at least two thefts. Because of these problems, Their Ladyships have ordered us to search the belongings of all the maids living in the garden. So if you"—Wang Shan's Wife indicated the maids lined up behind me—"will get out all your chests and boxes and open them up, we can carry out Their Ladyships' orders."

My maids seemed bewildered, but I told them to comply. They each brought out their own chests and boxes and, acting in concert, also brought out Amber's. One by one, each maid opened her chests and boxes, and the five older women went through the contents, item by item. The women found nothing suspicious.

Finally, the five women came to Amber's chests and boxes. "Whose are these?" Wang Shan's Wife asked.

"Those are Amber's," I said. "I'll get the key."

"What about Amber herself? Doesn't she live here? Where is she?"

"She's ... not feeling well tonight. She's in bed."

"Oh," said Wang Shan's Wife, drawing out the word and lifting her eyebrows. "The young lady isn't feeling well. Maybe we should go get a look at her, see whether we need to bring in the doctor. As a matter of fact, wasn't Dr. Wang here just a few weeks ago to see Amber? Is she sick again? Let's go have a look."

Just at this moment, Amber emerged from her bed. Over the weeks of her illness, I had grown accustomed to her pallor and emaciation. Seen in the spotlight of the night's inquisition, however, her sickly appearance sent a shock through the room. Without a word, she went over to her chests and boxes, unlocked and opened them, turned them upside down, and dumped the contents onto the floor.

Wang Shan's Wife had lost all interest in the chests and boxes. "My, my, what do we have here? Looks like this young lady is seriously ill. I wonder if this has been properly reported to Their Ladyships."

I said nothing. Amber stifled a cough.

"Well, if it hasn't been, it certainly will be tomorrow morning,"

After a thorough search of Amber's belongings, which turned up nothing, the five women left.

The rest of that night was gruesome. Amber's condition worsened: she coughed up blood all night. I tried desperately to think of a way to prevent news of Amber's illness from reaching Mother, First Aunt, and Grandmother, but could not.

Meanwhile, news kept arriving from other parts of the garden. At the cottage of my half-sister, Tingting, she and Wang Shan's Wife had gotten into an argument, and Tingting had slapped Wang Shan's Wife in the face!

Good for Tingting! was my first thought. Then I realized the extent to which Tingting's courage reflected badly on me. Why, when the five women had first shown up, had I not simply told them to go away? I clearly outranked them: I was a master; they were mere servants.

The more I thought about it, the more ashamed of myself I became. Tingting was a girl and the child of a concubine. I, on the other hand, was "Second Master"—in Confucian theory, the second highest-ranking member of the family. Yet it had been Tingting, not me, who had stood up to Wang Shan's Wife.

Later, a junior maid scurried over to tell us that at the cottage belonging to my cousin Lotus, an incriminating letter had been found in a box belonging to a maid named Chess. I barely knew Chess, but still the news saddened me—the fall of another young girl just starting out in life. Besides, what sort of "incriminating letter" could one of our junior maids possibly possess?

Early the next morning, Grandmother summoned me. Some old friends of the family were visiting from Nanjing, and she wanted me to meet them. When I dutifully showed up, my aunt was present, but my mother was not. Nothing was said about any search of the garden. I deduced that whatever was going on, my mother was in charge. I greeted the family friends as politely as I could but left the gathering as soon as proper manners allowed.

As I was hurrying back to Happy Red Court, I encountered a small but sad procession. In the procession were the maid Chess—she of the incriminating letter—and four older women servants, two of whom I recognized from the night before. Chess was dragging a cotton bag behind her and crying uncontrollably.

I went up to the procession. "What's going on?"

"This is none of your business, Second Master," one of the women replied. "You should get back to your books."

"What has she done?"

"We're just carrying out Her Ladyship's orders, your mother's orders. If you want to ask questions, you should ask her."

Chess threw herself onto her knees in front of me. Her round face and upturned nose made her look pitiably young. "It's not their fault, they're just following orders. But Second Master, could you please go to Her Ladyship and beg her to forgive me?"

"Stop bothering him and get a move on," the older woman said. "You're not a maid here anymore. If you don't obey, I'll beat you." The four women yanked Chess away from me and pushed her ahead.

In an ideal world, I would have gone to my mother and

pleaded Chess' case. I was not living in an ideal world. I was desperately worried about Amber and could think only about getting back to Happy Red Court.

I entered to find my mother seated at my small table, calmly sipping a cup of tea. Standing behind her were several older women, including Wang Shan's Wife, a smug smile on her face. Opposite Mother was Amber, now unable to stand on her own, being held up by two older women. Amber was sweating and coughing; she looked emaciated and white as a bone; her hair was a tangled mess. Several of my junior maids were hurriedly stuffing her clothes into a cotton bag.

"I have dismissed Amber," Mother said in an icy tone. Though presumably speaking to me, Mother did not look at me. "I am appalled this sickness has gone on for so long and has become so serious without my being told about it. Certainly Amber and you and everyone else in this cottage have shown absolutely no sense of responsibility to the other residents of the garden. Your irresponsible conduct has placed their health in serious danger.

"I have also told Amber that, even if she recovers her health, we do not want her back in our employment. You may think that, because I live in my own courtyard and rarely go into the garden, I do not know what goes on here. I assure you, I do. I know only too well, Baoyu, that this whore standing before me has, ever since she entered your service, made it her sole mission in life to corrupt you and lead you astray. Bitch that she is, she has succeeded only too well.

"You are the only son I have left, Baoyu. I do not intend for you to spend your life consorting with whores."

Ten breaths of absolute silence followed. Then Amber had a coughing fit. One of the junior maids brought over a spittoon, and Amber spat up bloody phlegm.

Mother's tirade dumbfounded me.

Why now? Before Amber became sick, she and I had been intimate for nearly two years. If Mother had objections to our relationship, she should have voiced them earlier. Not now, when Amber was dying.

Who was this callous, hate-filled woman, sitting at my

table and drinking my tea? She looked exactly like my mother, yet my mother had always been gentle, kind, loving. Or at least so I had perceived her. Mother was perhaps not the brightest person on Earth, perhaps she spent too much time reading obscure Buddhist sutras. Never before, however, had I seen her vindictively destroy the life of another human being, as she was now doing to Amber.

Or had I? I remembered Goldie, the poor maid who had ended up at the bottom of a well. Had I seen my mother's true character in her cruelty toward Goldie, repeated now in her cruelty toward Amber?

I did not challenge my mother. So inculcated was I with the ideology of filial piety, so much was I a prisoner of the idea one must always obey one's parents, without question and without whimper, that I would no more have challenged my mother than I would have challenged the sun's right to shine in the sky.

After my beating, I had puffed out my chest and boasted that if my father tried to kill me again, I would stand up to him. I did not have the courage to stand up even to my mother. I claimed to be a rebel, a nonconformist. In truth, I was a coward.

Mother looked at Amber and the two women holding her up. "Get her out of here. Hold her at the gate until her cousin comes to pick her up." The women began dragging Amber out of Happy Red Court. Her feet slid along the floor as she was pulled forward. Another older woman picked up the bag with Amber's belongings and followed. Soon, the group was gone.

Mother next fixed her angry gaze on my junior maids—around fourteen of them, all stupefied, their mouths agape. "Let this be a lesson to the rest of you. I know everything that goes on here. If any of you step out of line, if any of you try to seduce my son, you will suffer the same fate as Amber."

Finally, Mother looked at me. Her face and eyes bore cold contempt. "You get back to your studies."

Mother took another leisurely sip of tea. Then she got up from my table and, with her entourage of older maids and manager's wives, slowly walked out of Happy Red Court.

For several minutes after Mother left, all of us at Happy Red Court were paralyzed with shock. When finally we came to life again, we began conferring about what we could do to help Amber.

"Don't worry, Second Master," said Pansy, who had taken over as my chief maid. "We maids were already talking about it this morning, while you were gone. Several of us have money we've saved up that we can give her. And Mrs. Song, the woman at the west gate who was always such a good friend of Amber's, has agreed to take everything over to Amber's cousin's house. But we can't do anything during the day: too many busybodies would be spying on us. Mrs. Song will go over right after sunset."

I agree to contribute money and what was left of the bird's nest Baochai had provided. I wanted to be more than simply a donor, however. I wanted to see Amber. I resolved to let several hours elapse after sunset, enough time for Mrs. Song to complete her mission. Then, I would go to Amber's cousin's house myself.

To prepare for my nighttime journey, I asked around about the cousin. I learned he had once worked for our household, as a cook. He had proved to be a drunkard, and we had fired him. He was now a bondservant in another household.

The cousin was married. Presumably, if anyone was going to take care of Amber, it would be the cousin's wife. I therefore made inquiries about her.

She had never worked for us but was known to many of our servants by reputation. The reputation was for sexual promiscuity. The cousin's wife even had a nickname. She was known as "the Mattress."

I remembered the time Amber had tried to convince me her relatives wanted to buy her out of servitude. She had portrayed her relatives—I had thought at the time there were more than just this one cousin—as respectable free men and women, distressed that one and only one family member remained in servitude. What bravado it took for Amber to fabricate such a story. How worried about my feelings for her must she have been to feel the need to fabricate.

Two hours after sunset, I slipped out of Happy Red Court, by myself, into a brutally cold night. The freezing air stung my face, my breath turned instantaneously to white smoke. I decided not to take a horse; taking a horse from our stable would attract too much attention. Plus, I would need a guide to Amber's cousin's house, which would mean taking two horses. Instead, I headed to our mansion's west gate on foot.

I hoped to find there Mrs. Song, Amber's friend. When I arrived, though, I didn't see her. Instead, three elderly, gap-toothed, rough-skinned women I didn't recognize guarded the gate. The women, bundled in layers of shabby clothing, huddled over a brazier.

"Where is Mrs. Song?" I asked.

"Not here," one of them answered.

"Do you know where she is?"

"Nope."

"By any chance, would any of you know how to find the house where my maid Amber was taken? The house belongs to her cousin, the man who used to work here as a cook."

The reddish light from the brazier accentuated the deep creases in the women's faces and the numerous gaps in their mouths where teeth should have been. Two of the women shook their heads no. The third cocked a rheumy eye at me and asked, "Why would you be wanting to know, young master?"

"I want to go visit her, but I don't know the way. I need a guide to take me there and bring me back."

The old woman rubbed her hands over the brazier and pursed her lips. "Why, young master, if I was to guide you there and anybody found out, I'd be fired quick as a wink, no ifs, ands, or buts about it. I can't afford to be your guide. It all comes down to money, don't it?"

I pulled out a string of two hundred fifty copper coins and held it in the flickering light of the brazier.

"Yes, I'd be fired quick as a wink," the woman went on, "and I don't have nowhere to go. Nobody's going to take in an old woman like me. Two fifty wouldn't do me much good then. Why, two fifty is barely enough to buy a pot of hair pomade."

I pulled out another string of two hundred fifty copper

coins and held it up beside the first.

"I've worked for this family for thirty years, never got into no trouble yet. Don't figure I should start now, at my age." The woman leaned toward me, so close I could smell her foul breath. "You know, seems like a good-looking young master like you would have some silver on him. Don't you have some silver you'd like to show me?"

I reached deep into my coat and pulled out a tael. The silver, reflecting the reddish light of the brazier, looked like an exotic form of gold.

The woman's hand reached out and grabbed the tael and the two strings. "Let's go. It's just going to get colder." She rose arthritically from her stool.

We turned left on the street that ran in front of our mansion. The path was difficult: it had rained that afternoon, turning the dirt of the street into mud, and now the mud had frozen into a rough, uneven, but still glassy-slick surface. No moonlight penetrated the overcast night.

After about fifteen minutes on main streets, we headed into hutongs. The stench of urine and excrement enveloped me. Smoke from a myriad of cooking fires stung my eyes. Piles of debris filled corners and oozed over the dirt paths. Behind thin walls I could hear people talking, cooking, arguing, singing, making love, caring for babies.

My aged guide led me through a maze of hutongs, one turn after another, a new turn every few steps. The width of the hutongs narrowed as we burrowed farther and farther in, to the point where with my arms outstretched I could touch the houses on both sides. Finally, in front of a small one-story brick building that looked exactly like all its neighbors, my guide said, "This is it."

I reminded the old woman of her duty to wait for me so she could guide me back to the mansion, then knocked on the door.

No one answered.

I knocked again. Again, no answer.

I gave the door a push. It opened with a rusty creak.

The narrow, dimly lit room smelled of coal dust and

garbage. At the back was an earthen kang covered with a reed mat. On top of the mat was Amber.

Her eyes were closed, she seemed asleep. Fortunately, she was wrapped in her bedding from Happy Red Court. Mrs. Song must have brought it. I looked around. No one else was in the room.

I went up to Amber, took her hand, and softly called her name. She opened her eyes and gave my hand a faint squeeze. "I didn't think I'd ever see you again."

Amber was chalky white. She had lost so much weight her skin now hung flaccidly over protruding bones; her once-alluring high cheekbones looked like poles holding up a collapsed tent. The room felt frigid, but she lay bathed in sweat.

She broke into deep, hacking coughs. "Merciful Buddha," she said when her coughing subsided. "You've come just in time. I thought I was going to die of thirst. I keep calling out, but no one ever answers. Can you please bring me some tea?"

I looked around and saw a dilapidated brick-and-mud stove built against the wall. On top of the stove was a grimy earthenware pot with a small amount of orange-brown liquid at the bottom. For a cup, the only thing I could locate in the shadowy room was a bowl, much larger than a normal teacup, sitting on a table next to the stove. Rancid oil covered the bowl. I found a tub of water and tried to wash the bowl, using my silk handkerchief as a towel, but the oil was crusted on, and I wasn't sure the water itself was clean. Nevertheless, I poured the orange-brown liquid into the bowl.

I took a sip. The liquid tasted bitter as a cypress seed, nothing at all like proper tea. Amber must have seen my frown, for she said, "You can't expect my cousin to have the kinds of fine tea we had at Happy Red Court." I handed her the bowl, and she downed the foul liquid as if it were the finest Hangzhou tea.

"How are you?" I asked, sitting down on the kang.

"What can I say? It's just day to day, hour to hour. I know I'll be gone in a few days at most." She coughed violently, and as she put aside her spittoon, I could see her phlegm saturated with blood.

"The horrible thing is, I can't die content. I still can't get over those things your mother said about me. Called me a whore. Am I your whore, Second Master?"

"No, of course not. Mother was .... She wasn't herself that day." I took hold of Amber's hands; they felt like bundles of dried twigs.

"If I'd known things would end up like this," she said, "I might have acted different. But I was fool enough to think we'd always be together."

I had intended to maintain a cheerful face, but these words set me to crying. Another coughing fit overtook Amber, and again she spat up bloody phlegm.

Amber still had on some of her jewelry—a pair of silver bracelets on either wrist. Thin as her wrists were now, the bracelets were far too big. "Better take these off," I said. "You can wear them again when you're better." She nodded yes. I took off the four bracelets and put them under her pillow.

Again I took hold of her hands. "You still have your two long red nails, don't you?"

She held her hands up to her face and stared at the nails. Suddenly she put the long nail on her right hand into her mouth and bit it off at the base. Blood oozed from where the nail had once been attached. Amber next put the left-hand nail into her mouth and bit that one off too.

She pulled my hand toward her and dropped the nails into my palm. "Here. Something to remember me by."

My throat was so tight, I could say nothing. I put the two long red nails into my pouch.

Amber struggled to rise from her lying position. Sweat flowed off her face in rivulets. Her raspy breathing sounded like a rake scraping over gravel.

Once she was slightly raised on her elbows, she began to take off the red silk chemise she wore next to her flesh. With superhuman effort, she managed to pull it off. Her shriveled, sweat-covered upper body was now naked.

Amber was so winded she could no longer talk. With one hand she held out the chemise to me and with the other pointed at me and made a beckoning motion. I knew what she wanted.

I took off all the layers of coats and shirts with which I had armed myself against the cold, until I was stripped to my undershirt. Then I took it off and handed it to Amber. I put Amber's red silk chemise on myself, next to my own flesh.

Amber was trying to put my undershirt on but was so weak and exhausted she could not. "Help me," she whispered. I lifted her part-way up, eased her arms into the undershirt, wrapped it around her stick-like torso, and buttoned it up. Then I gently laid her back down on her bedding.

Neither of us said anything. Amber coughed and struggled to breathe. At last she said, "Now, when I'm lying in my coffin, it'll be like I'm still at Happy Red Court."

My breath caught, my eyes filled with tears, I couldn't speak.

"Go, Second Master," Amber said. "This place is filthy, and it isn't good for your health. The important thing is we were able to see each other again before I died."

I began putting my shirts and coats back on. As I did, Amber said, "If anybody asks you where you got your red chemise, tell them the truth. I've already got a bad reputation, may as well have something to show for it."

When I was ready to go, I bent over and kissed Amber. "I'll see you tomorrow." Up close, I could feel her fever, the heat of her disease.

I straightened up, turned around, and began to head out. But someone was blocking my way.

She was a woman I'd never seen before, with hard features, exaggerated by thick makeup—ghoulish eye shadow; garish, caked-on lipstick. Her clothing exposed oversized breasts. Her breath smelled like alcohol.

"Is this the famous young master from the Jia palace?" the woman said in a rough voice. "What are you doing here? Poking around in a servant's bedroom? Seems like you'd have better things to do than that."

The woman had to be Amber's cousin's wife—"the Mattress."

She reached an arm toward me and began pinching my cheek. "I know. You've heard about *me*. You've heard about how much fun I am, and you've come to get in on some of the action yourself." She leered at me.

"Amber was my chief maid," I said primly. "I came here because I was concerned about her health."

The Mattress smiled and nodded. "They always said you was nice to the girls. Now you can be nice to me. Ain't often I get the chance with somebody as young and good-looking as you."

She took hold of me with both hands and began wrestling me toward a door I hadn't noticed before. She pushed me through the door into a windowless room, pitch dark, that stank of piss and shit.

Next, she circled around, grabbed me from the front, and began pulling me down. She was lowering herself, back down, legs spread, onto a kang and drawing me on top of her.

With one hand she kept hold of my shoulder, with the other she reached for my genitals. "How's your pecker, boy." The hand discovered my limp penis and grabbed hold of it. "Not much going on down there."

The hand then seized my balls and started squeezing. A lightning bolt of pain shot up my groin. I screamed.

"People talk about you being a lady's man. Far as I'm concerned, you're a firecracker that ain't got no powder."

I reached for the hand that was holding my balls and grabbed it. The Mattress squeezed even harder. I writhed in pain. Finally I managed to pry her fingers off, then punched her other hand off my shoulder.

I groped my way out of the dark, stinking inner room. In the outer room, Amber seemed asleep. I left her alone, opened the front door, and stepped out into the hutong.

I looked to the right: the old woman who was supposed to be waiting for me was not there. I looked to the left: she was not there either. I took a step and immediately slipped on the ice. It took several attempts to get back on my feet, and I now had a pain in my right side from the fall.

I continued to look for the old woman. I called, walked up and down. She had disappeared.

The door to Amber's cousin's house opened. The Mattress

stuck her head out and said, "You know that old hag that was here, supposed to be waiting for you? I told her to go home, said I'd take you back to the Jia palace myself. But if you think I'm going to do anything for you now, after I seen what a faggot you are, you're fucked in the head." She slammed the door shut.

It was close to midnight. The residents of the hovels that hugged the sides of the hutongs had extinguished their candles and lanterns, leaving everything in total darkness. The wind had picked up, making the bitter cold even more punishing. With every step I took on the slick surface, my feet threatened to fly out from underneath me. Worst of all, the dense maze of the hutongs offered no clue as to how to get out.

After walking in circles for several minutes, I encountered a man returning to his house from a public privy. In a thick Beijing accent, dripping with exaggerated *r*'s, he gave me directions to the nearest main street. I still blundered into a couple of dead ends, but eventually found my way out.

During the long walk back to the mansion, I recalled tender moments Amber and I had shared. I particularly remembered the day we first made love. Earlier that day I had experienced my strange dream in Crimson's red bedchamber, and Amber and I fell into lovemaking as I was trying to describe to her the erotic parts of my dream. I would always remember that day as the one on which I lost my virginity, and Amber as the girl to whom I lost it.

I also thought of the morning we ate dragon eyes at my small table and—something almost unheard of in the Jia household—talked openly and honestly about our future together. I thought of the night when, even as she was dying, she stayed up all night to mend my peacock cape.

I arrived back at Happy Red Court to find my maids frantic with worry. Never before had I stayed out so late; never before had my whereabouts been such a mystery. My appearance and demeanor by the time I arrived home were no help either. I was trembling from a combination of cold and fright, my lips were blue. Passing my closet on the way to my bed, I caught a glimpse of the peacock cape and broke out crying.

I went to bed immediately but couldn't sleep. Images kept

thrusting into my mind, despite my best efforts to block them. I saw Amber lying on her reed-covered kang—pale, emaciated, dying. I saw the Mattress—her drunken leer, her garish makeup, her bared breasts. I felt her rough hand squeezing my testicles.

Toward morning, I drifted into a state halfway between sleep and wakefulness. I saw Amber walk into Happy Red Court—not the Amber I had seen a few hours before; rather, Amber at the peak of her health, with peach-bloom cheeks, firm flesh, and a glint in her eye. She kept walking toward me, step after step, but never seemed to get any closer. She was saying something, but I couldn't make out the words, I could hear only sounds. It was as if she were talking to me from underwater. Finally, by concentrating as hard as I could, I was able to decipher what she was saying. It was: "Goodbye, ... Baoyu, ... goodbye."

11

I AWOKE THE NEXT MORNING feeling fuzzy-headed and feverish. I knew it. Spending half the night outside in freezing weather had given me a cold.

I wanted to visit Amber again. That meant getting out of bed, whether I felt well or not. I started to raise myself up.

Nothing happened.

I tried again.

Again, nothing happened.

I seemed paralyzed. The connection between my brain and body seemed to have disappeared. I began sweating and breathing in short, shallow breaths. What had happened to me? The more anxious I became, the weaker I felt.

After several attempts, I managed to push myself across my satin sheets to the edge of my bed. I lowered my legs to the floor, lifted my torso, and ... promptly crumpled to the floor. I didn't have the strength to stand up.

"Second Master! What happened?" The four maids on duty rushed to my side. Once recovered from their initial shock, they helped me up and put me back in bed.

I remained there, with the curtains closed, for the next two hours. For the first half hour, my entire body trembled. Later, a leaden stillness took over.

I felt deeply ashamed, even angry with myself. I had failed Amber and embarrassed myself in front of my maids. My extreme physical weakness frightened me.

By noon, some of my strength had returned, and I was able to get out of bed and stand up. By mid-afternoon, I was able to think about going out. Tealeaf had located an older nurse—a pleasant, honest woman, not the greedy one from the night before—who could guide me to Amber's cousin's house. The two of us set off together.

When we arrived at the house, the door was shut and locked. I banged and pushed, but the door would not budge. I was too late.

I later learned that Amber had died around dawn—the same time as my dream in which I heard her say "Goodbye, Baoyu, goodbye." Her cousin and the Mattress had quickly come to our mansion to ask for money to bury her. My family, eager to put the matter to rest, had given them five taels, on condition that Amber's body be immediately removed from the city and cremated, a reasonable requirement given Amber's consumption. By the time I arrived at the cousin's house, the cousin and his wife had already taken Amber's body to the crematorium.

I doubted whether Amber's cremation had taken place with any semblance of dignity. I could easily imagine her cousin and the Mattress dropping her body off at the cheapest open crematorium, hurriedly paying the proprietor (probably only two or three taels and pocketing the rest), then immediately leaving.

I felt guilty I had not been present at Amber's cremation. Even more, the fact Amber had been denied any ceremonial closure to her life weighed on me like a stone. I searched my mind for a way to commemorate her with the dignity she deserved.

I decided to begin by writing a poem—an elegy. I brought out paper, brush, and ink. Once again, though, the blanket of lethargy that had settled over me betrayed my good intentions. I wrote only a few mediocre lines. Then, feeling exhausted and cloudy in the head, I skipped dinner and went to bed.

Despite how tired I felt, I couldn't sleep; I tossed and turned most of the night. As I did, a rancid feeling of self-loathing enveloped me. Why had I not stood up for Amber against my mother's harshness? Or for Goldie? My father was right: I was as worthless as a sewer rat.

When dawn came, I was more tired than when I'd gone to bed. But I didn't have a cold.

I remained immured inside my canopy bed for hours, unable to face the frightening prospect of another day. When I finally emerged, my glance fell on the barely started elegy to Amber on my writing desk.

I managed to write a few more lines that afternoon. When dusk came, however, the same pattern repeated itself: I stumbled into bed exhausted, I couldn't sleep.

The following day, one of Grandmother's junior maids appeared at Happy Red Court. Grandmother wanted to know why I had not been to see her in several days. I told the maid I had been busy and would be over to see Grandmother that afternoon.

I cleaned myself up—my personal hygiene had deteriorated since Amber's death—and trudged over to Grandmother's courtyard. She was with my mother in the sitting room. They had news.

First Uncle had arranged a marriage for my cousin Lotus. She would be marrying a man named Sun. Because she was now engaged, she would be moving out of the garden.

I had never met this Sun, but the fact Lotus would be leaving the garden turned my somber mood even more leaden. Seven of us had moved in, now we were only six.

I also worried for Lotus. This was the end of her youth. Soon she would be living a new life, one that might be tolerable or not, depending on her new husband, her new household, her new in-laws.

While I was absorbing the news about Lotus, my mother shocked me a second time. "I suppose you've heard about Baochai."

"No. What?"

"She's moved out of the garden too."

I felt as if I'd been doused with cold water. "Why?"

"She's moved back in with her mother. Her mother's been sick lately, and their only two reliable maids have also been ill. She decided to return home to help." Mother, obviously pleased with Baochai's filial piety, smiled.

As a practical matter, Baochai's departure from the garden made little difference. Her mother's residence, Pear Tree Court, was part of our mansion. Baochai's mother, when she was well, visited my mother, her sister, almost every day. Baochai probably would too. Given the mordant pessimism that had come over me, though, Baochai's desertion of the garden struck me as tragic.

Originally we had been seven. Now, apparently, we were only five. Before that moment, I had never considered that our idyllic life in the garden, with its beauties, its freedoms, its unclouded friendships, would someday end, and we would all be marched off to the fates in store for us as adults. The garden was my youth, and it was fading.

Over the following three days, bad health continued to plague me, but I managed to complete the elegy to Amber. In a neat hand, I copied it onto a translucent silk handkerchief that had been a particular favorite of hers. That night, after the moon rose, I went out into the courtyard of Happy Red Court, carrying with me the handkerchief, some charcoal in a little burner, a cup of tea, and a spray of oleander and winter sweet. My maids followed.

First, I declaimed the entire poem out loud, in as resonant a voice as I could muster. Then, using the charcoal burner, I set fire to the handkerchief. Once it had burned, I poured out the tea as a libation and scattered the flowers.

At last, I had said a proper goodbye to Amber.

Two days after my nighttime homage to Amber, I forced myself to rise before noon and allowed my maids to wash me and oil and rebraid my queue. Then, slowly, I headed to Bamboo Lodge for a long-delayed visit to Daiyu.

When I knocked on the door, Swallow answered. I asked to see Daiyu.

"She's not feeling well today. But to be honest, these days she never feels well. If you're not going to see her on a day like this, you'll never see her. I'll go and ask her if it's all right."

Swallow disappeared, leaving me to absorb her foreboding words. When she returned, she said Daiyu wanted to see me and led me through the beaded curtain into Daiyu's dayroom.

The room had a stale smell, like wet paper. Daiyu's kang had been turned into a bed, and she was lying in the bed, beneath a green coverlet. Her face, which was all I could see of her, was ghostly white, cruelly emaciated, and covered in sweat. Her black hair, once so lustrous, was dull and matted. To the side of her bed, resting on a garden stool, was a spittoon. Next to the spittoon was a handkerchief streaked with red stains.

I felt as if every fiber of my body had turned to ash.

Daiyu too had consumption. She was dying, just like Amber. I had loved two girls in my life. Soon both would have died, pathetically young, of consumption.

I began to cry, but for Daiyu's sake, tried to stifle it. She already had tears in her eyes.

I sat down on the edge of the kang and looked around. Daiyu's dayroom reflected the intelligence and taste I had always loved in her. Behind her pillow at the head of her bed stood a bookcase filled with volumes of poetry. On the opposite wall hung a calligraphy scroll bearing the words of a Tang dynasty poet. Beside the bed was a lattice window backed by parchment, and on the parchment the bamboo forest outside created a constantly shifting shadow play of muted sunlight and darker leaves.

At the center of this scene of quiet and beauty was a fifteen-year-old girl struggling to stay alive.

I could think of nothing to say. For several minutes, Daiyu and I simply stared at each other, a despairing and unbreakable silence hanging between us. From time to time, she coughed.

Finally, Daiyu said, slowly and in a voice made hoarse by coughing, "Baoyu, can I ask you a question?"

"Of course."

"*Bao* means *precious*, and *yu* means *jade*. How are you precious, and how are you like a jade?"

At first I was bewildered. Then I realized: she wanted to

have another of our Zen conversations. She could no longer fly kites, she could no longer paint, she could no longer play Go, but she could still converse in aphorisms and literary allusions.

I searched for a creative response to Daiyu's questions, but in my sleep-deprived stupor, my brain was slow to respond. "I am not precious," I said. "Nor am I like a jade. But what about you, Daiyu? *Dai* means *black*, your name means *black jade*. You are like a black jade because black jades are precious and rare and the most beautiful of all jades."

Daiyu smiled. A moment later, she had a coughing fit. When she'd recovered her breath, she drew one of her hands out from under the coverlet and stared at it. The hand was pathetically thin, the shrunken remainder of a hand. She rotated it—left, right, back left again. Still staring at her hand, she said, "Alas, I cannot hold the moonlight in my slender hand."

I recognized the passage. It was by one of Daiyu's favorite poets, Zhang Jiuling.

I recalled some lines from Nalan Xinde: "If only you could recover like the moon, from the half to the full."

Daiyu put her hand back under the coverlet. She sighed deeply. "There's no stopping the chill rain at dawn, or the shrill wind at night."

I struggled not to break down and bawl. Somehow I managed to recall and recite: "To express everything I feel for you would be as difficult as plucking the flower from the mirror."

"Oh Baoyu." Daiyu broke down crying.

A moment later a violent coughing fit overtook her. She covered her mouth with her handkerchief and spat out phlegm. I looked away, knowing the phlegm would be bloody.

By now Swallow had stepped forward and was comforting Daiyu. "You should probably go now," Swallow said to me. "We don't want to tire her out."

"No, I don't want to go. I want to stay with Daiyu. I don't want to leave her alone like this. I want to be with her forever." I threw myself onto Daiyu and wrapped my arms around her. She felt, as Amber had, like a bundle of dried sticks.

Another coughing fit seized her. Because I was embracing her, she could not get her handkerchief to her mouth in time, and she expelled strands of red-streaked phlegm into the air. Several strands fell back onto her, one hit my cheek.

"Second Master!" said Swallow. "Please control yourself. Have pity on my mistress. Let her rest in peace."

When I didn't move, Swallow, a big, strong girl, grabbed me by my shoulders and pulled me off Daiyu's bed. Weak as I was from not sleeping, not eating, and from grief, I collapsed onto the floor.

12

FOR DAYS, I BARELY EMERGED from my canopy bed. Then, one morning my maids invaded my privacy to report that my half-sister, Tingting, had come to Happy Red Court to visit. Though I felt vile, I couldn't turn away my sister.

The moment Tingting saw me, a look of puzzled concern came over her face. "Big Brother, what's happened to you? You don't look yourself."

"I've been ... ill."

I sat on the edge of my bed, my feet dangling. I thought about trying to get up and move to my table but wasn't sure I could make it and didn't want to embarrass myself. "Get my sister a stool and bring it over here," I instructed my maids.

Tingting sat down on the stool. She continued to stare at me, slowly shaking her head. "Big Brother, I hate to say this, but you look terrible. What's been going on?"

I sighed. "It began with the death of Amber. You remember her, don't you? ... And some things that happened in connection with her death.... Then, Daiyu. Have you seen her lately?"

Tingting grimaced. "Yes."

"I saw her a few days ago. Before that, I hadn't seen her for a while. I had no idea ...."

We both remained silent for five or ten breaths. Then Tingting forced a half-smile and said, "We just have to remember: she's been living with this disease a long time now. She's always managed to keep it at bay before, and we have to hope she can keep doing that."

"You think she's had consumption for a long time?"

"Oh yes. Ever since she came back from that journey to the south, to bury her father. She was so thin when she arrived back, and I noticed her coughing all the time."

I thought back to the time shortly after her return when I climbed over a ridge and found her looking pathetically thin, crying, and burying fallen blossoms.

"It crossed my mind at the time," I said, "but I guess ... I just tried not to think about it."

After another long period of silence, Tingting said, "I'd like to get back to *your* health problems. You're so thin. And your skin doesn't look healthy, it's all dry and red. What's the matter with you?"

I looked at my hands, which were inexplicably chapped and raw. I shut my eyes and searched for words. "It's very hard to describe."

"Can you try?"

I took a deep breath and looked at the ceiling. "I ... feel exhausted all the time. But when I try to go to sleep, I can't. Then in the morning, I can't get up. It's too frightening for me to open the curtains to my bed and face the world. Even when I do get up, it's like ... I'm not here. For example, I haven't felt like eating for days."

I squeezed my eyes shut, opened them again. "I don't know. I just seem to have ... left my body."

Tingting looked at me warily. "Have you been coughing?"

"No, no, I don't think I have consumption, if that's what you're asking."

"You say you can't get to sleep at night. Can't you just lie there in bed, calm and relaxed? That way, you'll either go to sleep eventually, or even if you don't, you'll still get a good night's rest, because lying in bed calm and relaxed is almost as good as sleeping. See? That's what I do when I have trouble sleeping."

I covered my face with my hands. "No, no. When I lie in bed, I can't be calm and relaxed, because I feel like I'm locked in a room, and the room is fiery hot. I need to get out of the room immediately: the heat is suffocating me, asphyxiating me. But I *can't* get out. There's no exit. All the escape routes are blocked."

Tingting stared at me, her brow furrowed.

After a few breaths, she said, "What are you doing to get over this ... problem of yours? Are you taking anything? How are you planning to get out of this mess you're in?"

I slowly shook my head. "I'm not."

Tingting said nothing. I wanted to fold back into my purple canopy bed and close the curtains. But I felt obligated to say *something*.

"I live only in the present. All I can think about is getting through the night, then getting through the day, then getting through the night again. Moment to moment. I remember Amber saying something like that when I visited her the night before she died. Something like, 'It's just day to day, hour to hour.'"

Another long silence. At last Tingting said, "Big Brother, I've known you my whole life, and I thought I knew who you were. What you're saying today has me totally mystified. You used to be the most energetic person in the Jia mansion: everywhere at once, talking to everybody, jumping up and down, flirting with every maid under twenty. You were always so good-looking and so vibrant. Now you've become this gloomy, emaciated recluse who can't even get out of bed. Who are you, Baoyu? Who are you?"

The silence that followed seemed endless. I hung my head in shame.

"I don't know."

Tingting's glum look made clear her disappointment.

"I can tell you only one thing," I said. "I'm not the same person I was a few months ago."

"Second Master, it's a beautiful day outside, warm and sunny. Don't you want to get up and take a walk in the garden? It could be a short walk, just a few minutes."

My maids had seized on the first warm day of spring to

make a concerted effort to lift me out of my stupor. They had even sewn a new set of clothes for me to wear, since anything I had previously worn now hung loose and flapped about my limbs. The maids' blandishments were so well-intentioned and heartfelt that, despite my forebodings, I said yes.

I could barely get out of bed. Not only was my body frail, it was also clumsy, disjointed. Trying to walk, I lacked coordination; at best, I could shuffle. When I tried to speak, my speech was slow and halting.

The maids and I went out the moon gate of Happy Red Court into the garden. As we walked along a path leading to the river, I looked up at a young elm tree. An aggressive vine had almost completely taken it over. The vine had wrapped itself around most of the tree's trunk and lower branches and was obviously smothering it. Parts of the tree were already dead.

I realized this was what was happening to me. Something was taking over my mind, my body, my soul, and it was crushing me, squeezing the life out of me. Soon I would be dead, like the young elm tree.

I shuffled a few more steps along the path. From out of nowhere, a huge, flapping bird—a pheasant—flew up directly in front of us with a loud whir. My maids all screamed and scampered back.

Fear gripped me. I felt as if the air around me had crystallized, had somehow transformed itself into a solid, like water freezing into ice, and I was entombed inside this solid, unable to move, unable even to breathe. Had I been buried alive? Or was I even alive?

The next thing I knew I was lying on my back, on the pebbled path, my maids hovering over me, all of them talking at the same time, all of them panic-stricken. In a frightened, disorganized manner, with eight maids tugging and pulling on me in eight different directions, they lifted me up and helped me half-crawl, half-stagger back to Happy Red Court. Once sealed back inside my canopy bed, I lay down, closed my eyes, and placed my arms over my chest.

A queasy feeling came over me. Something was wrong.

I ran my hands over my chest.

Where was my jade?

I ran my hands over my chest again. I couldn't find it!

I snatched the five-colored silk cord on which the jade hung, pulled it over my head, and peered at it. The jade wasn't there!

I patted down all the clothing I was wearing. I examined every corner of my bed. I carefully went through all my clothing a second time. I dug into every nook and cranny of my bed again.

Nothing.

I had lost my jade.

Shock waves pummeled my body. My mouth went cottony dry. For several minutes I couldn't move, couldn't even think.

Eventually, I was able to put together a few simple thoughts. The jade had probably come off in the midst of all the tugging and pulling that had taken place after I had collapsed on the garden path. It was probably somewhere on or around the path. The sooner it was found and retrieved, the better.

Unfortunately, I was in no condition to search. I would have to send my maids, which meant informing them of the catastrophe. I was loathe to do this: the news would trigger another eruption of panic and disorganization. I had no choice, however.

My maids reacted exactly as I had expected: they cried, held their heads, lurched about the cottage, and repeated over and over, "We can't let Her Old Ladyship hear about this. We can't let Her Old Ladyship hear about this."

Finally, Pansy began to organize a search. They would bring in all the junior maids, and the entire group, fourteen in all, minus one left to remain by my bedside, would go to the path and comb the entire area.

"What if someone asks what we're doing?" one of the junior maids asked.

Pansy thought a moment. "Tell them Second Master lost a pouch with ten taels in it, and we're looking for that."

After all the maids save one had left, I retreated into my canopy bed, enjoyed the silence, and anticipated the prompt reappearance of my jade. Day turned into dusk, however, without any word back, and after sunset my maids returned to Happy Red Court, looking as frightened as if they'd seen a ghost. "We couldn't find any trace of it," Pansy said.

That night was hellish. My maids, going without sleep, brought out every piece of clothing and unfolded every item of bedding in Happy Red Court, shaking everything out. They moved every piece of furniture, upended every vase, emptied every drawer. They got down on their knees and peered into every corner, behind every curtain. It was all in vain: the jade was not to be found.

The noise, confusion, and commotion the search entailed only worsened the misery I had been feeling for days. I felt as if someone were splitting my head open with an ax, every blow forcing the blade in deeper.

The next morning, Pansy sent out a smaller party to search the path again. Shortly after it left, Rosebud appeared at Happy Red Court to inquire why I hadn't visited Grandmother for several days. My maids, now without the leadership of Amber, responded to Rosebud's question with terrified silence.

Getting no answer, Rosebud decided to see for herself. She came over to my canopy bed and pulled open the curtains.

She drew back in shock. "Second Master, what's come over you? You don't look well. You've lost so much weight!" She hastened out of Happy Red Court.

An hour later, at the head of a large entourage, Grandmother herself appeared. When she saw me, she gasped. "Baoyu, I can't believe this!" She bent over and embraced me. "Oh, Baoyu, I warned you about your frail health. I warned you time and time again. Now look what's happened."

Grandmother turned to the phalanx of maids standing behind her. "Get a litter ready. He's coming back to my courtyard."

It had been only a year and a half since I, along with the other six, had moved into the garden. At that time, I had pranced in, brimming with optimism, certain my every moment would be filled with happiness. Now, unable to care for myself, or even walk, I was being carried out in a litter. All my dreams had been shattered; the girls I had loved were dead or dying; and my mind and body had been reduced to piteous wrecks.

I sensed I would soon die. I looked forward to the event.

No one dared tell Grandmother my jade was lost. When she and her entourage swept into Happy Red Court, all my maids remained mute, their heads lowered.

Grandmother was not long in discovering the ghastly truth. Just after a group of maids had hoisted me into the bed in my old room in her courtyard, she began embracing and comforting me. Soon her hands were patting down my neck and chest. "Baoyu, where's your jade?"

An agonized silence followed. Finally:

"It's lost."

"What?"

"It's lost."

Grandmother gazed up at the ceiling, her mouth and eyes wide with horror. She squeezed her eyes shut and let out a long, loud wail.

Next she homed in on me. "Baoyu, how could you? Your life depends on your jade. That explains why you're sick. You lose your jade, and this is what happens. Oh, Baoyu, how could you?" She began weeping.

I would have been subject to even more recriminations had not our family doctor, Dr. Wang, appeared at that moment, accompanied by his usual quartet of pages. Grandmother had sent for him while still at Happy Red Court. Dr. Wang proceeded to take my pulse, first the left wrist, then the right. He didn't ask me any questions.

"What's the matter with him, doctor?" Grandmother asked.

Dr. Wang furrowed his brow. "The left distal pulse is deep and agitated. That indicates a febrile condition arising from the weak action of the heart. The left medial pulse is faint and deep. That is due to anemia caused by a sluggish liver. The right distal pulse is faint and feeble. That comes from debility of the lungs. The right medial pulse is slight and lacking in energy. That arises from a wood element in the liver that is too strong for the earth element in the spleen."

"Oh," said Grandmother.

"I shall write a prescription." His pages produced a pink form.

Dr. Wang's prescription must have included many ingredients, for he wrote for a long time. I had no interest in looking at the prescription. Nor did I intend to take it once it was compounded. I didn't want to live. I wanted to die.

The next morning Grandmother and Mother appeared at my bedside, their faces full of hope. "We have a fortune-teller outside," Grandmother said. "He'll help us find your jade. Once we get your jade back, you'll be healthy again."

The fortune-teller was an old man dressed in a black gown and a hat that made his head look square. He strode in bearing his cylinder full of bamboo sticks. Bowing deeply before me, he said, "Young master, we shall pose to the heavens the question of the current location of your jade."

He shook the cylinder until a red-tipped bamboo stick fell out. With a sweep of his arm, he reached down to pick up the stick, drew it close to his eyes. "The character chosen by the heavens is *shang,* meaning *to reward.*"

He stared at the stick silently for ten or fifteen long breaths. Then he said, "The top half of *shang* is similar to the character *dang,* meaning *to pawn.*"

Once again he stared at the stick. "If we add the character *ren,* meaning *man,* to the left-hand side of *shang,* we have the compound character *chang,* meaning *to redeem.*

"Therefore, the answer to your question is obvious: you must go to a pawnshop, find the man in charge, and redeem the master's jade."

Grandmother and Mother erupted with joy. "What a miraculous prophecy," Grandmother said. "We should have Baoyu's jade back in no time." The fortune-teller bowed, a self-satisfied smile on his face.

The fortune-teller's prophecy led to a process almost as

obnoxious and painful to me as my maids' turning Happy Red Court upside-down for an entire night had been. What the fortune-teller, Grandmother, and Mother had failed to take into account was that Beijing had not just a few pawnshops, but scores, and each pawnshop had at least one, and more often five or ten jade pieces on hock. For the next several days, every time I tried to settle back into my bed, one or another of our family's managers would barge into my room and demand I look at a boxful of jades. None of the jades the managers brought were mine.

Perhaps it didn't matter. I was starting to believe the disappearance of my jade made sense. It had long since lost any magical powers it might once have possessed. Losing the physical object was simply the last stage.

Soon after Grandmother moved me back to her courtyard, two family members who had been away for a while returned to our mansion. The first was my cousin Lotus; she was making her first visit back after having married the man named Sun. A group of maids helped me walk the short distance to Grandmother's reception hall to see her. On the way, the maids told me Lotus had previously stayed two days with her mother and father; this was her opportunity to see the rest of the family.

When I arrived, a large group had already assembled: Grandmother, Mother, Baochai's mother, Baochai herself, and all the girls from the garden except Daiyu. Everyone was in tears. Lotus herself seemed the most grief-stricken. I greeted her with a warm embrace. "Why are you crying?"

Lotus wiped her eyes. "I've been telling them what a terrible situation I'm in. My husband, Sun Shaozu, is a horrible man. He cares for nothing but women, gambling, and drinking. He has affairs going on with practically all our maids. The one time I complained to him about his affairs, he cursed me for being jealous and said I must have been steeped in vinegar."

Lotus had another crying spell, then blew her nose.

"My husband also claims he loaned my father five thousand

taels," she continued. "Father was supposed to pay it back, but instead spent the money. My husband's gone to Father several times to demand the money back, and each time, Father refuses. Whenever that happens, my husband comes home angry with me. He says, 'Don't put on those fancy airs with me. I paid five thousand taels for you. Your father sold you, I bought you. As far as I'm concerned, you're nothing but a slave. If you don't behave, I'll send you back to sleep with the other slaves.'

"But the worst thing"—Lotus squeezed her eyes shut and shook her head—"is that he beats me. He's done it several times now. He beats me with a bamboo rod." She broke into tears again.

I remembered what it was like to be beaten with a bamboo rod. I wanted to say something consoling to Lotus, but, devoid of optimism, I remained silent.

Grandmother appeared to be crying but in truth was just patting her eyes with a silk damask handkerchief. Real tears were in short supply.

"No doubt you're married to a nasty man," she said to Lotus. "But you *are* married to him. I'm afraid there's nothing that can be done about it now. It's your fate, dear girl.

"I was uneasy when your father first proposed this marriage. In retrospect, I probably should have said something, but"—Grandmother pursed her lips and shook her head—"your father was so determined to go through with it. Oh well, it's too late now. It's your fate, Lotus, you've just got to accept that."

Grandmother's cold remarks reduced everyone in the room to another round of anguished weeping. Among those weeping were three girls—Baochai, Tingting, and Peony—whose "fate," to use Grandmother's term, was still to be decided.

After a long period in which no one spoke, Peony, Lotus's younger half-sister, asked her, "You just spent two days with Mother and Father. What did they say about your husband?"

Tears flooded out of Lotus's eyes. "In the whole two days I was there, they never once asked me how my husband was treating me or whether I was happy in my new home."

"Did you ask Father about the five thousand taels?"

"I didn't dare. I knew how angry he'd get with me."

After another grim interval, my mother asked Lotus, "Where would you like to sleep tonight?"

"Could I please sleep in my old cottage in the garden? I look back at my time in the garden as the happiest period of my life, and I don't know if I'll ever get back here again. If I could just spend one more night in the garden, then I can die content."

"Now, now, you don't need to make it sound so tragic," Mother said. "Most young married couples have their squabbles. You just have to be patient and try to please your husband. But I can understand your wanting to sleep in the garden tonight, and yes, we can arrange that."

I shambled back to my room, feeling more desolate than ever. The universe punished people who were good and decent, like Lotus. Why were we all condemned to live in a universe so cruel? There had to be some way to escape, but I had no idea how to find it.

Two weeks later, news of another arrival reached my sickbed. My father had returned. His term as provincial examiner was up, and he was now living in the adjacent courtyard. He wanted to see me.

My reaction to this news was surprisingly muted. A year before, right after my beating, I would have envisioned my next encounter with my father as an event fraught with emotion, my hatred of him pitted against his loathing for me, a test of malevolent wills out of which only one would emerge alive. Now that the event was about to take place, I was indifferent.

I was curious how Father would act toward me. Would a year of having been a high-ranking government official surrounded by dozens of fawning assistants have made him even more of a bully? Or would the humiliations he had suffered in the aftermath of my beating have made him more circumspect? I wondered whether he would bring up the beating, and if he did, what he could possibly find to say.

In the end, though, none of these questions mattered. If Father were to give free rein to his emotions and kill me, it would give me exactly what I wanted. To be dead.

I was certain Father would pressure me about taking the

Imperial Examination. But wasn't it obvious I was in no condition to do that? I had not attended Jia Clan School for a year, ever since Grandmother, after my beating, had excused me. I had written nothing since I had belatedly finished my elegy to Amber, and with my mind as sluggish as it was now, I wasn't sure I could write even a single character. Father could rant and rave all he wanted; it would not change the fact that sitting for the examination in my condition would be pointless.

My maids spent half a day fixing me up: washing me, oiling and rebraiding my queue, outfitting me in clean clothes. Once that was done, they helped me make the short walk to my parents' courtyard.

I entered their sitting room slowly, supported by a maid on either side. When Father first caught sight of me, he recoiled. I stared at the slate floor.

"You look horrible," Father said. A gracious way of greeting me, after having not seen me for a year.

I said nothing. Silence hung in the air. My mother, who was also in the room, put a handkerchief over her mouth.

"I still expect you to take the Imperial Examination," Father said. "To do that, you are going to have to pull yourself together. I am appalled by what I see before me today. I cannot fathom how anyone could let himself fall apart as completely and in as pathetic a manner as you seem to have done.

"Let me be clear as to what I expect of you. Another Imperial Examination will take place in two years. You will be eighteen then, and you will take that examination. When you enter the examination compound, you will be well prepared. Very well prepared, in fact. Is that clear?"

I continued to stare at the floor. A maid on either side propped me up.

Father labored to breathe. He cleared his throat, waiting for me to reply, waiting for something I could not give him. At last, he said, "Get out of my sight."

With my maids assisting me, I shuffled out.

Father's talk about events two years in the future had drifted past my ears like smoke. In two years, I would be dead.

13

"CONGRATULATIONS, SECOND MASTER!" I was lying in my bed, in a stupor. Rosebud had stuck her head in. "Your father is choosing an auspicious date for your wedding. Doesn't that make you happy?"

I shook my head. Something had to be wrong with my hearing. "What?"

"Your father is choosing an auspicious date for your wedding. You're sixteen years old, and it's time. You're getting married."

I stared open-mouthed at Rosebud, not knowing what to make of her sudden appearance, her giddy talk about a wedding.

"You'll be marrying your cousin, Miss Daiyu. Aren't you glad?"

"I'll be what?"

"You'll be marrying your cousin, Miss Daiyu."

I was speechless. One part of me was radiant with joy. Another part, curdled with suspicion.

What was going on? Had Daiyu's health improved? Had I been wrong in assuming her imminent death?

Or was my family acting out of pity, granting Daiyu one final wish: to become my bride, even though everyone knew the marriage would be short, and Daiyu would soon be dead?

Rosebud interrupted my thoughts. "But Second Master, listen to this. Your father says you can marry Miss Daiyu only if you start acting normal again. You can't marry her if you keep on acting the fool."

What was this threat? What was I supposed to do? What *could* I do, given the malignant force that had overtaken my mind and body?

Amidst the turbulence of my thoughts, one idea gained control. I started to get out of bed. "I need to go see Daiyu."

Rosebud pushed me back. "You can't do that. A bride and bridegroom aren't supposed to see each other before the wedding. Don't worry, Miss Daiyu knows all about it."

I fell back into bed. Rosebud was right: traditionally a couple about to be married avoided seeing or even communicating with each other.

"I'm sure the happy day will be here soon. Isn't that right, Second Master?"

"I ... guess."

"Good." Rosebud left the room.

My mind was a battleground of joy and suspicion, hope and anxiety. I felt as if I'd swallowed both sugar and vinegar and couldn't tell which flavor predominated.

In my joyous moments, I was delirious. My lifetime dream was about to come true! A few hours before, I had no reason to live; now I had the best of all possible reasons. Even if Daiyu was dying, even if our marriage lasted only an hour, the marriage would give meaning to our lives, validate our youthful love, and join our fates in heaven. I yearned for marriage to Daiyu, yearned at a time I thought I had lost the capacity to yearn.

Suspicious moments came just as often. Was the news true? Would I soon be marrying Daiyu?

Something about the way the news had been conveyed didn't seem right. Rosebud had said my father was making all the decisions, but if that was the case, why didn't he, or at least one of his pages, contact me? Why was Rosebud, who worked for Grandmother, the messenger? Behind Rosebud's talk about Father choosing this and Father wanting that, I detected the hand of my grandmother. If that was the case, however, why didn't she herself come and tell me about Daiyu's and my betrothal?

Also, what was the business about my "acting normal"?

Was I being judged on my "normalness"? If so, how? By whom?

I wondered ceaselessly about Daiyu's health. Had she staged a miraculous recovery? It sometimes happened that a young person on the brink of death from consumption suddenly recovered. I shouldn't get my hopes up, though. I remembered how feeble she had looked the last time I had seen her at Bamboo Lodge. If she was still as sick as that, how would she look for our wedding? Would she even be able get through the ceremony?

Despite the welter of conflicting thoughts in my head, I gradually convinced myself the marriage would take place, or at least the likelihood of its taking place was great enough I should prepare myself. Over the next several days I began a regime of trying to put myself back together. I forced myself to get out of bed in the morning, instead of staying hidden past noon. I allowed, even encouraged, my maids to clean me. Even though I didn't feel hungry, I forced food down my throat. I started to exercise, first by walking around my room, then by walking around the veranda of Grandmother's courtyard.

Most of all, I tried as best as I could to act "normal." I made special efforts to focus on other people and respond to them when they spoke to me. I stopped complaining about my insomnia and pretended my health was fine. Still, it wasn't clear I was being watched: Father never summoned me, and Rosebud never came back. If I was being tested for "normalness," who was the judge?

Eight days passed, with no more word about a wedding. Then, on the morning of the ninth, Rosebud again bustled into my room. Fortunately, I was up, having only moments before forcing myself to leave the womb of my bed. "Better start getting ready. Your wedding's going to be tonight."

My heart leapt. It was true! I was going to be marrying Daiyu!

"Second Master, there's one thing I need to tell you."

I cringed. Was Rosebud about to take it all back? "Yes?"

"You probably haven't heard, but the Grand Imperial Concubine—not your sister, but the Emperor's number one concubine—died last month, and the Emperor proclaimed six months of mourning for the entire country. That means we can't do a full wedding ceremony, with a banquet and opera scenes. It's going to be a small wedding, with just a few close family members present. When the six months are up, we can have another ceremony and invite all the relatives and friends."

I breathed a sigh of relief. I didn't care about feasting or music or how many people were present. I cared only that Daiyu and I would be married.

That afternoon, my maids washed, oiled, and rebraided my queue and secured it with a half-dozen bejeweled gold clasps. I donned my wedding gown—bright red with a delicate yellow floral border.

My mother came to see me in my wedding finery. "Why do we have to wait till dusk?" I asked her. "Cousin Daiyu lives just a few steps away in the garden. She can come over now."

"Tradition, son, tradition. Dusk will be here soon enough."

When dusk finally came, my maids took me to our mansion's main courtyard to watch the arrival of the bride. In the street, a crowd of neighborhood children had gathered, while at the back of the courtyard, an ensemble of flutes and gongs stood ready to play. Soon the bridal procession appeared, making its way slowly down the street to our triple gate. Fireworks exploded, the musicians began to play, servants threw copper coins at the children, and the children lunged for the coins. As the fireworks and children's shouting peaked, the wedding procession—a bright-red palanquin, followed by twenty-four maids, each carrying an oversized, red-and-yellow palace lantern—passed through the gate and entered our courtyard.

When the fireworks were over and the coins gone, the mistress of ceremonies—a professional hired for the occasion—signaled for everyone to quiet down. It was time for the bride to emerge from her palanquin.

I trained my eyes on the palanquin's door to get my first glimpse of Daiyu. She would be veiled, I knew; I would not be able to see her face. Yet I could probably tell from the way she moved, the way she walked, how healthy or sick she was.

The first thing that struck me was that the maid standing

beside the palanquin's door was not Swallow, but rather one of Daiyu's junior maids, a girl whose name I couldn't even remember. Why was Swallow not with Daiyu? Swallow and Daiyu were as tight as lacquer and sizing. Swallow was distrustful of me, I knew that, but was she so hostile she wouldn't even participate in Daiyu's and my wedding? That seemed unlikely. What other explanation, though, could there be for Swallow's absence?

The mistress of ceremonies invited the bride to emerge from the palanquin. The door opened, and, assisted by the mistress and junior maid, Daiyu stepped out. I started to breathe again. Daiyu moved well and seemed to have no trouble standing on her own. In fact, she even seemed to have gained back some of her weight, though perhaps that was an illusion created by her thick, multi-layered wedding gown.

The gown was an intense, pure red; not a red compromised by any tinge of pink, yellow, or orange, but a red the essence of red. Over Daiyu's face, completely covering it, was a large, opaque, square cloth. The cloth was the same brilliant red as Daiyu's gown, and embroidered in yellow on it, in exactly the place Daiyu's face would have appeared had the cloth not been covering it, was the round, stylized character for "Double Happiness."

The mistress of ceremonies directed me to move to the steps at the back of the courtyard. Then she and the junior maid guided Daiyu, who couldn't see because of the cloth over her face, to a position beside me. Daiyu walked well, even seemed sturdy. Her health had apparently improved dramatically. I had been wrong—blessedly wrong—in thinking she was doomed to die.

Daiyu and I knelt side-by-side on the top step, facing the entrance to our main reception hall. Directed by the mistress of ceremonies, we kowtowed three times to Heaven and Earth. Grandmother came over to stand before us, and we kowtowed three times to her. Then, we did the same for my parents.

Once our obeisances were over, the mistress of ceremonies led Daiyu and me into the mansion, through our main reception hall, and along a series of corridors leading to a room that my family, unbeknownst to me, had completely renovated. It was now a bridal chamber for Daiyu and me.

I felt something I had not felt for months—joy. This was like the day we had moved into the garden, the realization of a fantasy. Daiyu and I were side by side, sharing the experience as one. Despite my weakness, I felt as buoyant as a bird in flight.

Our bridal chamber blazed with multiple shades of red. Scarlet silk draped all four walls, and a maroon carpet covered the floor. A carmine canopy covered an enclosed wedding bed, which gleamed with ruby lacquer.

Grandmother, Mother, and Rosebud stood opposite the wedding bed. Behind them stood my father, First Uncle, First Aunt, and Baochai's mother. All the other people in the room were servants.

The mistress of ceremonies led Daiyu and me, clad in our matching red gowns, to the foot of the bed. We stood next to each other, Daiyu still veiled. A small group of children scampered in, and while the mistress read a silly poem—something about the north, south, east, and west sides of the wedding bed—the children pelted Daiyu and me with dried fruit.

When this was over, the mistress of ceremonies helped Daiyu sit down on the bed. I remained standing. This was the moment I had been waiting for. This was when I could remove the veil from Daiyu's face and finally see her.

I slowly lifted the veil. A face appeared. It was not the face of Daiyu. Instead, it was the face of—

Baochai!

The world around me shattered into shards of glass. My mind went blank, I couldn't think.

Baochai sat motionless, her eyes fixed straight ahead, her face resolutely formed into a smile. With strands of pearls and turquoise hanging from pins in her hair, with her features buffed and rouged to perfection, Baochai looked delicious, like a ripe peach.

Her beauty made no difference. She was not Daiyu.

I wondered whether I was dreaming. I vaguely remembered the dream I had had two years before in Crimson's bedchamber. In that dream too a room had been decorated entirely in red. In that dream, too, a face had changed from Daiyu to Baochai. My mind was too stupefied to remember any more details of the dream or to decipher its obscure meaning. I had energy only to ask whether I was once again dreaming, or whether something had happened to me in so-called reality.

Baochai, her face now flushed with embarrassment, continued to stare ahead. I turned and saw Grandmother, Mother, and Rosebud watching me intently.

"What is going on?" I asked.

The three of them looked at each other uneasily. Forcing a smile, Grandmother said, "It's your wedding day. We have a new Second Mistress."

"Who is that?"

Again, the three of them exchanged worried looks. Grandmother replied, "Miss Baochai, of course."

"I wanted to marry *Daiyu*. Not Baochai. *Daiyu*."

"Hush yourself, child. Your father decided Miss Baochai would be the best choice for you. If you keep on talking like that, you'll make him angry, and we don't want that, do we?" Father was standing behind Grandmother but had said nothing and looked as if he was trying to make himself as small as possible.

"You told me I was marrying Daiyu. Everybody told me I was marrying Daiyu."

"Baoyu, Miss Baochai is sitting right behind you. You have no business talking like that in front of her."

I started to walk away. "I need to see Daiyu."

Grandmother's face hardened into an imperious mask. She whispered something to Rosebud. Rosebud signaled to several maids in the room, and before I knew it the maids had surrounded me and were dragging me out of the bridal chamber. I was too weak, too dazed, too confused, to resist.

The maids brought me back to the same bedroom and bed I had been occupying ever since Grandmother moved me out of the garden. Grandmother, Mother, and Rosebud followed, supervising the maids' every move.

At another signal from Rosebud, the maids brought in

a large incense burner and a type of incense I'd never seen before. They lit the incense. Grandmother, Mother, Rosebud, and the maids stepped back as smoke began to fill the room.

A scent I didn't recognize enveloped me. I collapsed onto my bed. My mind clouded over, consciousness drifted away. The last thing I could ever remember from that night was the sweet, vanilla-like smell of the incense.

14

I AWOKE THE NEXT DAY feeling as if a sandstorm had hit me. Grit encrusted everything—my mind, my memory, the outside world. My throat felt raw, my head ached. The air in my room smelled acrid and looked yellowish brown. I was alone in my bed. It was midday.

Slowly, the events of the previous night trickled back into my mind. I had been married, but not to Daiyu; instead, to Baochai. My dream of spending the rest of my life with Daiyu had been destroyed. Everyone in my family had deceived me. Even Grandmother—my beloved Grandmother, my champion, my protector—had deceived me.

The hopelessness of my situation crushed me. Live as long as I might, I would never again know happiness. I wanted to die.

I also wanted to see and to be with Daiyu. In the days leading up to my wedding, I had entertained the fantasy Daiyu had recovered from her consumption. I now realized I had been the victim of a deception; she was, as I had previously thought, dying. So too was I, however, and that was yet another thing we had in common. We needed to be together, if only to die together.

I wondered whether Daiyu knew about my marriage to Baochai, and if so, how she had reacted. I feared I knew the answer to the last question: in her weakened condition, the news would have destroyed her.

I pushed with my elbows to raise myself. Somehow the

strength I had worked so hard to build up in the days leading up to my wedding had slipped away overnight. I could barely sit up. I certainly could not get out of bed and walk the substantial distance to Bamboo Lodge.

I needed an intermediary, someone who could keep me informed of Daiyu's condition and relay messages between the two of us.

I hadn't seen Tealeaf or any of my other pages—normally my most reliable allies—since well before my wedding day. I suspected Grandmother and my parents were deliberately keeping them away from me.

I thought of Pansy. She was now one of many maids attending me. It wasn't clear whether she still worked for me or worked for Grandmother; I wasn't sure I still had any maids of my own. Pansy had always been a friend, however, and I assumed she still was.

I waited for a moment when I could talk to Pansy alone, without anyone overhearing. This proved elusive. Dr. Wang returned that afternoon—Grandmother was unhappy that his previous prescription had obviously failed—and my room again filled with a crowd as he took my pulse and wrote out another prescription. After Dr. Wang left, four maids continued to hover around my bedside. Finally, toward the end of the day, the other maids disappeared, leaving, as far as I could tell, Pansy and me alone.

"Pansy, could I talk to you?"

She came over and poked her head into my canopy bed.

"What do you know about Daiyu? Has she heard about my marriage? Is she crying her heart out?"

Pansy averted her eyes. Her lips parted slightly, but no words came out. Finally she said, "Miss Daiyu is ... ill."

"Could you please give her a message for me? Could you please tell her I think of her every moment, and I'll be with her as soon as possible?"

Pansy bit her lower lip. "I'll ... see what I can do."

"One more thing. I want you take a message from me to my grandmother. Can you please explain to her that Cousin Daiyu is dying, and I'm dying too, so Daiyu and I are the same, we're both dying, see? But we're dying in different places. Can you tell Grandmother it would make much more sense for the two of us to be together, in the same room? That way, the same maids could attend both of us while we're still living, and when we die, you can lay us out together. Please tell Grandmother—"

"Stop that ridiculous talk, Second Master." A voice from behind Pansy. The voice of Baochai. My wife.

"You seem to be seeking out death. What makes you think you have the right to do that? You've always been your grandmother's favorite; she's doted on you your entire life, and now she's over eighty. Don't you think it would hurt her terribly if you were to die now, at such a young age? What about your mother? She gave you life, yet what would become of her if you died young? Finally, what about me? I didn't seek out this marriage, and I now realize how unlucky I am, but I don't want to spend the rest of my life a widow.

"That's three people whose lives you would destroy if you were to die now, as you seem to want to. I can't believe heaven will allow you to die."

By this time Baochai had yanked open my curtains and was looming over me. Her presence repelled me. I could accept her claims that she hadn't sought out our marriage and now considered herself unlucky. I could *not,* however disassociate her from the horror I had felt when, on my wedding night, I had lifted the red veil and seen, not Daiyu's face, but hers. She was a wife I did not want, had never wanted.

"I'll tell you another thing," she said. "The reason you're sick is because you *want* to be sick. I've seen how you turn away food and only pretend to take Dr. Wang's prescriptions. If you'd start eating again and taking your medicine, and maybe get out of bed from time to time and get some exercise, I'm sure within a week or two you'd be good as new."

I lay back in my bed, closed my eyes, and took a deep breath. Baochai reminded me of my father. I searched for a way to get rid of her. After a long silence, I opened my eyes and said, "You know nothing about me."

Baochai reared back. Her jaw tensed, her eyes narrowed. "I think it's time to stop pampering you and tell you the truth. Daiyu is *dead.* Do you understand? Daiyu is *dead.*"

Baochai's eyes exuded spite. A slight tick infected her left cheek. Behind her stood Pansy, cringing in fear, her hands over her face. Behind Pansy hovered four other maids, their jaws slack with apprehension. The room was dark; even though it was daytime, the curtains had never been opened. It was also deathly still.

Baochai hated me, that much seemed clear. Maybe she was just trying to make me suffer. "You're lying," I said.

"Believe what you want. Someday you're going to have to face the truth. She died yesterday, on our wedding day. You can ask anybody."

Like a tree branch snapping, I suddenly realized Baochai was telling the truth: Daiyu was dead. She had died on the same day I had married Baochai.

I felt as if all the life inside me had been sucked out, my very existence extinguished.

By now four months had passed since Amber had died and an evil spirit had overtaken my mind and body. Strangely, even though throughout that period I had felt profoundly sad, I had cried little. The effort of crying had seemed beyond my powers: I was too parched.

Now, though, I cried—cried profusely, endlessly, uncontrollably. I cried through the night, through the next day, through the next night. My eyes became sore from the effort of manufacturing vast quantities of tears. My face became chapped from the ceaseless flow of salty water.

I ate virtually nothing and as a result lost more weight. I even started to smell bad: my body seemed to give off a dank, moldy smell, and my piss stank unbearably.

When I was not crying, I told anyone who would listen that I wanted to go to Bamboo Lodge to pay my last respects to Daiyu's coffin. Grandmother, Mother, and Rosebud told me that was impossible: I was in no condition to make such a trip. Their response only made me ask again.

When my uncontrolled crying continued into a third day, Grandmother decided she had had enough of Dr. Wang. Clearly, his prescriptions were not working. Grandmother brought in a new doctor, and I was surprised at her choice. Pompous

Dr. Wang, with his staff of pages, was the most expensive physician in Beijing; his face was familiar even in the Forbidden City. My new doctor, Dr. Bi, was a poor fellow who lived in an abandoned temple on the outskirts of town.

Dr. Bi, dressed in a well-worn tea-colored robe, came into my bedroom, sat down, and quickly took my pulse. Then, unlike Dr. Wang, he talked with me. He asked me how I felt. He asked me what was on my mind.

I told him about Daiyu, about Amber, about my marriage. I talked at length.

After I finished, Dr. Bi thought for a moment, then said to Grandmother, "I ascribe the young master's sickness to two causes, one external, the other internal. From the outside, he has been subjected to sudden transports of joy and grief, and these shocks have deprived him of his senses and his appetite. On the inside, he suffers from congestion caused by pent-up anger."

Amazing! I thought. After all these months, someone had finally said something that made sense.

Grandmother, Mother, and Rosebud looked at each other uncomfortably.

"I will make out an appropriate prescription," Dr. Bi continued. "One other thing. My prescription will be much more effective if the young master is allowed to express his emotions as he feels necessary. He is grieving, and the more he can act upon his grief, the sooner he will recover."

"He wants to mourn beside his cousin's coffin," Grandmother said. "We all thought that would be a mistake. Would you advise it?"

"Yes, definitely."

The next morning a group of pages brought a bamboo chair into my room, helped me into it, and carried me to Bamboo Lodge. Grandmother, Mother, Rosebud, and Baochai accompanied me.

I cried all the way over. Kneeling beside Daiyu's fig-wood coffin, though, I felt a deep sense of relief. Finally, I was by her side. And for once, I was not the only person in the room crying; everyone else was too.

I wanted to know what Daiyu's last days were like, and for that purpose I asked to see Swallow. She was outside, avoiding the family gathering. When she was brought in and saw me, a look of disgust crossed her face and she turned away.

As politely as I could, I asked Swallow if she would be willing to talk about Daiyu's last days. Swallow grimaced and said nothing. Then she noticed Grandmother, Mother, and Rosebud watching her with ears cocked. "All right," she said.

"Did Daiyu know I was marrying Baochai?"

Swallow nodded. "I'm sure she did, though we never discussed it. I can't tell you *how* she learned about it—certainly not from me. But I think I know exactly *when*. About a week before she died, she went out for a walk in the garden, and when she came back from that walk, she was a different person. She vomited up blood, took to her bed, and barely moved. She was never the same again."

"What were her last words?"

Swallow took a deep breath. "It was terrible at the end, just terrible. On the day she died, for most of that day she didn't say anything. She just lay there, in a sort of coma, trying to breathe. Then, late in the afternoon, her breathing changed. She'd have these long breaths out, but when she breathed in, it was like nothing was happening. I knew she was close to dying.

"I sent for Mrs. Silk and Miss Tingting to come, and when they got here, we touched my mistress' hand. It was already starting to get cold. I had the junior maids bring water over, and we started wiping her face with a flannel cloth. While we were doing that, the most awful thing happened.

"We heard music. There was a band, and it was playing wedding music. Mrs. Silk, Miss Tingting, and I didn't say a word to each other, but we all knew what was going on. It was the start of your wedding to Miss Baochai.

"I didn't think my mistress was conscious; she hadn't opened her eyes or moved for hours. But just as we were wiping her face and the band was playing the wedding music, she opened her eyes—wide, like she'd seen a monster—and in this strange, hoarse voice cried out, 'Baoyu, Baoyu, you betrayed me!'

"Right after that, she broke into a cold sweat, and her body started getting colder and colder. We told the junior maids to put up her hair and dress her in her grave clothes, and to do it fast. Even before they were done, my mistress stopped breathing."

Swallow looked at me with hatred. "So, Second Master, if you want to know what my mistress' last words were, that's what they were: 'Baoyu, Baoyu, you betrayed me!'"

I crumpled to the floor, enveloped in black, hating myself, wanting to die. I felt a noose around my neck, a millstone on my chest, shackles on my legs.

With her dying words, Daiyu had cursed me.

Grandmother's voice floated in from afar. "Baoyu, we need to get back. This is bringing you bad luck. We need to get you out of her ... You four, go pick him up. Baoyu, let them help you up."

The pages lifted me, set me into the bamboo chair, and carried me out.

As I was being carried back to my room in Grandmother's courtyard, I could think of nothing but suicide. I longed for death, longed for it with a hard, physical craving, as if I were gasping for air underwater.

My problem, I now realized, was I had been too passive. I had expected death to come to me. Death was not something that was going to happen on its own, though. I needed to make it happen.

The issue was how. I thought of four possible ways of committing suicide. I could jump into a well, like Goldie. I could hang myself. I could get a knife from the kitchen and stab myself. Or I could swallow arsenic.

All these ideas ran up against the fact I was constantly attended to by at least three maids, who watched my every movement. I could no more jump into a well unnoticed or fabricate a noose and hang it from a rafter unnoticed than I could fly to the moon. Plus, I was very weak. I could barely walk, I certainly couldn't outrun anybody.

Lying catatonic in my canopy bed, I went over the alternatives one by one. I realized three of the alternatives—hanging myself, stabbing myself, and poisoning myself—required some piece of equipment other than my own body: a noose, a knife, a bottle of arsenic. Throwing myself into a well had the salient advantage of requiring nothing beyond my own arms and legs. It was a one-step process; all the others were two-step processes.

I resolved to die like Goldie, by throwing myself into a well. But when?

The obvious answer was: at night, when most of the household was asleep.

By now I knew the nightly routine in my room like the back of my hand. Three or sometimes four maids watched over me. In theory, all three maids were supposed to stay awake throughout the night, to make sure nothing bad happened to me and to respond immediately to any request I might make. As a practical matter, however, the maids all drifted off to sleep as the night wore on. They slept on the kang, often in a tangle of young female bodies. Lying in my bed, plagued by insomnia night after night, I had learned to recognize the sounds produced as one maid after another fell asleep.

That night, three maids remained to watch over me. That was a lucky break: sometimes there were four. I disappeared into my canopy bed, they hovered around the kang. I stayed awake—hardly a challenge for me, since I was rarely able to go to sleep, even when I was trying—and listened for the sounds of maids dozing off.

A rhythmic wheeze gave evidence one maid had fallen asleep. Slow, full inhalations and exhalations—barely audible, except to someone as familiar with the sounds of the room as I was—marked the second. Finally, raspy breathing punctuated by occasional snores signaled the third. It was time for me to make my move.

With all the stealth and care I could muster, I slowly rose up, parted the curtains of my canopy bed, and slid out. I began to tiptoe across the pitch-dark room, pausing between each step, holding my breath as much as I could.

As I was about two-thirds of the way from my bed to the door, I took another step, put my foot down, and ... encountered something soft. A scream pierced the air. I tripped and fell.

For reasons unknown, one of the maids had decided to spend that night, not on the kang, but curled up on the slate floor. I had stepped on her shoulder. Her scream awakened the two other maids, and they too began screaming. The screams of the three maids brought in others from down the hallway, and soon alarmed maids filled my room.

The maids picked me up off the floor and put me back into my bed. By their grim faces and added numbers, I could tell they were determined to keep me there. My plan had met with utter failure.

I lay in bed, half-asleep, half-awake, plunged into deeper despair than ever. Toward dawn, I found myself walking down a dark road. I could see a long way ahead, but above the road, black clouds blotted out the sky. I was alone, and I was lost.

An old man approached me from the opposite direction. He was bald, with a few scraggly hairs on top of his scalp, and had a sleepy, heavy-lidded look.

"Excuse me," I said to the old man. "I'm afraid I've lost my way. Could you please tell me where I am?"

"You're on the Road to Hell. But what are you doing here? Your allotted time on Earth is not yet up."

"A friend of mine died, and I was looking for her. Somehow I lost my way."

"What was the name of your friend?"

"Her name was Daiyu."

The old man's sleepy eyes turned angry, and he spat onto the dirt road. "Your yearning for Daiyu is endangering your soul. If you wish to see her again, you must accept the fact of her death and end all thoughts of suicide. If you do that, you will see her. If you commit the crime of suicide, you will go to Hell. You may see your parents there, but you will never see Daiyu."

The old man pulled a stone from out of his sleeve, cocked his arm, and threw the stone at my heart. I felt a sharp pain in my chest. The pain jolted my eyes open.

I saw the inside of my canopy bed—the enveloping folds of purple silk brocade that served as my refuge. I was not on the Road to Hell. Instead, I was in a bed, in a luxurious mansion, still in that vain world we call reality.

From that point on, I realized suicide was not a way out. My dream echoed Baochai's rational arguments, and Baochai's arguments echoed my dream. I could not, would not, kill myself.

Still, I could not endure a life following along the path on which I was currently set. I needed to escape, to start over. Finding the way to do that became the purpose of my life.

15

My sickness had come over me like a tidal wave—suddenly, with overwhelming force. It left me in the way a slow drip of water, given enough time, can wear away even the hardest of stones.

My recovery took months. Months for the tragedies I had experienced—the deaths of Goldie, Amber, and Daiyu; my betrayal by my grandmother and parents; my fraudulent marriage; Daiyu's cursing me with her dying breath—months for those tragedies to recede far enough into the past that they no longer hurt like open wounds. Months for my mind and body to fight off the evil force that had taken possession of them.

I often thought about my dream, the one in which I was on the Road to Hell and met the old man. Suicide was not the answer, the dream had taught me. My future was here on Earth, living out my allotted lifespan.

Thinking led to reading, and when I started to read again, I read mainly the ancient sage Zhuangzi. This proved to be the fulcrum on which my journey turned.

I had long dabbled in reading Zhuangzi: his Taoist irreverence provided the perfect foil to the Confucian writings I was forced to memorize every day in school. Before my illness, however, I had read Zhuangzi for his wit, the poetry of his writing, and his unique perspective on the human condition. Now I read him because, even though he had lived more than two thousand years before me, he seemed to speak straight to my heart.

Zhuangzi taught me there was an alternative to always obeying my family's dictates. I could say no, and if I did, I was not a fool, I was not an evil person, and I was not alone.

Did my father want me to pass the Imperial Examination and become a government official? Here's how Zhuangzi handled a similar request:

Zhuangzi was fishing in the Pu River when the King of Chu dispatched two senior officials to visit him with a message. The message was: "I would like to trouble you to administer my lands."

Zhuangzi kept a firm grip on his fishing rod and said, "I hear that in Chu there is a sacred tortoise that died a thousand years ago. The King keeps the tortoise's shell in his ancestral temple, wrapped in layers of cloth. Tell me, did this tortoise want to die and leave its shell to be venerated? Or would it rather have lived and continued to crawl about in the mud?"

The two senior officials conferred. At last they said, "The turtle would probably rather have lived and continued to crawl about in the mud."

"Shove off, then! I will continue to crawl about in the mud."

Zhuangzi also provided a model for how I should lead my life. Both in his teachings and his own personal conduct, he emphasized detachment—avoiding intense yearnings for persons or things. Doing this, he taught, a man could keep an even emotional keel. If a man has the right understanding, he is "at ease with both calamity and fortune, takes care as to what he approaches or avoids, and therefore nothing harms him." This was what I wanted: to be beyond the possibility of harm.

Before my illness, strong personal attachments had dominated my life. I had been attached by love to Daiyu, by lust to Goldie, and by both love and lust to Amber. Yet those attachments had led to nothing but tragedy—both for the girls and for me. Daiyu, Amber, and Goldie had all died miserable deaths: Goldie at the bottom of a well, Amber in a hovel in the hutongs, Daiyu cursing me with her dying breath. As for me, those deaths had plunged me into paroxysms of grief, near-fatal illness, and attempted suicide.

I concluded that tragedy and misery were inherent in personal attachments. If I was to avoid tragedy and misery, if I was to place myself beyond the possibility of harm, I needed to avoid personal attachments.

A surprising change accompanied my recovery. I lost my interest in sex. I was an anomaly: a sixteen-year-old boy not obsessed with sex.

I will admit that, prior to my illness, I had had too much interest in sex: witness my role in the tragedies of Goldie and Amber. Now I had swung to the opposite extreme. Even the comeliest young maid in our household no longer excited me. I was married to Baochai, a girl generally thought exceptionally beautiful, and I was certainly expected to have sex with her, to produce an heir. I had absolutely no interest.

I was a different person than I had been before my illness. I was more even-tempered and imperturbable. I was more at peace with myself.

These gains came, however, at a considerable cost. Before my illness, I had thrown myself into Grandmother's lap, my mother's arms, Daiyu's heart, Amber's vagina, Goldie's mouth, the games and gossip of my cousins, the lives and psyches of dozens of serving girls. Now, a coldness had crept into my heart. I kept everyone at arm's length.

Was it better to open my heart to others, knowing that any personal attachments that might result would lead inevitably to tragedy?

Or was it better to seek peace of mind and personal salvation, knowing that, to be successful, I would have to make myself impervious to the needs for human affection of those around me?

I wished I didn't have to choose, but since I did, I had chosen the latter.

One afternoon, about three months after my marriage, my half-sister, Tingting, dropped by my room. I was sitting on my kang, reading Zhuangzi.

"You're looking much better these days, Big Brother."

"Thank you."

Tingting looked around the room. "This is the same room you lived in before you moved into the garden, isn't it?"

"Yes."

Tingting continued to survey the room. "It looks so impersonal, compared to Happy Red Court. There, with all your vases and books and rocks and things, the whole place seemed like a reflection of your personality. Here, there's almost nothing."

She was right. With all the chaos in my life over the past few months, I had done nothing to decorate my room. The only addition I had made was a small shelf of Taoist and Buddhist books above my desk.

"I hope you don't mind."

"Not at all. I'm just happy to see you looking so much better. I'm curious, have you thought about moving back to the garden?"

"I've thought about it, but ... for now there are too many unhappy memories."

"I can understand that."

Tingting's expression turned unsure. "I guess I should congratulate you on your marriage."

I let out a half-laugh. "Should you?"

"Well, I should at least acknowledge the fact you're married."

"You weren't at my wedding."

"I wasn't invited."

"You weren't? Why not?"

"I wasn't part of the inner circle. They didn't trust me."

"Really? Why not?"

"I think it went back to ... Do you remember the night a group of older women servants went around the garden demanding to see the belongings of all the maids? I took offense at that and ended up slapping Wang Shan's Wife in the face. I think that was it. After that, they never trusted me."

"'They' meaning ... ?"

"Grandmother and your mother. The people in charge."

"What about my father?"

Tingting laughed.

"Why do you laugh?"

"You really are off in your own world, aren't you? I thought I was isolated, but you're a lot more so. Well, to bring you up to date on developments in the Jia family, ever since that time Father went berserk and beat you to a pulp, he's been afraid of his own shadow. Grandmother and Mother make all the decisions. He just goes along."

"Is that right?" It was gratifying news that Father was paying a price for his cruelty to me. Once again, I couldn't help thinking that Confucius would be appalled at the Jia household, where the women ruled, and the eldest male groveled on his knees.

Tingting, I remembered, had witnessed Daiyu's death. "Because you weren't at my wedding, you ended up at Bamboo Lodge, right?"

Tingting's face fell. "Yes."

"Was it true what Swallow said, that Daiyu's last words were: 'Baoyu, Baoyu, you betrayed me!'?"

For ten breaths, Tingting looked at me silently. Finally she said, "Yes, that's true, but you've got to put it in context. Daiyu didn't know what was going on. Very few people did, I didn't either. There was so much secrecy during that whole period; everything was conspiratorial. Grandmother and your mother had their tight little circle, and if you weren't part of that, you didn't hear anything. It was only later that things started to leak out."

I shifted on my kang, trying to absorb what Tingting had said. At last I asked, "Why did Grandmother and Mother decide to marry me to Baochai?"

Again, Tingting took her time before answering. "I think they were absolutely panicked about your health. I don't know what your memories of that period are, but you looked horrible, and you came across like you'd lost your mind. Grandmother and Mother were desperate for some way to restore you back to health, and at some point they became convinced the way to do that was to marry you off. Looking back at it now, it may seem like a terrible idea, but I think at the time they thought marriage would be a kind of salvation for you."

Tingting raised her eyebrows and shook her head.

"Then, once they'd decided to marry you off, the question was to whom. I know right at that time Grandmother made a trip to Bamboo Lodge to see Daiyu. She came back convinced Daiyu was going to die, and die soon. Of course, she was right. That meant if the purpose of marrying you off was to restore you to health, Daiyu was the worst possible choice.

"Meanwhile, I think your mother always favored Baochai. Why shouldn't she have? Baochai's mother is her sister; the two of them were always close, and they'd become even closer since Baochai's mother moved back to Beijing. With Daiyu out of the picture, Baochai was the obvious choice."

I stared at the carpet covering my kang, a pattern of white chrysanthemums against a blue background. Tingting's explanations made sense.

Then I remembered the deception that had been practiced on me. "If the plan was to marry me to Baochai, why did they tell me I was going to be marrying Daiyu?"

Tingting raised her hands and pushed my question away. "Don't ask *me*. It certainly wasn't *my* idea."

She seemed lost in thought. Finally she said, "You've got to understand: during that period, everybody was a little bit crazy."

With my finger I traced the outline of one of the white chrysanthemums on my carpet. I looked into my heart to find forgiveness for Grandmother and Mother. I did not find it.

"You've been asking *me* all sorts of questions," Tingting said. "Can I ask *you* a question?"

"Of course."

"What was the matter with you during that period? Did you ever figure it out?"

Now it was my turn to take a deep breath. I wondered whether Tingting would understand, but since by now she seemed my only true friend in the family, I decided to be open with her. "It was a stage."

"A stage? A stage in what?"

"My spiritual growth."

Tingting looked suspicious. "What do you mean?"

"Before my illness, I was a purely sensual being. I let my senses govern my life. Everything I did was done for love or lust or gratification of the senses. I needed to get out of that stage and ascend to a higher stage. I did, and as it turned out, the higher stage was a period of nothingness, a period in which my former sensual self was obliterated, but nothing else took its place. Fortunately, I think I'm now getting out of that nothingness stage and making my way to an even higher stage."

Tingting looked puzzled, but not hostile. "I remember when we talked a few months ago, I asked you if you knew who you were. You said no, you didn't. Do you know who you are now?"

After thinking a minute, I said, "Can I tell you a story?"

"It's up to you."

"All right. This story is from the *Book of Zhuangzi*. Once upon a time, Zhuangzi dreamt he was a butterfly, flitting around and enjoying himself. He had no idea he was Zhuangzi. Then suddenly he woke up, and he was Zhuangzi again. But he could not tell: Had he been Zhuangzi dreaming he was a butterfly? Or was he now a butterfly dreaming he was Zhuangzi?"

A long silence followed. I smiled. Tingting looked bewildered. "What does that mean? Are you worried you might be a butterfly?"

I laughed. "Not exactly."

"What does it mean, then?"

"It doesn't suggest anything to you?"

"Not enough."

I leaned back on my kang. "How about this? Even a great sage like Zhuangzi has trouble knowing who he is. Why should I, a mere boy of sixteen, not have trouble too?"

A few days later, I was sitting at my desk, studying the "Autumn Floods" chapter of the *Book of Zhuangzi*. Baochai came into my room, stood beside me, and looked at what I was reading. She said nothing but continued to stare at the book and at me.

Baochai and I did not live together. She had her room, I had mine. It was unusual for her to come into my room. It was even more unusual for her to stand beside me and stare.

"Why are you staring at me like that?"

She cleared her throat. "I think we can agree that our becoming husband and wife did not reflect either your personal wishes or mine. That having been said, the fact remains: we *are* husband and wife. That in turn means I have to rely on you for the rest of my entire life.

"You are always in here reading your friend Zhuangzi. However, the wisest of the ancient sages all said that man should strive for virtue, and by virtue they meant filial piety, family responsibility, carrying on the family lineage, service to the Emperor."

I stiffened. "What the ancient sages said was that man should strive to keep the heart of a newborn baby. What did they mean by that? A newborn baby has no cravings or hatreds, no greed or envy. As soon as we're born, though, we start to sink into the mire of lust and greed, anger and passion. What the ancient sages advocated was avoiding the snare of worldly attachments."

Baochai's goose-egg-shaped face tightened with resentment; her voice became razor-sharp. "Despite what *you* think, what the ancients saw when they looked into the heart of a newborn baby was loyalty and filial piety, not detachment from humanity or escape from the world. For Confucius and Mencius, love and sympathy were basic facts of human life.

"Don't you remember Mencius' definition of what it means to be human? A human being, he said, is someone who cannot bear to see pain or suffering around him. Mencius and Confucius, the Duke of Zhou, Kings Yao and Shun—all of them spent their entire lives trying to help other people and make the world a better place. What they meant by the heart of a newborn baby was simply a love of humanity. Whereas you are so cold-hearted you seem willing even to reject your own family. I ask you: what kind of world would this be if everyone were to think and act as you do?"

I groaned and rested my elbows on my desk, my head on

my hands. Baochai's grating voice conveyed the rote assurance of someone who had never, even once, doubted anything she had been taught.

She was erudite, no doubt about that. She could keep on countering my rational arguments with rational arguments of her own, until we both fell over in exhaustion. And she would.

The problem was our differences transcended the realm of rational argument. We came from different spiritual universes.

When I thought about questions of individual morality, I viewed them in the context of human suffering and the need to escape the endless cycle of birth and rebirth. These concepts meant nothing to her. Instead, she placed her faith in loyalty and filial piety.

I knew what those principles meant. I had studied them for years. After sixteen years growing up in the Jia household, however, I could no longer believe in them.

I decided to take a different tack. "Throughout the history of this country, there have been hermits and recluses, men who dropped out of society and followed their own spiritual paths. Society has always respected the choices made by those individuals and allowed them to pursue their spiritual goals in peace. Did your beloved Duke of Zhou go out and arrest all the recluses and hermits and force them to become government bureaucrats? Did Kings Yao and Shun do that? Why can't—"

"If you study those hermits and recluses," Baochai interrupted, "you'll find that all the respectable ones took up that path in times of trouble, when the Empire was in decline, or the government was corrupt. That isn't remotely the case today. Our Empire is at the height of its glory. Our government has never been more virtuous. Plus, our family is deeply indebted to the Emperor; we've received innumerable favors from him.

"Look at *you*." Baochai pointed her silk-clad arm at me, thrust her right index finger, with its perfectly buffed, red-painted nail, directly in my face. "Your grandmother has doted on you your entire life. Your parents have treated you like a jewel. What possible justification do *you* have for going off and becoming a hermit?"

My parents had treated me like a jewel?

My father had beaten me so badly I was bedridden for months. My mother had treated a girl I loved with appalling cruelty. The two of them, in conspiracy with Grandmother, had lied to me and tricked me into an unwanted, loveless marriage. Baochai's rewriting of my life story appalled me.

I smiled and said nothing. I was never going to win an argument with Baochai.

Given opportunity by my silence, Baochai said, "I see you've run out of arguments. I'm not surprised. I just hope you'll take to mind what I've said today and start putting your life together again."

I sighed. "What is it you want me to do? Do you want me to be like Laolaizi, that paragon of filial piety, who dressed in baby clothes, even when he was sixty years old, just because it amused his parents?"

"Don't be ridiculous. What you need to do is simple and obvious. You need to buckle down, start studying again, and prepare to take the Imperial Examination in two years. If you could only do that—pass the Imperial Examination. I know your father has a lot more plans for you after that, becoming a government official and so forth. But if you could just pass the examination, then, even if you stopped there and did nothing more, you would at least have repaid your debt to your grandmother and your parents, repaid your debt to your ancestors, and repaid your debt to the Emperor."

Baochai stood over me, her eyes like daggers. Despite how estranged from her I felt at that moment, something she had said echoed in my ears: "If you could just pass the Imperial Examination, then, *even if you stopped there and did nothing more,* you would have at least repaid your debts."

The idea was new, and it intrigued me. Was this a possible compromise between what I wanted and what everyone around me wanted?

Notably, Baochai had not said anything about consummating our marriage or fathering a male heir.

I looked up at Baochai. She was strikingly beautiful, even though her looks were now contorted by anger. "Are you saying that if I passed the Imperial Examination and then stopped there, did nothing more, to use your own words, you would be happy?"

"At this point, yes."

I lowered my head and said, quietly, "Let me think about that." After a few minutes of silence, Baochai left my room. I remained lost in thought.

One of our managers poked his head into my room. "Excuse me, Second Master, do you mind if I bother you a minute."

"No. What is it?"

"We have sort of a strange situation. Outside our triple gate right now's a Buddhist monk and a Taoist priest. The odd thing is, they have a jade medallion, and they claim their medallion is the one you lost. Now I know you had a lot of problems earlier about being shown one jade piece after another and none of them being yours. So I wouldn't normally bother you just because two characters show up off the street saying they've got your jade. But with these two being a Buddhist monk and a Taoist priest, it made me think they might not be lying. I went to see your father, and he said I should find you and show you the jade.

"I went back to the gate and told the monk and priest I'd take the jade back and show it to you. But they said nothing doing, they weren't going to let go of the jade without their money. Oh, I guess I need to explain: they're asking ten thousand taels for the jade."

"A Buddhist monk and Taoist priest are asking ten thousand taels for returning my jade?"

"Does seem strange, doesn't it? And wait till you *see* these two." The manager furrowed his brow and shook his head.

"Anyway, the point is, I need you to go out there to the gate, look at the jade, and see if it's yours or not. I hope this isn't asking too much, Second Master."

"I'll go."

Waiting at the left side door of our triple gate—with a sextet of Jia family pages lined up in front of them, blocking their way—were two of the ugliest, scruffiest individuals I had ever seen.

On the left, the Buddhist monk had numerous large scabs on his shaved head. A bulbous nose and long, unruly eyebrows dominated his pudgy face. Bare feet poked out from under a moth-eaten maroon robe.

The Taoist tilted to one side: he was lame, one leg shorter than the other. His long, tangled hair fell over his shoulders, while mud and dust caked his once-blue robe. He wore straw sandals.

I couldn't believe my eyes; they were so uncouth. Then I remembered an ancient saying: "He who has attained the Way makes no show of it. He who makes a show of it has not attained the Way."

"Baoyu, your precious jade is back!" the monk shouted at me in a booming voice.

How did he know my name?

I went up to the Buddhist. The rank smell of unwashed clothing and bodies assailed my nostrils. The monk held out a jade piece. I took it and immediately knew it was mine. Touching it was enough.

"It's mine," I told the manager.

"Where's our ten thousand taels?" the monk said.

"Yes, we need it immediately," the Taoist said. "We have a very busy schedule." He doubled over in laughter.

The manager looked appalled. "I'll ... go talk to First Master." He hastened away, leaving me alone with the monk and priest.

For a minute, the Buddhist, Taoist, and I simply stared at each other. Soon curiosity got the better of me. "Where are you two from?"

The Buddhist waved his hand in the air. "Whence we came, thither we shall go. We're here to return your jade. Can you tell us where *it* came from?"

Without thinking, I said, "It came out of my mouth."

Both the Buddhist and the Taoist roared with laughter. "The stone came from out of his mouth," the Taoist said between giggles. "That's a good one."

"All right then, if you want to know where we came from," the Buddhist said, "we came out of our mouths too." They laughed even harder.

Just then the manager returned. Beckoning the monk and priest, he said, "First Master will see you in his study." To me the manager said, "First Master said you should get back to your studies."

The monk and priest headed off, the Buddhist swaggering, the Taoist limping. Whether by design or forgetfulness, they left the jade with me.

Later that day, the entire family gathered in Grandmother's reception hall to celebrate the return of my jade. By now, the jade was once again hanging from my neck, secured by its woven silk cord of five colors.

The cord's slight pull on my neck and the jade's faint weight against my chest felt good. While I had long since lost faith in the jade's ability to protect me from harm, its return seemed a good omen. I couldn't help reflecting that the manner of its return—by the scabby-headed monk and lame priest— was as bizarre as the manner of its first appearance—in my mouth, at birth.

"Baoyu," Grandmother said, "now that your jade is back, you should be able to throw off that horrible mood that's been plaguing you for so long. That's been your problem all along. Your health depends on your jade; without it, your health falls apart."

Apparently Grandmother had not noticed I had already recovered my health.

"Another thing," Grandmother continued. "Now that your jade is back and you're going to be healthy again, you need to start preparing for the Imperial Examination. You haven't been to Clan School for a while, so you're going to have to work twice as hard. But we all know you can do it." My father nodded in agreement.

Grandmother's words startled me. After my beating, she had told me I didn't have to go to Jia Clan School anymore. I assumed she was signaling she didn't care whether I stood for the Imperial Examination or not. I now realized I was mistaken.

I should have known. She may have wanted to brighten my spirits at a time I was racked with pain, but in the end she was matriarch of a great noble family and just as much a Confucian as Father and Baochai.

My father told the assembled group of his dealings with the Buddhist and the Taoist. "When they first came into my study, they immediately and in no uncertain terms demanded their ten thousand taels. Then, without being invited, they both sat down. I took that to mean they weren't going to leave until they got their money. I tried to engage them in small talk. I asked them what monastery they were from and where they found the jade. They pushed aside my questions and kept demanding their ten thousand taels. I told them they would get their money, but it might take a few minutes. They told me to hurry up. At that point I left, leaving a few pages to guard over them as they sat in my study.

"I came back and talked with my wife. We didn't know what to do, since obviously we don't have ten thousand taels just lying around the house. We talked about what we could pawn to pay the two characters off. Finally, my wife suggested that, to gain time, I should go back and entertain them. Entertain them? I thought. I'm no entertainer—"

On that point, I had to agree with my father.

"—and those two didn't seem in the mood for entertainment. Since I didn't have any better ideas of my own, though, I followed my wife's advice and headed back to my study. When I got there, the two were gone! The pages said they'd just gotten up and left, without saying anything. And of course, without having gotten their money." Father raised his eyebrows and shrugged.

"I can't believe a Buddhist monk and a Taoist priest would do something solely for money," I said.

"I wonder where they found the jade," my mother said.

"Judging by the way they came and left," Baochai said, "I suspect they didn't *find* it, they *took* it."

"But it was lost here in our mansion," Mother said. "How could those two have taken it?"

"If they could bring it back, they could have taken it," said Baochai.

Three days later, I heard a servant talking in front of Baochai's room. "The monk and priest are back, demanding their ten thousand taels. First Master is away, and First Mistress doesn't know what to do. She asks if Second Mistress can come to her sitting room to discuss how to handle things."

My mother wanted to consult with Baochai, not me. She trusted her daughter-in-law more than her own son.

I decided to take matters into my own hands. I went to our mansion's triple gate and once again found the scabby-headed Buddhist monk and lame Taoist priest, looking as ragamuffin as before. A phalanx of pages blocked their way.

"Baoyu," the monk shouted when he saw me. "Maybe you can help us get our money."

I motioned to the pages to step aside and ushered the pair into our main courtyard. "If you'll take a seat for a few minutes," I said, "my mother will have the money ready." I had no basis for that statement, but it was the first thing that came to mind.

"That won't be necessary," the Buddhist said. "We came just to talk with you."

"What?"

"We came to talk with you. We'll be seeing you again, someday."

"You will?"

"Yes, we're looking forward to some good times together," the Taoist said.

"You are? Where?"

"You don't need to worry about that," the Buddhist said. "Just submit to fate, and things will take their natural course."

I gaped at them.

"One other thing," the monk said. "I have a word of advice for you."

"Yes."

The monk approached me, cupped his hands, and spoke into my ear. "All earthly ties of affection are bewitchments. They are obstacles blocking your spiritual path."

With that, the monk and priest turned around, walked out of our courtyard, and headed up the street. The monk swaggered, the priest limped, and both were laughing and poking each other in the ribs. I stared at them, dumbfounded.

16

Soon after the return of my jade, two changes took place at the Jia mansion. My father left Beijing to take up a new post—imperial grain commissioner of Jiangxi province. Simultaneously, I sat down to study and prepare for the Imperial Examination.

Father was honored by his appointment; provincial grain commissioner was an important and lucrative position. The function of a grain commissioner was to enforce and administer the grain tribute, the requirement that agricultural landowners contribute fixed quotas of husked rice to be shipped north to Beijing to feed its vast and hungry population. To meet his expenses, a grain commissioner was entitled to charge landowners a cash fee for each picul of rice collected.

Father left within two weeks. Once again, I was excused from accompanying him on the first stage of his journey to the Pavilion of Parting. The reason given was my poor health, even though by now this was a transparent excuse.

In buckling down to prepare for the Imperial Examination, I was bowing to the inevitable. Not only were my father and Baochai adamant that I take it, Grandmother was too. I had thought a great deal about what Baochai had said: that if I could just pass the Imperial Examination, then, *even if I stopped there and did nothing more,* I would have repaid my debts to my family, my ancestors, and the Emperor. Baochai's proposal seemed to offer a way out of the bind between my own desires and those of my family.

The goal of passing the Imperial Examination was daunting. Every three years, five thousand two hundred candidates took the test. By rule, only ninety-eight passed—no more, no less. In other words, the odds of passing the Imperial Examination were worse than one in fifty.

There was also the problem that I had not attended Jia Clan School, or even cracked open a Confucian text, in more than a year and a half. I did not look forward to returning to school.

Jia Clan School, supported by and limited to members of our extended Jia clan, was relentlessly grim. Located a short horseback ride from our mansion, the gray brick edifice had no kangs, no braziers, no heat of any kind. During winter all of us students (there were generally eight or nine of us) recited our lessons through a cloud of steam—our breath. We sat facing a gargantuan Confucian altar, an elaborate wooden enclosure in the center of which hung ten tablets, each with large gold characters on a brilliant red background listing generation after generation of Jia family ancestors. On the top of the altar, even larger characters proclaimed a Confucian motto: "Filial piety and brotherly obedience are the roots of humanity."

The instructor was a Jia family member who, though from a minor branch, had the undeniable prestige of having passed the Imperial Examination. A gaunt, white-haired man, he seemed to us students old enough to have studied with the ancient Confucius himself. He could flawlessly recite from memory the entire Confucian corpus yet could never remember any of our names.

My studies at Jia Clan School consisted entirely of memorization. I started with the first of the *Four Books*, the *Analects*. My task was to memorize the entire work, passage by passage. A passage was thirty characters when I started, many more as my studies advanced. The instructor and I would go over the passage character by character, to make sure I understood each character's meaning. Then, I would recite the passage one hundred times: fifty while looking at the book, fifty with the book turned over.

I found Jia Clan School boring, but I was an excellent

student. I had a knack for memorization. Within weeks I could memorize two hundred characters a day, on some days even three hundred. Soon I was through the *Analects* (which was only about twelve thousand characters) and onto the other three of the *Four Books*. Still, I did not find Confucius and Mencius edifying—quite the contrary, I found their sententious moralizing annoying—and I failed to see the need for me to spend my youth memorizing volume after volume of their writings.

A serendipitous discovery saved me from a return to Jia Clan School. I was rummaging around our back storerooms, looking for copies of the *Four Books* and *Five Classics*. I had burned my old copies after Grandmother had told me I didn't have to go back to school. In a dark corner, I came upon a dust-covered wooden chest. Opening it, I found stacks of papers. They turned out to be past examination questions and answers. Not only that, the answers were explicitly identified as having been *successful*.

I took the papers back to my study and pored over them. From that point on, I looked at preparation for the Imperial Examination in an entirely new way.

The standard wisdom was that a candidate needed to memorize, in their entirety, nine works: the *Four Books*—the *Analects, Great Learning, Doctrine of the Mean,* and *Mencius*—and the *Five Classics*—the *Book of Changes, Book of History, Book of Poetry, Book of Rites,* and *Spring and Autumn Annals.* All told, the nine works were said to amount to around four hundred thirty-one thousand characters. I wouldn't know, I never counted them.

The papers in the wooden chest revealed, however, that examination questions tended to repeat and focused on only a few select passages from the *Four Books* and *Five Classics*. That made perfect sense. Examiners were men like my father, who *had been* an examiner a year earlier. These men were unimaginative, not-terribly-bright bureaucrats who would prefer to reuse questions they knew had worked in the past rather than come up with new questions of their own.

This meant I did not have to memorize the *Four Books*

and *Five Classics* in their entirety. My younger self had been right: it *was* a waste of my youth to attempt that. All that was needed was to focus on the passages that popped up again and again in examination questions and analyze how the successful answers treated those passages. I breathed a sigh of relief. My preparation was now manageable.

My discovery of the papers in the wooden chest also answered a question that had long baffled me: How had my father, in my opinion not the brightest of men, managed to pass the Imperial Examination, managed to surmount the one in fifty odds. I now knew how—knew with a certainty, for marginal notes in his calligraphic style were scattered throughout the papers.

Father had never informed me of the existence of this treasure trove. I wondered why not. It couldn't be because he had forgotten about it. He must have spent years using the questions and answers to prepare for the Imperial Examination, just as I was planning to do. They were what had launched his career. He had also probably used them to devise questions for his recent stint as a provincial examiner.

Only one conclusion was possible: Father had deliberately concealed from me his secret to passing the Imperial Examination.

I decided to ignore this sad fact. Since I had discovered the wooden chest on my own, what difference did Father's spitefulness make?

I soon settled into a comfortable routine. Every day, all morning and afternoon, I sat at my desk in my room, poring over old exam answers, referring back to the Confucian classics, and composing answers of my own. In the evening, I put down my Confucian studies and took up works I found personally meaningful—Zhuangzi, or more and more as time went on, the teachings of the Buddha.

My life was simpler and calmer than it had been for years. Baochai and I continued to live separately, rarely together except for family gatherings, and a polite formality seemed to suffice for our marital relations. My father was stationed a journey of many weeks away; I had nothing to fear from him.

I still thought about Daiyu, about Amber, about Goldie, but by now I was able to contain my grief. I didn't find my Confucian studies interesting, but at least there was a purpose to what I was doing. My greatest satisfaction came from the evenings I spent immersed in Buddhism.

The Imperial Examination was given once every three years, in the years of the ox, dragon, sheep, and dog. It had last been given in the year of the ox, and thus a year and a half remained before it would be given again, in the year of the dragon. I anticipated spending this entire period in the study routine I had created for myself. Once again, though, as when I had moved into the garden, events soon made a mockery of my optimism.

Four months after I began preparing for the Imperial Examination, I heard a babble of alarmed voices outside my study door. I went to investigate. Maids informed me that Grandmother and Mother had been summoned to the Forbidden City; they were now putting on their ceremonial attire. A eunuch was waiting in our main courtyard to accompany them.

I rushed to the courtyard, where I learned the eunuch had brought news about Spring. She was seriously ill. On the verge of death.

Grandmother and Mother emerged, weeping. Ill at ease in their stiff official robes and heavy official jewelry, they walked slowly, as if trying to balance a great weight. Maids supported Grandmother on either side, and the lines around her eyes looked even deeper than before. "I can't understand it," she said. "The last time we saw her she looked so healthy." Grandmother and Mother disappeared into separate palanquins and, led by the eunuch on horseback, headed to the Forbidden City.

Grandmother and Mother did not return for eight hours, until well into the evening. When they stepped out of their palanquins, their faces told the sad news faster than words could have. Spring had died.

Back in her sitting room, Grandmother, her face sagging with exhaustion, told a story of tragedy made even worse by disrespect. "When we got there, they told us we couldn't go in to see Spring. The reason they gave was that some of the other imperial concubines might be coming in to see her, and it would be improper for us to see them. So they put us in a small sitting room outside and made us wait.

"We sat there for five hours. Nobody told us anything. Then we saw them bring in the Imperial Astrologer. I knew what that meant: they were already choosing an auspicious date for Spring's funeral. But I didn't say anything, and nobody said anything to us. Finally, an hour or so later, a little eunuch—younger than you, Baoyu—came in and said, 'Her Majesty, the Jia Concubine, has passed.' He didn't say anything more, just turned around and walked out."

Grandmother paused, closed her eyes, and shook her head from side to side.

"We stayed in the room, waiting, but nobody else came out to talk to us. After an hour, we left."

I was in a state of shock. I knew Spring; at one time I was as close to her as anybody in the world. She was the most vibrant, energetic, healthy girl imaginable. She was only twenty-five. How could she possibly be dead?

I spent a sleepless night grieving for Spring. Memories came unbidden: Spring and I seated on a kang, teacups between us, while she patiently taught me my first characters. Spring, at a birthday party for Grandmother, reciting poetry she had written, all of us in awe of her poetic talent. The most vivid memory of all: Spring's nighttime, lantern-lit visit to our magnificent new garden, created especially for her.

The next morning, I realized I was once again losing control of my emotions. I needed to get back to the principles of detachment and keeping an even emotional keel. I limped over to my desk and began reading Zhuangzi and the Buddha.

By the end of the day, I had regained my composure. Spring had merely gone on to another life. Since she had been an exemplary person in the life she had just left, her karma was excellent, and her new life would be better than her previous one.

I was able to sleep that night and resume my studies the next day.

During the month following Spring's death, Grandmother, Mother, First Uncle, and First Aunt traveled to the Forbidden City almost every day to attend funeral rites for Spring. Because I had no official rank—I did not have a title of nobility, as First Uncle did, nor did I hold an official position, as Father did—I was unable to attend any of these ceremonies. My father too missed all the rites for Spring. The Imperial Astrologer had set the date for Spring's funeral solely by the stars, not by how long it would take for Father to travel from Jiangxi to Beijing.

The more time Grandmother and Mother spent in the Forbidden City, the more frustrated and upset they became. Spring was so young. Grandmother and Mother, who were permitted to visit her in the Forbidden City a few times a year, had seen her only two months before, and she had seemed in perfect health. Why had she died? No one offered any explanation.

Adding to their discontent, Grandmother and Mother felt a distinct coldness every time they went to the Forbidden City. Their relationship to Spring was respected: at the various ceremonies, they were always placed in a proper, front-row position. But no one spoke to them; it seemed as if everyone was avoiding them.

"They certainly make it clear they're Manchus and we're Chinese, don't they?" Grandmother said one day after returning home.

"They do have that *line* they insist on," Mother said.

Grandmother and Mother were referring to a fact all of us in the Jia family preferred to think about as little as possible. The Emperor and the inner circle of the Imperial Court were Manchu. We were Han Chinese.

Not only that, in strict legal terms, we were no more free than were the three hundred or so servants who staffed our mansion. They were bondservants owned by us. We were bondservants owned by the Emperor.

Chinese bondservant families like ours could scale extravagant heights of wealth and power, as we had. Everything depended on imperial favor, however, which could change in an instant, or on a whim.

"I still can't get over the fact they've never told us why Spring died," Grandmother said.

"I keep thinking we should ask," said Mother.

"I'm afraid. That Forbidden City intimidates me."

Mother looked at Grandmother skeptically. "That isn't like you, to be intimidated."

"I know. It's just ... all those Manchus and eunuchs. And those horrible robes we have to wear. Whenever I go there, I can't even open my mouth."

"Maybe when my husband gets home, he can get to the bottom of it."

"He's certainly more used to dealing with them than we are. The trouble is we don't know *when* he's coming home."

As the days passed, another worry came to the fore. Normally, when an Imperial Concubine died, she was given a posthumous title of nobility. We heard nothing about a title for Spring, absolutely nothing. Why not? Again, Grandmother and Mother were too timid to ask.

Three weeks after the conclusion of Spring's funeral rites, more devastating news arrived. We first heard the news from a distant relative of ours who worked in the Imperial Secretariat. He told my uncle, who went immediately to the Ministry of Civil Affairs to see whether the news was true. It was.

My father had been impeached. The governor of Jiangxi province had filed a complaint against him, alleging he had failed to control his subordinates, who had requisitioned extortionate amounts of grain and demanded excessive fees. My father had been relieved of his position and ordered to return to Beijing to defend himself.

Grandmother and Mother broke down crying. Baochai, dutiful daughter-in-law that she was, tried to comfort them. I too tried to console them but was so dazed by the news I could hardly say anything.

"I've had a bad feeling about that grain commissioner post for a while," my mother said, wiping her eyes with her handkerchief.

"What do you mean?" Baochai asked.

"For one thing, grain commissioner posts are supposed to be so lucrative. But your father-in-law hasn't sent a single tael back ever since he arrived in Jiangxi. He's written to me several times asking me to send *him* money. He says he needs it down there. Anyway, I've sent him just about everything we have."

Mother's words jolted me. I thought we were rich. Apparently, we were not. Of course, I'd never thought to ask.

"Another thing," Mother went on, "you remember those men he took with him when he went to Jiangxi, the ones he called his secretaries?"

I had always called them his cronies.

"I keep seeing their wives at social events, and every time I see them they've got more jewelry on, more gold, more silver, fancier clothes. I've had a queasy feeling for some time that those men have been stealing your father-in-law blind."

"I've always felt those provincial posts are too risky," Grandmother said. "Your husband's an honest man, but he's not good at managing people, and sometimes he's a little naïve. I don't think he was ever cut out for a provincial post."

"He wanted one so badly."

"I know, I know, they all do. But he would have been much better off passing his life quietly here in Beijing, as a junior official." She sighed and lowered her head.

I sat in stunned silence. Never before had I heard Grandmother and Mother calmly and rationally discuss my father's flaws. They had, of course, screamed at him after his beating of me, but their words then had been neither calm nor rational. Today, their violation of filial piety was matter of fact.

"I just hope this god-awful mess doesn't result in our losing the Rongguo title," Grandmother said. She was referring to the hereditary title of nobility our family held—Duke of Rongguo. First Uncle, elder brother to my father, currently held the title. Grandmother was right, however: a scandal involving my father could result in punishment of the entire family.

Two months later, Father arrived back at our mansion. He looked older than I remembered, with gray streaks in his hair and more lines in his face. Drained after a long, difficult journey, he said little and fell into bed.

The next morning, he sacrificed meat, rice, fruit, and wine in our family's ancestral temple. Then he sent to the Forbidden City his acknowledgement of culpability, which he had composed during his journey. Three days later, he appeared before the Emperor in person to acknowledge his guilt.

When Father returned from the Forbidden City, he avoided our eyes, his shoulders slumped, he walked like an old man. The family gathered in Grandmother's reception hall to hear his report.

"The eunuchs took me to the upper library," he began. "When I first entered the room, the Emperor was bent over a pile of papers, with around twenty eunuchs standing guard. For a minute, he didn't look up or say anything. I assumed he was looking over my file, so I stood there as still as I could. Then he looked up and said, 'Your name is Jia, right?'

"I said yes.

"'Are you related to Jia Fan?'

"That's when I knew I was in for a bad time. Jia Fan, who's only distantly related to us, was a magistrate in Suzhou. A year or so ago, he killed another man in an argument over a slave girl. After that, he was impeached, found guilty, and executed. So you can see it was a terrible omen the Emperor was associating me with Jia Fan. But what could I do? I had to answer the Emperor's question and answer it truthfully. I said, 'He's a distant kinsman.'

"The Emperor shook his head and snorted in disgust. 'How could any respectable family raise a man who would do something that vile?'

"The Emperor stared at me. I didn't dare say anything. I was so terrified I could barely stand up.

"Then the Emperor said, 'Wasn't there a Jia Hua who was minister of war for a time and then demoted?'

"By now, I could barely breathe. But again, I had to answer the question. 'The only Jia Hua I know of,' I said, trying to keep my voice steady, 'is a senior imperial tutor. I'm not aware of any member of the Jia clan who's ever been minister of war.'

"The Emperor looked at me as if he didn't believe me. Then he looked back down and started shuffling through his stack of papers again. Finally he looked up and said, 'You can go.'

"With that, I left."

A long silence followed Father's report. All of us were lost in thought, grappling with the realization our family's days of imperial favor had come to an end.

"It's unfortunate your case came up so soon after Jia Fan's," First Uncle said. "It's just coincidence, but it looks bad. The trouble is, our Jia clan has grown so large over the years there are dozens of Jia officials. And in every family's cooking pot, there's at least one black spot."

Once again, everyone lapsed into a morose silence.

"I have the feeling all this is somehow tied in with Spring's death," Grandmother said. "If she were still alive, at least we'd have someone close to the Emperor to put in a good word for us. It's even more than that, though. I can't get over how they never told us what Spring died of, and how cold to us they were during all the funeral rites, and how Spring to this day has never been granted a posthumous title. I don't know how, but I have a sense it's all related."

"What about those two eunuchs who used to come by and tell us all the palace gossip?" Father asked. "Do we still hear from them?"

"The last time was about six months ago," First Uncle said. "They came to our gate and asked for another loan. I told them no. They haven't been back since."

Everyone in the family looked down.

I myself had mixed feelings. On the one hand, I regretted that so many people close to me—my grandmother, mother, father, wife—seemed on the verge of losing everything they held dear. On the other hand, *what* they held dear—wealth, power, official position, a hereditary title of nobility—were things on which I personally placed no value.

More than anything else, I felt the rift between my family and me.

Normally, the return of a provincial official to his home in Beijing was the occasion for an elaborate banquet, including opera performances. Because we were still in mourning for Spring's death, we could not put on opera performances, and in light of my father's unsure status, an elaborate banquet was inappropriate. Grandmother and Mother wanted to do something for Father, however, and they decided on a modest dinner to which only family members and some of our closest friends would be invited. The afternoon event would take place in our main reception hall ten days after Father's return.

Despite the initial talk about modesty, the Jia family's penchant for extravagance soon took over. Grandmother, dressed in an eggplant-colored gown, and my father, clad in gold and orange, sat in the center of a raised platform, in front of four gold-flecked vertical scrolls filled with calligraphic odes to family happiness. Sixty or so guests ate at small tables below, and dozens of green-liveried servants hurried about to keep platters and glasses full. Rows of red lanterns hanging from the ceiling lent everyone a rosy glow, a musician strummed cheerful tunes on a zheng, and the air tantalized with the smells of roast duck and plum sauce.

We were just finishing a course of abalone with peas and fish paste when one of our managers hurried in and whispered something in my father's ear. Father looked alarmed, quickly rose, and began following our manager toward the reception hall's door. Before Father and the manager could reach the door, a man I had never seen before burst through.

A peacock feather, indicating high rank, adorned his round metal hat. His face bore a fierce expression. Soon, six other men appeared. They wore metal helmets topped with red plumes, and their bodies were covered with brown leather armor. They were soldiers.

"Are you Jia Zheng?" the man with the peacock feather asked my father in a peremptory tone.

"Yes." My father's voice shook.

"I am Commander Zhao of the Imperial Guard. I have ordered that all gates of this mansion be sealed. No one is to leave."

When the Commander said "Imperial Guard," everyone in the reception hall cringed. The Imperial Guard was an elite military unit under the personal command of the Emperor. Historically, it had been used to crush the ruling monarch's political and dynastic opponents and carry out secret executions.

In the silence that followed Commander Zhao's announcement, we could hear footsteps—many footsteps. Through the still-open door to the reception hall we saw squadrons of soldiers march by. The Jia mansion was under military occupation!

"I have two orders from the Emperor," Commander Zhao said. He held up two sheets of paper and began reading from the first. "Jia She, Jia Zheng."

First Uncle and Father stepped forward.

"Kowtow to the Emperor."

My uncle and father went down on their knees and kowtowed to the Commander, as the representative of the Emperor.

"By order of the Emperor, Rongguo Mansion is to be searched, and anything illicit or contraband, and any evidence of criminal activity, is to be confiscated."

First Uncle and Father again kowtowed.

Hearing the words "Rongguo Mansion" made a terrifying situation even worse. Rongguo Mansion was the proper legal name for what we always thought of as our Jia family mansion. But the name reminded us of a fact we preferred to ignore. We did not own our mansion. The Emperor did.

The mansion had been assigned to us when we were granted our hereditary title of nobility—Duke of Rongguo. Presumably, if the title were taken away, so too would be the mansion.

First Uncle and Father remained on their knees. The commander held up the second sheet of paper.

"Jia She, Jia Zheng, Jia Rong, Jia Baoyu—"

Me!

"—Jia Lan."

My head spun, I started trembling. Why were they

summoning *me*? I hadn't done anything.

My cousin Rong and my nephew, Lan, moved forward. I followed. We went down on our knees, joining First Uncle and Father in a straight line in front of the Commander.

"Kowtow to the Emperor," he ordered. We kowtowed in the direction of the Commander.

As we were kowtowing, I realized why I had been summoned, why even little ten-year-old Lan, son of my sister-in-law and deceased older brother, had been too. The order had named every male member of the Jia family who resided in the mansion. For once, I envied my loathsome half-brother, Huan, who had been kicked out.

Satisfied with our kowtows, the Commander continued to read from the second order. "By order of the Emperor, you are to surrender to the custody of Commander Zhao of the Imperial Guard, to be detained in the Temple of the Prison God pending full investigation of the activities of your family and the results of the search of Rongguo Mansion."

Had I heard the word *prison*? Were we being imprisoned?

A group of ten soldiers marched into the room. They carried two pairs of stocks and a long rope. The soldiers carrying the stocks rushed to First Uncle and Father. One group thrust First Uncle's neck and wrists between the thick wooden boards of one set, then clamped and locked the boards shut. Another group did the same to Father. Father's and Uncle's heads and hands poked out pathetically in front of their stocks, body parts without a body.

Meanwhile, the soldiers carrying the rope surrounded Rong, Lan, and me and tied us together in a line, with Rong in front, me in the middle, and Lan behind. An extension of rope in front of Rong ended in a loop. We could be led along, like donkeys.

The Commander ordered us to leave the reception hall and walk to our triple gate. Father and First Uncle staggered under the weight of the heavy stocks into which they were locked. Rong, Lan, and I had it easier: we simply had to move at the same pace and in the same direction. Looking back over my shoulder as we shuffled out, I saw the other dinner guests—the female members of our family and our close friends—reeling from fear and shock.

As we passed through our main courtyard, sounds assailed us from all sides. Heavy boots trampling on stone floors. Orders being shouted out. Vases being smashed. Furniture being splintered.

Outside our triple gate, three wagons awaited. Each wagon was an improvised prison cell, with bamboo bars enclosing all four sides and the top. Soldiers pushed Father into one wagon, First Uncle into another, while Rong, Lan, and I, still roped together, went into the third. Soldiers locked the gates to our wheeled prison cells, and our procession headed off.

Gawkers and passers-by filled the late-afternoon streets. Rong, Lan, and I slumped down into the bed of our wagon to avoid being seen. Father and First Uncle, imprisoned in their thick stocks, did not have that option. Jeers and catcalls came from Beijing residents delighted to see what appeared to be a group of aristocrats getting their comeuppance.

I thought back to a previous occasion on which I had been part of a procession through the streets of Beijing. Then, I had been mounted on a magnificent white horse, ensconced in a saddle decorated with opals and agates. Crowds dressed in rags and straw sandals had gazed up at me in awe. I had felt guilty: I had so much, they had so little.

No need to feel guilty today. Today the crowds were free, I was a prisoner.

We traveled in the wagons for more than an hour, from the city into the countryside. My back hurt, my head ached, my eyes itched, and I needed to piss.

As the journey dragged on, I seethed with anger. For years, I had vowed I would never become part of the world of government officialdom and imperial politics. Now, at age seventeen, I was already a victim of that world. And I had done nothing! Bile rose in my throat.

I gave my jade pendant an angry squeeze. What a useless piece of rock it had become.

I worried about little ten-year-old Lan, who looked

extremely pale, said nothing, and for most of the journey kept his eyes shut. I hoped he would survive whatever ordeal awaited us.

In far worse shape was twenty-year-old Rong. He bawled like a baby, and from time to time blurted out, "We're ruined. We're ruined."

"Why are we ruined?" I asked at one point. "We haven't done anything."

Rong grimaced, baring his betel-stained teeth. "You fool!"

We stopped in front of a large ceremonial gate painted in Taoist imagery. A plaque on top read: "Temple of the Prison God."

The soldiers led us into a large hall, bare except for a huge, twice life-size, painted-wood statue of a ferocious-looking deity. The Prison God, I guessed. The deity had reddish-orange skin, red hair, long fangs, and a collection of writhing snakes at his feet.

They pushed us through the hall into a large open area surrounded by high walls. In the center of this area stood a fortress-like stone building, with an iron door and thick iron bars over all the windows. Soldiers armed with halberds, maces, and battle axes guarded the building on all sides.

In front of the iron door, the soldiers who had brought us from our mansion turned the five of us over to a new group of soldiers. The captain of the new group unlocked the iron door and pushed us in.

Inside was dark. Dark and smoky. The air reeked of rancid oil, rotting vegetables, and coal dust.

As my eyes adjusted to the darkness, I realized we were under the overhang of a small, gloomy courtyard. Piled along one side of the courtyard were scores of decaying cabbages. On another side, a stooped, elderly man with only one eye was cooking something over a portable stove.

The soldiers led us through the courtyard to a dark corridor lined with prison cells on either side. Thick bamboo poles separated the cells from the corridor. The only light came from small windows covered with iron bars, one window to a cell.

The soldiers unlocked and removed Father's and First

Uncle's stocks and shoved them into one cell. They untied Rong, Lan, and me and pushed us into another. The soldiers closed the cell doors, secured each door with three locks, and left.

For almost a year, I had been making good progress on my resolve to keep my life on an even emotional keel, to remain detached, to avoid the extremes of elation or depression. This new development overwhelmed my youthful resolve. A net of despair tightened around me, a poisonous mood the color of verdigris enveloped me. It was one thing to say I placed no value on wealth, rank, or power. It was another to say I didn't care whether I was in prison or not.

17

A STRAW FLOOR teeming with vermin. A wooden bucket in the corner of the cell, where the three of us pissed and shat.

Two meals a day. Each and every one a bowl of rice and a bowl of cabbage soup with a few bits of sour pork thrown in. All prepared and delivered to us by the stooped man with one eye.

No books. Even if I had books, no light to read them by, for the single window in our cell admitted its dim, smoky light only a few hours a day.

To look at, only grotesque monsters, for painted on the walls of our cell were hideously ugly, half-human figures with long horns popping out of the tops of their heads and jagged fangs protruding from their mouths. This was the Temple of the Prison God, and these, I guessed, were the Prison God's disciples. In the dim light of our cell, they seemed as real as our own bodies.

All the while, I was elegantly dressed. To attend my father's welcome-home banquet, I had donned an embroidered white silk gown and on top of that a red velvet archer's jacket. This costume—increasingly dirty and smelly—remained my only clothing for the duration of my stay in the Temple of the Prison God. White, I can attest, does not take dirt well.

After a week of eating only cabbage and rice, all three of us—Rong, Lan, and I—developed diarrhea. The stench inside our cell became unbearable. Flies arrived in hordes. It seemed as if my nose and mouth were covered with a rag soaked in shit.

I began to lose weight. My white gown, which had fit perfectly the day of the banquet, became baggy. I had experienced an extreme weight loss once before, during my breakdown following the death of Amber. Afterwards, people told me I had wasted away almost to the point of death. In the Temple of the Prison God, I feared I was again following that dangerous path.

To complete my list of health woes, I developed an itchy red rash in my private parts. Soon scabs covered the entire area, then the scabs began to break. I suspected I had acquired the rash from my straw bed, rife with tiny vermin.

My two cellmates offered no consolation. Lan, with whom I had spent little time previously, was a mystery. He spent much of his time staring at the straw on his bed and arranging it so that all the blades pointed in the same direction.

"What are you doing that for?" I asked.

He didn't look at me, instead he continued to work on his straw. "I can't sleep if the straw's not all lined up."

I tried to talk to Lan, comfort him, assure him I would protect him. I felt doubly obligated to do this, since Rong showed no concern whatsoever for him. Lan ignored me, however, and didn't seem to want to talk. After a few days, I gave up.

Rong, even though the oldest, was coping the worst. He cried for long periods and talked only to bemoan his fate.

Three days after our arrival at the Temple of the Prison God, Rong was standing at the front of our cell, crying and squeezing the bamboo poles with his sweaty hands. I went over to comfort him. "I'm sure something will work out. We have many friends, many relatives in powerful positions. I'm sure they're all working to get us out of here. We have to have faith they'll be successful."

Rong turned to me, his face enraged. "What do you know, you simpleton? As far as that goes, what do you care? You know *you're* going to come out of this just fine." He sneered. "Like the lotus rising out of the muck."

"Cousin Rong, don't get angry at *me*. I'm in this mess just as deep as you are."

Rong's knuckles turned white as he squeezed the bamboo

poles. "Don't make me laugh. You don't have anything to worry about. Everybody knows Grandmother's going to leave all her money to you, and you can go on being the spoiled rich brat the rest of your life. But the rest of us have to make our own way."

I said nothing, drew back. I suspected he was saying to my face what others had long said behind my back. They were wrong, though, and I resented the insult. I didn't lust for Grandmother's money, I didn't lust for money from any source. My future aspirations lay in an entirely different direction. I never tried to comfort Rong again.

The outside world occasionally penetrated the Temple of the Prison God. A distant relative of ours knew one of the soldiers guarding us, and the relative was able to slip into the prison building from time to time and bring us up to date. The news he brought was not good. Our mansion had been ransacked and most of our treasures and art objects either destroyed or carted away. Our basement vaults lacked money to pay our servants; many were drifting away. Grandmother, Mother, Baochai, and the other women were still living in the mansion, coping as best as they could.

One day the relative brought news that made life in my cell even more difficult. During the search of our mansion, soldiers had found usurious promissory notes, and they had been found ... in the room of my cousin and cellmate, Rong.

After hearing that news, Rong became even more maudlin and self-pitying than before. "My life is ruined," he repeated, banging his head against the bamboo poles.

When I was younger, I had looked up to Rong. He was three years older, had always held himself out as infinitely more worldly and sophisticated than I, and had snared the beautiful Crimson as his wife at a time when I was still a virgin. How times had changed.

Imprisoned with members of my family, I thought many times of a passage from the *Book of Zhuangzi*: "When the springs dry out, the fish are stranded on the earth. To keep themselves damp, they wet each other with their slime. But it would be better if they could just forget about each other and swim in the rivers and lakes."

Prior to being incarcerated, I had practiced Buddhist meditation informally, by reading Buddhist texts and thinking about them afterwards. According to the texts, meditation could take many forms, and reading followed by reflection was one. Now, with endless amounts of time on my hands and a heightened need for emotional stability, I decided to make my meditation practice more formal.

Every day, often several times a day, I sat down on the straw floor beside my bed, facing the wall, with my back to Rong and Lan. I arranged my legs in half-lotus, sat up straight, and closed my eyes. I looked inward rather than outward. The paintings on the walls of the cell, the fiendish monsters with their long horns and jagged fangs, disappeared.

The first stage of meditation is the calming phase, and for this I used a technique recommended by the Buddha himself: I focused on my breathing. The inhalation. The short pause at the top of the inhalation. The exhalation. The short pause at the bottom of the exhalation.

I tried to stay focused on my breathing, but inevitably other thoughts intruded. My upset stomach. Rong. Grandmother, Mother, and Baochai, back at the mansion. Lan. The maddening itch around my penis. The death of Spring. The possibility of execution. The reek of shit.

I struggled to prevent these extraneous thoughts from worming their way into my mind, but being only human, I did not always succeed. When unwelcome thoughts did intrude, I tried to view them dispassionately, as if from a distance. They were like clouds in the sky, eventually they would move on. Meanwhile, I focused on my breathing. The inhalation. The short pause at the top. The exhalation. The short pause at the bottom.

Usually, after ten or fifteen minutes, my mind had stilled; fewer and fewer extraneous thoughts were making their way in. I was then ready for the next stage—insight meditation.

For that, I usually began by focusing on the Buddha's Four Noble Truths, the subjects of his first sermon, the one he preached to the five ascetics in Sarnath deer park.

The first of the Four Noble Truths was: All life is suffering.

Everything I had seen and experienced in my short life substantiated this. Daiyu, Amber, and Goldie had died horrible deaths at tragically young ages. My sister Spring and my older brother had also died young. The remaining male members of my family were rotting in prison, begging for their lives. The female members were back in our mansion, desperately trying to deal with the collapse of our family's power and wealth. My cousin Lotus was married to a man who beat her. Baochai was trapped in a loveless marriage. Everyone I knew had suffered or was still suffering.

There could be no clearer proof of the ubiquity of suffering than my own life. I had been born with every possible advantage: wealth, social position, good looks, a doting grandmother. Yet I too had suffered. From the wrenching deaths of Daiyu, Amber, and Goldie. From a beating so brutal it took me three months to recover. From a debilitating illness that almost killed me. From being tricked into a fraudulent, unwanted marriage. From being arrested and incarcerated.

Once, I had believed a vast gulf lay between wealthy people like me and poor people. Mounted on a white horse, seated in my saddle encrusted with opals and agates, looking down at people clad in patched clothing and frayed straw sandals, I had thought: I am so fortunate.

The scales had now fallen from my eyes. I could see good fortune was an illusion. Everyone suffers. No one is immune. All life is suffering.

The second of the Four Noble Truths was: The cause of suffering is desire.

I had suffered from the deaths of Daiyu and Amber because I had desired them. Other girls—perhaps thousands around the world—had died around the same time as Daiyu and Amber. I had not suffered from those other girls' deaths, however. Why not? Because I had not desired them.

My family members now suffered because for years they had thirsted for wealth, power, and social standing. If my family had not wanted to live like great lords and ladies, if they had not yearned to live as extravagantly as possible, they would not now be plunged into misery. The cause of suffering is desire.

From this followed the third Noble Truth: To eliminate suffering, eliminate desire.

Which led to the fourth Noble Truth: The path to the elimination of desire is the cultivation of morality, meditation, and insight.

The Buddha said that he who understands these truths "becomes dispassionate toward all things. Being dispassionate, he becomes detached. Through detachment, he becomes liberated."

This was what I needed: dispassion, detachment, liberation.

My meditation and increased commitment to Buddhism gave me the strength to survive imprisonment. I was able to sleep at night and avoid a plunge into utter despair. The monsters on the walls of my cell were simply patches of paint. They did not control my mind or my emotions.

On the forty-first day of our captivity—I was counting by making scratches on the leg of one of the painted monsters—soldiers came to our cells, let us out, took us outside the stone building, and ordered us to stand in a straight line.

The sun blinded me. So long had I been inside the dark, smoky stone building that even with my eyelids half-closed the sun seared the backs of my eyes.

We stood shoulder to shoulder in our straight line—waiting, fearful. After many minutes, a eunuch arrived, carrying a sheaf of imperial decrees. I cannot say what was running through the minds of my four fellow prisoners. I kept repeating to myself: dispassion ... detachment ... dispassion ... detachment.

After we kowtowed, the eunuch held up the first decree. "Jia She."

First Uncle moved forward and kowtowed.

"You have been found guilty of abducting the wife of an honest citizen in order to make her your concubine. Your guilt is aggravated by the fact the young woman in question, Yu Sanjie, killed herself rather than submit to your lust."

Aiya! Over the years I had heard rumors First Uncle was a rampant womanizer, but I had no idea things were *this* bad.

"You have also been found guilty," the eunuch continued in his high voice, "of burying Yu Sanjie without notifying the proper authorities, the crime of clandestine burial."

First Uncle sank lower and lower into his kowtow.

"In view of the fact you are descended from one of the greatest generals in the history of our dynasty, we will forbear imposition of the punishment normally decreed for offenses of this gravity: to wit, execution. Instead, in our clemency, we will impose on you the following punishment: Your hereditary title of nobility, Duke of Rongguo, is revoked. All your property is confiscated. You are sentenced to penal servitude at a military post on the Mongolian border, where you may attempt to redeem yourself by diligent service."

Our mansion—gone. The garden—gone. Our aristocratic status—gone. Our annual stipend—gone. Everything Grandmother, Mother, and the rest of them held dear—gone. And we might never see First Uncle again.

A soldier rudely grabbed First Uncle by the shoulder and raised him up. Several soldiers then pushed him back into the stone prison building.

The eunuch returned the first imperial decree to his sheaf and pulled out another. "Jia Rong."

Rong whimpered as he moved forward and kowtowed.

"You have been found guilty of lending money at usurious rates of interest. You have also been found guilty of taking by force and violence a collection of valuable antique fans from a weak and defenseless individual; namely, Wu the Idiot.

"In view of the fact you are descended from one of the greatest generals in the history of our dynasty, we will forbear imposition of the punishment normally decreed for offenses of this gravity: to wit, execution. Instead, in our clemency, we will impose on you the following punishment: All your property is confiscated. You are sentenced to penal servitude at a military post on the coast, where you may attempt to redeem yourself by diligent service."

I felt little sympathy for Rong. Still, I cringed as soldiers dragged him back into the prison building.

The eunuch pulled out another decree. "Jia Zheng."

My father meekly moved forward and kowtowed.

I couldn't breathe. I shut my eyes and hunched my shoulders to brace myself.

"You have for many years held official posts in which you have served conscientiously and prudently. You are absolved from the consequences of your failure to control your subordinates in Jiangxi. All charges against you are dismissed."

Father had escaped! I started to breathe again.

"You are to be released from the Temple of the Prison God. You may keep all your property. You are hereby granted the hereditary title Duke of Rongguo with all its customary rights and emoluments. You are hereby reappointed a vice minister in the Ministry of Works."

Too great! Our family kept the Rongguo title, it was just transferred from First Uncle to Father. We still had our mansion, our annual stipend. Plus, Father had his old job at the Ministry of Works back, the type of job Grandmother said he could handle.

The eunuch put down the imperial decree. Father kept kowtowing to him, blubbering, "Thank you, thank you."

With a faint smile, the eunuch said to Father, "You may rise. Please stand over there while I deal with your son and grandson.

"Jia Baoyu, Jia Lan."

I trembled as I moved forward and kowtowed. Rationally, I had little to fear, but my body had not caught up with that fact.

"Since no charges were ever brought against you, you are to be released from the Temple of the Prison God."

Lan and I kowtowed. With difficulty, I restrained myself from saying: Since no charges were ever brought against me, why was I ever *in* the Temple of the Prison God?

A soldier came over to Father, Lan, and me and said, "We can arrange transportation for you back to your mansion. Please come with me." We followed the soldier as he led us back through the large hall dominated by the reddish-orange god with writhing snakes around his feet, then out to the street in front. He signaled to a nearby servant, who started hitching up a mule-cart.

I was lost in a swirl of emotions, trying to assimilate everything that had taken place over the past few minutes, not paying any attention to my surroundings, when suddenly before me appeared ... the Buddhist monk and Taoist priest who had returned my jade. They looked the same as before: the Buddhist had scabs on his shaved head, one of the Taoist's legs was shorter than the other. They both looked disheveled.

"Greetings, Baoyu," the Buddhist said, padding up to me in his bare feet. "Has life been good to you since the last time we met?"

"No!" I growled.

The Taoist limped up. "What's been the problem?"

"I've just been in prison for forty-one days."

The two looked at each other. Both had quizzical looks on their faces, as if they didn't believe me. "Forty-one days?" the Taoist asked the Buddhist.

The Buddhist furrowed his brow and scratched his head. "I thought it was a lot longer than that."

"Yes. Like seventeen years."

They shrugged, held the pose, then broke out laughing.

Suddenly I got the joke: I was seventeen years old. I joined the laughter. "You're right, seventeen years."

"We have to be getting along now," the Buddhist said, "but we'll be seeing you again."

The Taoist, lurching forward on his shorter leg, gave me a friendly punch on the shoulder. "That's right, it's getting closer."

The two headed down the street, the mangy monk swaggering, the lop-sided priest trying to keep up.

18

WE RETURNED TO A MANSION stripped of all its valuables, as if a hoard of bandits had passed through. Most of our artworks—vases, scrolls, jades, bronzes—were gone. So too were all our chests filled with gold and silver jewelry and bolts of luxurious fabrics. Even our better furniture pieces had disappeared, either destroyed or carted off. Our mansion had an empty, ghostly feel.

Grimmest of all was the situation in First Uncle's and Rong's courtyards. Government officials charged with implementing the orders of confiscation against their property were already there by the time Father, Lan, and I arrived home. There was little for the officials to seize in terms of inanimate objects: the Imperial Guards had stolen or destroyed most of those. The term *property* included servants, however, and between the two of them, First Uncle and Rong owned around one hundred fifty. The government officials were now confiscating them.

The officials had sequestered the servants in a storage shed at the back of our mansion. A large yellow poster forbidding entrance or exit without permission covered the door, and a squad of soldiers stood guard in front. The government officials were now going through First Uncle's and Rong's registers and sifting through their packets of servants' bonds to make sure all servants were present and accounted for.

In fact, many had vanished while the five of us were in prison. No wages had been paid during that period, and the threat of confiscation loomed large. Hence, for those with family outside, or who simply wanted to try their luck at creating a new identity, disappearance made sense.

For most, it was proving a false hope. The government officials were already sending out runners to track down and bring back the defectors. Once the officials had rounded up as many as they could, the servants would be marched off and, one by one, placed on the auction block and sold to the highest bidder.

The shed holding First Uncle's and Rong's servants reverberated with the sounds of weeping. These hapless souls dreaded what lay in store. On the whole, the Jia mansion was not a bad place to be a servant: the food was good, and almost anyone could find a cozy niche where he or she didn't have to work hard and could spend all day gossiping and playing games with friends. The household of a buyer at auction might be different. First Uncle's and Rong's servants feared the unknown, and with good reason.

I was able to talk with one of my uncle's servants: a girl—I believed her name was Snowgoose, though I wasn't sure—with whom, years earlier, I had flirted. She was crying so vehemently she could barely get her words out. "I was born in this household, I've never been outside. They say they're not going to be keeping families together, so I may never see my mother and father again. I keep having nightmares about being sold to a household where they beat their servants." I held her but could think of nothing to say to assuage her fears.

Things were not much better for the five female Jia family members who had been part of First Uncle's and Rong's households: First Aunt; Rong's wife, Crimson; my uncle's two concubines; and my cousin Peony. They now had no money, no servants, no way even to feed themselves. They were completely dependent on our side of the family.

From our standpoint, that meant we had more dependents, more allowances to be paid, more courtyards to be staffed with servants. This increase in obligations came at a disastrous time for us. We were deeply in debt: we had borrowed huge sums to pay bribes to get Father released from prison and First Uncle's and Rong's punishments reduced to mere exile.

Amidst all this misery, the only Jia family member who had not suffered major loss was I. The modest furniture in my little study-bedroom was still there. My papers and my books—my chest full of past successful examination answers and my shelf of Buddhist and Taoist texts—remained just as I had left them. Apparently, exam answers and religious texts did not interest the thugs in the Imperial Guard.

Still, returning to our mansion from prison, I felt as if a key part of my past had been ripped out of me. The garden had been abandoned.

Originally seven of us had moved in. Then, Daiyu had died; Baochai and I had ended up living, supposedly together, in the mansion; and Lotus had left to marry. When Lan was taken prisoner by the Imperial Guards, his mother, Silk, decided she no longer wanted to live in the garden and moved into her own small courtyard in the mansion. That left only Tingting and Cousin Peony. With winter coming on, the family decided they too should move back into the mansion.

Now the gates to the garden were kept locked, and the only full-time resident was an old male servant of ours who was too curmudgeonly to work around other people. He served as a twenty-four-hour watchman and lived in what had once been a garden shed. The exotic birds that had added color and music to Happy Red Court—those that had survived—had been moved to Grandmother's courtyard.

Three days after I was released from prison, I noticed one of the side gates to the garden open. A matron sat beside it.

"Is this gate always open?" I asked.

"No, it's usually shut. But today we were told Her Old Ladyship might want some fruit picked from the garden, so we opened it just in case."

"Can I go in?"

"You can do anything you want, young master."

I had not set foot in the garden for a year and a half. When I stepped inside, I winced.

Most of the original plants had withered or died; thistles

and brambles had taken their places. Brown leaves and stems lay everywhere, and the sour smell of decaying vegetation filled the air. Gouges and ruts defaced the pebbled walkways.

I passed by one of the cottages; it happened to be Baochai's old cottage, Alpinia Park. The paint was peeling from the walls. A roof tile had fallen and shattered into pieces.

I stood in the middle of the abandoned garden and surveyed the dereliction. As I did, images flooded my mind. Amber—pale, emaciated, standing upright only because maids on either side were supporting her, while my mother spewed invective at her. Daiyu—lying under a green coverlet on a bed in her dayroom, her face covered with sweat, a handkerchief streaked with red stains at her side. Rosebud—invading the privacy of my canopy bed at Happy Red Court to lie to me that I would soon be marrying Daiyu. Swallow—looking at me with hatred, saying Daiyu's last words were, "Baoyu, Baoyu, you betrayed me!"

A set of familiar—all too familiar—sensations came over me. Tears welled up in my eyes, my body started to weaken and tremble.

I did not collapse, though. I had strength enough to stagger back to my study-bedroom in Grandmother's courtyard. Once there, I sat down on the slate floor, positioned my legs in half-lotus, and focused on my breathing. The inhalation. The short pause at the top. The exhalation. The short pause at the bottom.

Half an hour later, I had recovered. I never went into the garden again.

A week after my release from prison, one of my father's pages appeared in my doorway. "First Master would like to know if you would be willing to accompany him tomorrow to the Pavilion of Parting, to see your first uncle and cousin off on their journeys into exile."

I was caught off guard. My father was *asking* me, rather than ordering me? I didn't know how to respond. Spending an entire day with my father was not an appealing prospect. On the other hand, for once he had approached me with a polite request.

The page stared at me.

"I ... was just reciting a passage from the *Four Books*. Would you mind coming back in a few minutes? I'll be done then."

Father could hardly criticize me for that.

As soon as the page left, I began analyzing arguments for and against going. Arguments against came to mind more quickly. Not only would I have to spend a long day with my father, I had few warm feelings for First Uncle, none at all for Rong.

On the other hand, if my father was willing to show me some respect, perhaps I should respond in kind. Also, I had never been to the Pavilion of Parting; it might be an interesting experience.

Most of all, my religious convictions pointed to saying yes. I remembered the Buddha had spoken of "the fire of hatred": it was just as bad as the fire of desire. If I needed to give up greed and lust, I also needed to give up hatred and anger.

When the page returned, I told him I would go.

The next morning, twelve of us—my father and I, First Uncle and Rong, four male servants who would accompany First Uncle into exile, and four who would accompany Rong—set out on horseback from our mansion. We traveled in a southwesterly direction, first through the Manchu city, then through the Chinese city, finally exiting at Broad Peace Gate. Half an hour's ride beyond the city walls, a wide river bisected the flat landscape. Spanning the river was a stone bridge lined by dozens of lion-topped marble pillars, and on the near side of the river, perfectly aligned with the bridge, stood an elegant two-story building with double flying eaves. The Pavilion of Parting.

Because of its fame, I had a fairly good idea of what to expect there. The one thing I had not anticipated was the wait.

The ritual lifting of cups of rice wine had to take place at a certain spot within the pavilion; otherwise, the perfect alignment of pavilion, bridge, and road beyond would be askew. That spot could accommodate only one party at a time. Several officials were leaving for provincial posts that day, and the other groups had apparently left Beijing before we had. We were last in line. We were also the only group whose departing members were headed to penal servitude, not high government position.

The group immediately ahead of us—a father and two sons, one about my age, the other a little younger—embodied all the high ideals the Pavilion of Parting was supposed to represent. The bond of affection between father and sons was palpable; their farewell embraces were charged with love and respect. The father seemed torn between regret at leaving his beloved family but also eagerness to take up an important new post.

What a contrast our group made. My uncle seemed in a daze; I suspected he had been drinking. Rong was his usual self—blubbering, crying, overwrought. Only my father and I carried ourselves with any dignity.

When our turn to occupy the coveted prime spot finally arrived, Father took charge. "We should all be grateful for the clemency the Emperor has shown our family. This clemency is entirely due to the noble deeds of our ancestors, and we must at all times try to live up to the excellent examples they set. Dear brother, dear nephew, the Emperor has given you the opportunity to redeem yourself by diligent service. Take advantage of the Emperor's magnanimity and devote yourself to service to the Empire. If you do, we shall soon be greeting you back, just as today we are bidding you goodbye."

Once my father had completed his homily, we poured the wine. First Uncle's hand shook, and soon he and Rong were bawling. The workers attached to the Pavilion of Parting looked on with disgust.

Once the farewell toast was over, First Uncle, Rong, and the servants rode off. Father and I watched them cross the stone bridge, then disappear into the distance. Eventually, First Uncle would veer off toward Mongolia, Rong toward the southern coast.

Father and I rode back to Beijing together, just the two of us. He rode ahead; I, a comfortable distance behind. One good thing about traveling with someone else by horseback: you're not expected to converse.

Even though I was no longer in prison, I continued my Buddhist meditation. Every evening I would retreat to a corner of my study-bedroom, sit on the slate floor in half-lotus, close my eyes, and meditate. I would begin with calming meditation, regulating my breathing, then proceed to insight meditation.

In prison, I had focused my insight meditation on the Buddha's teachings. Now I focused on his life, his personal story. More precisely, on the story of the young man who would become the Buddha—Siddhartha.

Siddhartha was a prince: his father ruled a kingdom in the foothills of the Himalayas. Siddhartha grew up amidst wealth, luxury, and sensual pleasures.

When he was sixteen, his father decided he should marry. His father chose a bride for him, and Siddhartha dutifully entered into the arranged marriage. Later, his wife bore him a son. Siddhartha named the son Rahula, meaning *fetter* or *constraint*.

Soon after his son's birth, Siddhartha experienced a spiritual awakening. He lost all interest in sensual pleasures and resolved to abandon his life of luxury. Instead, he would take up the life of a wandering monk.

He knew his father would never consent to his abandoning his royal heritage, so he resolved to leave secretly. In the middle of the night, he tiptoed through the palace to the stable, mounted his horse, and rode off, never to return.

In my meditation, I went over the story of Siddhartha again and again, each time finding more and more personal meaning. What I found in Siddhartha's story was something I had long been missing—hope. Like Siddhartha, I could flee my family and take up the life of a spiritual seeker.

Sitting on the slate floor with my eyes closed, my legs in half-lotus, I pondered that possibility.

Everything in my upbringing—the admonitions of my father, the teachings of my childhood textbooks, the family liturgies in which I had participated for years, the Confucian classics I was studying for the Imperial Examination—shouted that leaving my family would be an unforgivable violation of filial piety.

The story of Siddhartha offered a different perspective. Here was a man regarded as a moral exemplar by millions of followers over centuries. Yet he had abandoned his family to take up the life of a wandering monk. Siddhartha's abandonment had been even greater than mine would be, if I carried mine out. He had both a wife and a son; I had only a wife.

From this, I concluded that filial piety was a value, but not the only value in the moral universe. Other values a person might legitimately pursue included spiritual growth, the extinguishment of desire, and the end of suffering.

There was no point even asking my family for permission to become a wandering monk. Without question, they would refuse and simply increase their vigilance over me. I would be worse off than before. To become a Buddhist monk, I would have to emulate Siddhartha. I would have to escape.

It was a matter of courage. I needed the courage to give up soft silk sheets, pliant servants, and well-cooked meals delivered to my room. I needed the courage to venture into the unknown, to trust in fate. Most of all, I needed the courage to disobey my family.

Could I find such courage within myself? I pondered this question again and again.

19

BEFORE ANY ESCAPE, however, I intended to take, and hopefully pass, the Imperial Examination. While I had rejected filial piety as a value above all others, I still wanted to meet the challenge Baochai had thrown at me: If only you could pass the Imperial Examination, then, even if you did that and nothing more, you would at least have repaid your debts to your family, your ancestors, and the Emperor.

My preparation now focused on the literary requirements for examination answers—the intricate set of rules that mandated exactly how answers were supposed to be written. Examination answers had to be written "in the voice of the sage"; in other words, as if they had been written by Confucius himself, or Mencius himself. This meant, among other things, you could not refer to any event that took place or any person who lived after the death of Mencius. Mencius had been dead for two thousand years.

Requiring examination answers to be written "in the voice of the sage" would not have been so bad had it meant that answers should reflect the way the historical Confucius expressed himself—in comparatively simple, down-to-earth language. What it meant instead was that examination answers had to adhere to a rigid literary form—the notorious "eight-legged essay." The object was not to convey ideas or information; rather, it was to demonstrate mastery of this literary form.

Each answer had to be clearly divisible into eight parts, or legs:

First, breaking open the title.
Second, amplification.
Third, preliminary exposition.
Fourth, initial argument.
Fifth, central argument.
Sixth, later argument.
Seventh, final argument.
Eighth, conclusion.

Three of the eight legs—the fourth, sixth, and seventh—were subject to even more stringent rules. They had to be written in pairs of parallel phrases. In other words, in those legs every phrase had to be one of a pair, using the same grammar and syntax but different words.

Fortunately, by the time I returned to our mansion from the Temple of the Prison God, the Imperial Examination was still more than a year away—ample time to master the intricacies of the eight-legged essay. I scrutinized the successful examination answers I had found, focusing on their organization and structure. I diagrammed answers, I compared parallel sentences, I created new answers using different words. Gradually, I mastered the art of the eight-legged essay.

The year between my return from prison and my taking the Imperial Examination was, in general, calm and uneventful in the Jia household. After years of turmoil, I finally experienced some peace. Only one event that year interrupted my near-total concentration on my studies. That one event was, unfortunately, tragic.

We received word my cousin Lotus had died. The last time Lotus had visited us, she had been in tears during her entire visit and had said her husband beat her. Although we had no direct proof—we were told simply that Lotus had died and given no reason for her death—everyone in the family suspected she had been beaten to death.

I wept, I felt angry, but again I stopped myself from collapsing into inconsolable grief. I repeated my mantra: All life is suffering. The only remedy is to cultivate dispassion and detachment.

During the day I continued my intensive preparation for the Imperial Examination. When evening came, I resumed my meditation. I was two different people: by day a Confucian; by night, and in my heart, a Buddhist. I consoled myself with the thought: soon this will all end.

One day I heard from the maids that my parents had arranged a marriage for Tingting. Her fiancé was a young official who had passed the Imperial Examination two years before, in the year of the ox, and was currently stationed in Fujian province.

I was eager to hear what Tingting herself thought about the matter. Fortunately, the next day I encountered her on one of our verandas.

"Little Sister, I hear you're engaged."

She nodded.

"Should I congratulate you?"

She looked around the veranda. It was a cold, misty day; winter was coming on. "I'm hopeful. They are some good signs."

"Like what?"

Tingting pursed her lips. "For one thing, my fiancé's family isn't all that wealthy."

"You mean it shows our family isn't marrying you off for money? Or advantage at court?"

"Exactly."

"You may be the luckiest one of us all. You may be escaping the Jia family before things come crashing down for the last time."

She laughed. "That thought has crossed my mind."

"Tell me, who's the lucky man? I've heard he's an official and lives in Fujian."

"Right. He's a civil official in the military and works on coastal defenses."

"How did Father and Mother come to select him?"

"My fiancé's father is also an official, and he and our father are good friends. Our father has met my fiancé. He was impressed with him, says my fiancé is a serious and responsible young man. I guess that's a compliment."

"With Father, it's a compliment." We both laughed.

We sat down on the balustrade and drew our cloaks closer, to protect against the chill.

"Fujian province is a long way away," I said.

"Yes, I know. That part I'm not happy about. But maybe someday my husband will be reassigned to a post here in Beijing."

"When do you leave?"

"In three weeks."

"Three weeks? So soon?"

"Yes. It's better I go before the worst of winter sets in."

"How are you getting there?"

"By boat. I go to Tianjin by carriage; a boat will be waiting for me there; and then I sail down the coast, to Fujian."

"That's a long journey for a fifteen-year-old girl."

Tingting winced. "I know."

We both went silent. The gray bricks of our mansion, cold and damp, cast an aura of gloom. In the middle of the court-yard, fallen tree leaves covered the ground.

Tingting broke the silence. "You asked me why I was somewhat hopeful about my marriage. Another reason is I know Father and Mother are conscious of ... how should I put it? ... some of the mistakes this family has made in marrying off its daughters in the past."

"You're talking about Lotus?"

She nodded.

"You know," I said, "I believe First Uncle *did* sell her to that man Sun for five thousand taels."

"I agree."

Again, we both became silent, absorbed in our own thoughts. A quartet of maids passed by, smiling and bowing. As they disappeared, their footsteps clattered on the stone pavers and echoed off the brick walls.

"When we were growing up," Tingting said, "I had no idea First Uncle was doing all those things we now know he *was* doing. Did you?"

"Not really. From time to time I heard rumors, but I guess I never thought about them." I shrugged.

"When you talk about mistakes our family has made in marrying off its daughters," I continued, "I assume you're also talking about Baochai."

Tingting looked at me warily.

"No, we should talk about it. It's no secret: Baochai is unhappy to be married to me, and I'm unhappy to be married to her. I guess my question is: do our parents recognize they made a mistake?"

"Yes, I think so. Of course, in your case, it wasn't so much our parents; Grandmother played the biggest role in that disaster. For better or for worse, Grandmother isn't all that interested in me. But getting back to your question, yes, I think Father and Mother feel guilty about your marriage and the way it was handled."

I rubbed my tongue against the back of my teeth. What Tingting was saying was vindication. The irony was that I was no longer interested in vindication.

"What about Peony?" I asked, referring to my cousin whose father was now in exile on the Mongolian frontier. "Who's going to choose for her? Her father can't, and First Aunt seems helpless. What's going to happen to Peony?"

"I'm hopeful the current situation will work to her advantage. Certainly she'll be better off if her marriage is *not* arranged by her father. I'm hoping our parents will assume responsibility and arrange her marriage."

"Do you think they will?"

"I think so. I think they want to take care of me first, then turn their attention to Peony."

"I hope so. I hope she ends up with a better life than Lotus."

Tingting stared at the slate floor.

After a minute, she looked up. "Big Brother, I hear you've become quite the scholar. People say you're studying so much you practically never leave your room."

"That's ... more or less true."

"Tell me. What are you going to do after you pass the examination? And I'm sure you *will* pass."

My muscles tensed. This was coming too close. Even with

Tingting, my one and only confidant within the Jia family, I didn't want to share my future plans.

"I'll worry about that when the time comes."

Tingting seemed to accept that answer. After another pause, she said, "I hope that after I leave for Fujian, we'll see each other again."

My breath caught. The sad truth was: once Tingting left, we probably never would see each other again. I did not want even to hint at that fact.

"I hope so too. We have to trust in fate."

Tingting frowned. "You sound like Grandmother. Remember when Lotus visited that time, and all Grandmother could say was, 'It's your fate, dear girl, it's your fate.' I hate that word *fate*."

I had blundered into a thicket. I had not intended to endorse Grandmother's view that we should all dutifully accept whatever miseries are thrust upon us in life. Our conversation needed to end on a happier note. She was a fifteen-year-old girl heading off to an unknown future, and I should be trying to lift her spirits.

"I'm sure we'll see each other again. In this life, or another."

All along I had been acting on Baochai's words: If you could only pass the Imperial Examination—do that and nothing more—you would at least have repaid your debts to your family, your ancestors, the Emperor.

A thought kept nagging at me, though. Even if I passed the Imperial Examination, I would not have *completely* repaid my debts. There remained the issue of an heir. Baochai had not brought the subject up. I knew, however, that she and the rest of my family thought about it constantly.

I struggled to devise a course of action that would respect both my filial obligations to my family and my own spiritually-based need to separate myself from them. After wrestling with the question for several months, I decided that, in this area too, I would follow a "just that and nothing more" approach. I would have sex with Baochai. Once.

I had no idea what the chances were that a single sexual coupling would result in the birth of a child, let alone the birth of a male child, which of course was what everyone wanted. Obviously, not every coupling resulted in the birth of a child: otherwise, Amber and I, before we started using musk deer scent, would have become parents. What was the actual likelihood? I had no idea. As to the likelihood that any child born would be a son, that was presumably fifty-fifty. Thus, the chances that a single act of sex would result in the birth of a male child were less, probably considerably less, than fifty-fifty.

Ultimately, though, fate would determine the result. *Fate*, the word Tingting, and probably most of the girls I knew, hated. If Baochai and I were fated to have a boy, one act of sexual congress would suffice. If we were not, a thousand acts would not. In either event, by having sex with Baochai once, I would not stand in the way of fate.

One night a month before the Imperial Examination, I slipped out of my room and headed toward Baochai's bedchamber. Maids stared at me through eyes wide with surprise.

Reaching the room, I parted the beaded curtain and entered. It was the same room that had served as our bridal chamber, except that on that night every nook and cranny had been ablaze in red, whereas now the room was more subdued. The scarlet silk drapes that had covered the walls were gone; now the walls were simply white-painted plaster. The maroon carpet that had covered the floor had disappeared; now the floor was plain black slate. Only our wedding bed, with its ruby-colored lacquer and carmine canopy, recalled the redness of our wedding night.

The bed curtains were closed. Two maids were asleep on the kang.

I awoke the maids. Startled, they gasped and looked at me in terror, as if I were a barbarian invader come to rape and pillage. I asked them, as politely as I could, to leave. Cringing in fear, they did.

I parted the bed curtains. My eyes took time to adjust to the darkness, but soon Baochai came into focus. She was clad in a pink chemise, she was awake, and her head was half-raised. The porcelain perfection of her classic goose egg face astonished me.

Saying nothing, I drew back the bedcovers and began removing her chemise. She understood and began removing the garment herself. In the darkness I could barely make out her face, but I sensed suspicion and distrust.

She lay on her back, completely naked. The dim reddish light that peeked into her canopy bed from the candles outside only faintly illuminated the curves of her breasts, the depression of her stomach, the triangle of her private area, but even in darkness she radiated an almost unearthly perfection—an ideal of feminine beauty rarely seen outside a Tang Dynasty painting. The typical eighteen-year-old boy sitting where I was would have been consumed by lust.

Still saying nothing, I parted my robe, lowered myself, and joined our bodies together. Baochai's skin was peach-blossom soft, but her body was rigid and tense. I sensed she was holding her breath.

Despite Baochai's beauty, I was not completely hard; all the bitter memories associated with our marriage stood in the way. Using my hand, I labored to achieve a proper erection. At first nothing seemed to work. Then I shifted my focus to the one thing I knew would awaken my ardor. I thought of Daiyu.

I imagined Daiyu in the full bloom of her health, before consumption wasted her body. I imagined both of us naked, pressing our bodies together, our mouths united and our tongues intertwined, my sex throbbing against her smooth, soft torso. Soon I was ready.

I entered Baochai. As I penetrated her virginity, her body shuddered and she let out a brief moan, then suppressed it. After that, I continued to thrust but received no response in return. It was as if I were having sex alone.

As I was making my way toward climax, a thought entered my mind. It was one I had had before but had always been able to push aside. Now it overwhelmed me.

This was the only time in her entire life Baochai would have sex.

The sadness of that thought punctured my arousal. I lost my erection. I felt like crying.

I refused to allow myself to fail, however. I worked to suppress all thoughts of the tragedy of Baochai's life and refocused my thoughts on Daiyu, on the uninhibited physical intimacy between the two of us my imagination had conjured up. I imagined kissing Daiyu, exploring her with my tongue, my finger, my sex. The fact none of it had ever happened only added to my fervor.

Alternately, though, my thoughts gravitated to Baochai: to her immediate physical presence, as opposed to my gossamer dreams of Daiyu. Baochai's perfectly rounded breasts pressed against me; her elegantly formed abdomen melded into me; her goose egg-shaped face filled my vision. Baochai incarnated a physical ideal, she was a goddess. At that moment, I possessed her.

My mind went back and forth: Daiyu, Baochai, Daiyu, Baochai. I became hard again. I climaxed.

I lay still for a while. Sweat covered me. She remained motionless, rigid, distant.

I remembered the dream I had had, many years before, in Crimson's red bedchamber. In that dream, my inamorata, Two-in-One, had looked alternately like Baochai and like Daiyu. Perhaps that dream had been a prophesy.

I felt tired and wanted to be alone. I withdrew from Baochai, climbed out of our bridal bed, and walked out of our bridal chamber. Not once during the consummation of our marriage had either of us uttered a single word to the other.

The time had come for me to leave for the Imperial Examination. Earlier that day, servants had filled a mule cart with all the things I would need for the four days I would be spending inside the examination compound: my writing materials, food, bedding, curtain, large water jar, drinking cup, candles, matches, soap.

By late afternoon my horse was saddled and awaiting

me in our main courtyard. Ten servants also waited, lined up on horseback. They would accompany me to the examination compound's Great Gate.

My family gathered in our main reception hall to bid me goodbye. Pages carried Grandmother in a chair; by now she couldn't walk, though her mind was still sharp. My father, mother, and Baochai surrounded her. Behind them, lining the walls, stood servants. We now owned around two hundred, and every one of them, from every courtyard, was in attendance.

Grandmother spoke first. "This is your first examination, and tonight, after entering the compound, you'll be entirely on your own. You'll have to take care of yourself, and you'll probably be lonely. But I'm sure you'll be able to handle everything. Just remember, we'll all be thinking about you.

"When you get to Shuntian," Grandmother went on, using the examination compound's formal name, "there will be thousands of people there. I'm worried you might get jostled by all the people and all the horses. That's why I've arranged for ten servants to go with you, and the ones I've chosen are our top managers, the best and most experienced servants we have.

"When you're done with the examination, those same servants will be back, waiting for you outside the Great Gate. Come out as soon as you've finished your compositions and find them. Then come back here as quickly as possible, to put all our minds to rest.

"You can now pay your respects."

I approached Baochai. She stared at me warily. I had prepared words to say to her, inspired by the words Siddhartha had said to his wife and child before he fled his palace. As I started to open my mouth, however, Baochai burst into tears.

What was she thinking? Had she intuited my plan? How far had she penetrated the innermost regions of my mind?

I had no idea. Because I had never penetrated the innermost regions of *her* mind.

Baochai continued to weep. Grandmother and my parents looked at her with disapproval.

I decided to jettison the little speech I had prepared. Instead, trying to sound cheerful, I said, "I'll be going soon,

Cousin. Stay here with the family and wait for the good news."

Baochai managed to halt her crying and, in a strained voice, said, "You should be off. There's no need for you to make one of your long speeches."

Long speeches? Was I known for making long speeches? I thought about replying in kind, but my better instincts prevailed.

I turned to my father and mother. "Son," Father said, "I've been gratified by all the reports I've received over the past year that you've been applying yourself to your studies with diligence and discipline. I trust that your preparation will be duly rewarded when the examination results are announced, and that this examination will mark the start of an illustrious career in the service of the Emperor." He looked upon me with grave satisfaction.

Finally, I stood in front of Grandmother. To my surprise, I saw tears in her eyes. "Baoyu," she said, "I hope you realize how much this examination means to me. Of all my children and grandchildren, you're my favorite. I raised you from the moment you were born. I know there were difficulties along the way, but I always tried to do my best."

By now, Grandmother was crying. "If only you can pass this examination," she said in a choked voice, "it will make it all worthwhile. My life will be complete. I know you can do it, and just remember: all my hopes are with you."

Everyone remained silent for a minute. Grandmother wiped her eyes. Then, following Confucian ritual, I went down on my knees and kowtowed three times to Grandmother, three times to Father, three times to Mother.

For weeks, I had been thinking about what I would say at this point—my last words to my family. In the end, I had chosen words that were honestly felt but hid more than they revealed.

"Grandmother, Father, Mother, I can never repay all you've done for me. But if I can do this one thing successfully, if I can pass this examination, I will have at least given you some recompense for all the trouble I've caused you. I will do the best I possibly can, and I hope that in the end I will make all of you happy."

Father and Mother beamed with pride. Grandmother, recovered from her crying spell, smiled.

"Baoyu, people are waiting outside," Grandmother said. "You'd better be off or you'll be late."

I stepped back and took one last look at my family: Grandmother, Father, Mother, Baochai. If I kept to my plan, this would be the last time I would ever see any of them.

My throat tightened, my eyes began to moisten. I had been dreading this moment for months, fearing that when it came, I would give way to uncontrollable tears. Many times I had gone over in my mind what I would do, how I would avoid making a scene or giving away my secret plan. The only solution I had come up with was to leave as quickly as possible.

"I'm off," I said. I gave everyone one last bow, turned, and strode briskly out of the hall.

20

The Shuntian Imperial Examination Compound stood not far from our Jia family mansion: still within the Manchu city, just north of the Imperial Observatory, only a half-hour horseback ride under normal circumstances. Yet travelling there that night, I left one world and entered another.

For more than a year, I had been cooped up in our mansion. I had rarely gone out; I had rarely strayed from my study-bedroom. I had been a hermit, albeit one living amidst the hurly-burly of a large aristocratic household.

Now I joined a river of men, horses, and mules, all heading to the Great Gate of the examination compound. Five thousand two hundred of us were taking the examination, and we all had to be in front of the Great Gate, ready to enter, when it opened at one hour past midnight.

Some men were by themselves. Others were members of groups, often with banners proclaiming their home provinces or cities. A few rode horses, most walked. Some had horse or mule carts to carry their provisions. Most did not and served as their own draft animals. I saw no one else who had ten mounted servants plus a mule cart, as I did.

What shocked me was how old most of the candidates looked. I was eighteen. The youngest of the other candidates seemed to be in their mid-twenties, and most appeared even older—in their thirties or forties. Here and there trudged men truly elderly—in their sixties or seventies. Gray hair was common; walking sticks and canes, not unusual.

The examination compound appeared on the horizon as a cloud of orange-brown dust. Inside the cloud sprawled men, carts, horses, and mules, all crowded too close for comfort, arranged in no discernible order. The air smelled of horse and mule dung and the piss of nervous men.

Everyone faced north. There, beyond a large, roped-off swath of open space, stood the Great Gate itself—a three-tiered pagoda built of gray bricks with green tile roofs.

My servants and I searched for a patch of ground large enough to accommodate all of us, plus the cart. We found a spot within sight of the Great Gate but still behind a tangle of candidates who had arrived earlier. We dismounted and began our wait.

The murky late spring sun disappeared, darkness overtook us, and lanterns began to appear. My servants had brought two lanterns, which we lit. Clouds blocked the stars and moon; only the flicker of lanterns provided light. Faces appeared as vague shapes, lacking detail, more like tomb figures than real live men. Silence reigned; no one in the vast throng said a word.

I was still unnerved by how old all the other candidates looked, and another, related fear was starting to gnaw at me.

Most of these men had taken competitive examinations—district examinations, prefectural examinations, qualifying examinations, provincial examinations—many times before, probably at least five times. The reason they were standing in front of the Great Gate that night was because they had been successful in all those prior examinations.

I, on the other hand, had skipped any district examination, skipped any prefectural examination, skipped any qualifying examination, skipped any provincial examination. I was standing in front of the Great Gate that night because ... my father had purchased a place for me.

Technically, I was a student at Imperial College. It didn't matter I had never attended lectures there or even set foot inside. Several years before, my father had purchased, for one hundred taels, Imperial College student status for me, and that was all that mattered. As an Imperial College student, I was automatically entitled to take the Imperial Examination.

The more I thought about it, the more I felt like a lamb among lions. The thousands of men surrounding me were hardened veterans, victors in numerous prior struggles like the one about to take place. I was a complete novice.

Even the fact they were all men, no women among them, disconcerted me. I had spent my life mostly among girls, girls my own age. I had never had a close relationship with an older male, certainly not with my father, or First Uncle, or Rong. Now everyone around me was an older male.

Back at the Jia family mansion, secluded in my cozy study-bedroom, going over our family's voluminous collection of past successful examination answers, writing out my own answers over and over again, perfecting the art of the eight-legged essay, I had developed considerable confidence I would pass.

Now, standing in a dark dirt field with thousands of older men, breathing their dust, smelling their piss, sensing the thrust of their masculinity and the brute fact of their seniority, my confidence was crumbling. Five thousand two hundred of us were taking the Imperial Examination. Only ninety-eight of us would pass. Would I be among the ninety-eight? It hardly seemed possible.

Around ten o'clock, white silk lanterns, hundreds of them, began to appear in the open space in front of the Great Gate. The lanterns gradually coalesced into scores of small groups. The number and arrangement of lanterns differed for each group.

Days earlier, examination officials had assigned each of us a group number. The configurations of lanterns in the open field stood for those numbers. A single lantern meant one; two lanterns placed side-by-side, two; three side-by-side, three; and so forth. Five lanterns strung vertically meant ten. As soon as the ropes cordoning off the open space came down, we were all supposed to head to the configuration of lanterns that corresponded to our group number.

The crowd began to inch forward; the ropes were down.

I belonged to group seventeen, the Imperial College group. I located the configuration of five vertical and seven horizontal lanterns and, along with my ten servants and mule cart, pushed my way toward it.

Once united with the Imperial College group, I felt more comfortable. They were younger, mostly sons of government officials. I even recognized several of them, having met them at parties or family celebrations. We nodded hello, but no one felt confident enough to converse.

An examination official stood before us. After calling out several other names, he shouted, "Jia Baoyu."

"Here."

The examination official turned to a man standing beside him, someone I'd never laid eyes on before. "Can you confirm that Jia Baoyu is a properly enrolled student at Imperial College?"

"Yes."

I wondered how he knew.

At midnight, a single cannon shot boomed. Half an hour later, two cannon shots. At one o'clock, three cannon shots. The Great Gate of the Shuntian Imperial Examination Compound was now open.

We entered the compound group by group, group one first and so forth. Around the time group fifteen was called, my servants began the process of transferring my belongings from the mule cart to my back. They carefully arranged everything inside my rucksack to make it as comfortable as possible. Still, the weight staggered me, unaccustomed as I was to carrying much of anything.

An examination official came up to us and said, "Group seventeen, follow me." This was the point at which my servants and I would part company. From now on, I would be entirely on my own. I thanked the servants and said goodbye. They wished me good luck and promised to be there waiting for me when the examination was over. I did not tell them they might be disappointed.

Group seventeen began moving. Reeling under my heavy sack, I looked down to find my footing in the dim light. We headed to the Great Gate. Lit only by lanterns, it looked spectral, threatening.

Once there, we entered a long tunnel. Light gradually faded away. Total darkness enveloped us. Our walking slowed to a shuffle.

This was the point of no return. Once through the tunnel, we would be confined within the examination compound for the next four days—one move-in day and three examination days. Even if one of us died, his rotting corpse would remain within the examination compound until the four days were up.

I took a deep, slow breath, said a silent prayer to Buddha, and moved forward.

At the end of the tunnel, we emerged into an area filled with large sheds, covered on top but open on all sides. The official accompanying us herded us into one of the sheds, where a contingent of soldiers awaited us. They would search both us and our belongings.

The soldiers were dark-skinned, with haphazard teeth and coarse, bushy hair sticking out from beneath their military caps. They wore ill-fitting greenish-yellow uniforms. As we in the Imperial College group stumbled in under our heavy loads, the soldiers sneered. I heard a soldier near me say, in a thick country accent, "Now we get the rich kids."

If you grew up rich, as I did, you knew that rank-and-file soldiers, who by definition were poor, hated rich people. These soldiers had an added incentive to conduct rigorous searches. A soldier who found any book or piece of writing on a candidate received three taels. The guilty candidate himself was expelled from the examination, beaten on the back, and exposed to public view.

Two soldiers grabbed me. They groped every part of my body, jostling me, even deliberately punching me a couple of times. When they were finished, they pushed me away so hard I fell. Anger surged within me, and I had to order myself to remain calm.

Fortunately, the soldiers made no issue of my jade pendant, which I still wore. That was the one part of my old life I wanted to carry over to the new.

While I had been enduring my body search, two other soldiers had ripped apart my carefully arranged rucksack. They were now sifting through each and every one of my belongings. Almost immediately one of the soldiers came across the embroidered silk satin bedding my family had insisted I bring. The soldier held up the bedding, smirked, and said to his comrades, "Look at this. Fancy, fancy." The comrades snickered.

They opened all my bags of food and, with their dirty hands, handled everything I would be eating for the next four days. One soldier even cut open one of my buns, hoping to find inside a wadded-up piece of paper. To his disappointment, he found only bean paste.

In the end, the soldiers found nothing. As a last expression of their contempt, though, they stuffed my belongings back into my rucksack in the most disorganized way possible. With the soldiers' packing job, my rucksack was lumpy, and I had to carry two food bags in my hands.

By now my mood had turned black as coal. I was tired, my back ached, and I had had more than my fill of waiting and being pushed around. But I kept telling myself: Control your emotions. Don't get upset.

Emerging from the search area, I noticed faint gray light in the sky; sunrise was close. My journey into the examination compound was not yet over, however. I next needed to stand in a long line to get my entry certificate. At least this long line gave me an opportunity to repack my rucksack.

I noticed we were now being processed as individuals, not group members. I might never see my fellow members of group seventeen again; in the examination compound, our cells would be scattered. We were now competitors—enemies.

Dusty orange-brown sunlight colored the sky by the time the meticulous clerk handed me my entry certificate. The certificate told me, for the first time, precisely where I would be spending the next four days. It read "Harvest," the name of an alley, and "One Hundred Seventy-Nine," the number of a cell.

After passing through a long corridor, I finally arrived at the inner gate to the examination compound, the infamous Dragon Gate. It bore that name because on both sides bas-reliefs sculpted of glazed tiles depicted fierce yellow dragons. The two dragons had long pointed horns, bulging eyes, multiple legs, and on each leg, five sharp claws. The gate symbolized the fury that would be unleashed upon anyone caught cheating in the upcoming examination.

An examination official blocked my way. "Your entry certificate. Your search certificate."

I produced the two papers. He pored over them for what seemed an eternity, checking every seal, every attestation. Finally, "You can go."

I passed through the Dragon Gate.

I emerged onto a broad avenue, lit by full morning light, pointing straight ahead. In the middle of the avenue, a good distance away, stood a tall, three-tiered pagoda. Its upper two tiers were completely open except for a low railing, and soldiers packed those tiers, intently watching everything going on within the examination compound.

On both sides of the broad avenue ran low brick walls regularly punctuated with openings. The openings were the entrances to the alleys. The brick walls were the sides of the first cell in each alley.

I could see down the first few alleys. Cells ran in a straight, unbroken line perpendicular to the broad avenue. There were cells on only one side—the north side—of each alley; all the cells faced south, toward a blank wall. Down each alley, the line of cells extended as far as the eye could see.

The cells themselves were all identical, constructed of the same dingy gray brick, with the same crumbling tile roof, the same packed dirt floor. An individual cell consisted of two side walls, a back wall, the roof, and an open front—no door. Each cell was roughly three times as deep as it was wide.

The size of the cells shocked me; each was as small as a coffin. I wouldn't be able to move freely for the next four days. My larger-than-average body probably wouldn't fit into the cell lying down.

A gritty blanket of smoke and dust hung in the air. Hostile-looking soldiers walked up and down the alleys. The examination compound had not been used since the last Imperial

Examination, three years before, and the long neglect showed. The broad avenue and the alleys were rutted dirt, in places becoming mud. Weeds grew on top of most of the cells, a few had partially collapsed.

I had often heard descriptions of the examination compound. I knew in general terms about the broad avenue, the central watch tower, the rows of cells on either side. Still, I was unprepared for seeing the compound with my own eyes, knowing I would be spending the next four days there. A wave of nausea hit me. I closed my eyes, squeezed them shut, and tried to breathe deeply.

My next task was to find my cell. According to my entry certificate, my cell was "Harvest One Hundred Seventy-Nine." To locate Harvest Alley, I needed to recall from memory the first few lines of a children's book.

The *Primer of a Thousand Characters* was a poem a thousand characters long in which no character repeated. It had been around for more than twelve hundred years, and at some point every child learning to read encountered it. I had worked through it with Spring. As homage to the *Primer of a Thousand Characters*, or perhaps as a joke, the alleys in the examination compound were named in the exact same order as the first fifty characters of the *Primer*.

In my mind I recited the start of the *Primer*: "Heaven is dark; the earth, yellow; the universe, vast and boundless ...." Soon I came to "harvest." It was the twenty-second character in the poem.

I began trudging down the broad avenue, staggering under the weight of my rucksack. When I reached the twenty-second alley, a small sign confirmed I had indeed found Harvest. After figuring out that odd numbers were to the left, I turned into the alley.

Ahead ran a straight line of weed-infested dirt. On my right, the cells exuded a musty, rotting smell. Most of the cells were still unoccupied. Despite what had seemed an interminable entry process, I was among the first to make it into the examination compound.

Many steps later, I reached Harvest One Hundred

Seventy-Nine. It was tiny, shepherd's purse grew on its roof, and long, ugly cracks marred its walls. No sight could have been more welcome at the time, though. At long last, I could take off my rucksack, sit down, and rest.

21

FOR AN HOUR OR SO I SLEPT, the first sleep I'd gotten since
two nights before. I slept sitting up, slumped against the wall
of my cell. Soon, however, the bright midday sun and the noise
of candidates passing by and moving into nearby cells made
sleeping impossible. Though still tired, I decided to get up and
start organizing my cell.

I surveyed my new home. Its tininess frightened me. Of
the five thousand two hundred men taking the Imperial Examination that triennium, probably very few had spent time
in an actual prison cell. I had, and my cell at the Temple of the
Prison God had been at least ten times larger than the one I
was in now, large enough that I could pace back and forth.

Pushing these thoughts aside, I undid my sack, pulled out
my earthenware water jar, and walked to the communal water
supply at the head of Harvest. The compound was filling up;
more than half the cells were now occupied. Here and there
knots of candidates, probably friends from school, talked with
each other. I saw only one person I knew: someone I'd seen
at parties, who'd also been a member of the Imperial College
group the night before. We nodded to each other but did not
speak.

Back in my cell, I pulled my drinking cup out of my sack
and ladled water into my mouth. Slaking my thirst made me
realize how hungry I was; I had not eaten since the afternoon
before. I reached into my sack, brought out several bags of
food, and proceeded to stuff myself with buns, dumplings, and

pancakes. To top off my meal, I opened the lacquer box filled with candied fruits my family had insisted I bring and plucked out slices of pineapple and lotus root. After that, I fell asleep again.

The noise of someone moving into the cell next to mine woke me up. It was mid-afternoon, I realized with a start. I needed to set up my cell before darkness arrived.

My cell came equipped with just four things: three elm planks and an earthenware slop jar. The slop jar, located outside the cell in the alley, was best not thought about. The planks needed to be put to use.

Every schoolboy learned at an early age how the planks were supposed to be positioned. The planks were as long as the inside of a cell was wide, and the object was to fit them cross-wise onto narrow ledges built into the cell's brickwork.

One plank, the widest, fit onto ledges high up at the back of the cell. On that plank I placed all my foodstuffs and, for the time being, my bedding.

The second plank went onto ledges located about mid-thigh height in the middle of the cell. Once the examination began, this plank would be my desk.

The third plank fit onto knee-high ledges at the back and would serve as my bench. I would be looking out, toward the blank rear wall of the next row of cells.

On the middle plank, my desk, I carefully arranged all my writing materials—brush box, inkstone, ink sticks, water dropper, brush washer—leaving room for the things that would arrive tomorrow—answer sheets, draft paper, question sheet. By the time everything arrived, the plank would be quite full.

Though I had set up my cell correctly, the result was hardly convenient. The planks took up the full width of the cell. To get to my bench from the front, I had to lie down on my back, scoot backwards underneath my desk—taking care not to disturb any of the delicate writing materials on top—and emerge upwards between the desk and bench, like a fish jumping out of water.

I wondered how I would sleep. I was taller than the cell was deep. Assuming I slept with my head at the back, my feet would stick out into the alley, and my head would be directly under my bench.

Because these problems seemed insoluble, I decided to finish unpacking. I left my bench empty but placed my candles and matches underneath it. Utilizing hooks built into the brickwork, I hung my curtain over the cell's front opening. Finally, I tossed my rucksack, now empty, onto the high plank at back. I was all moved in.

By now both the cells next to me were occupied. The man in the cell to my right was older—in his fifties or sixties—with white hair and a long white beard. He talked to himself constantly and incomprehensibly. I said hello to him, but he ignored me.

The man in the cell to my left was a handsome fellow, probably in his late twenties, with an imposing brow and strong jawline. We talked in the alley, as other candidates brushed by.

"This is the second time I've taken the examination," he said, "but this time I feel much more confident."

"Why is that?"

"This time I had plenty of time to study. Last time I was working—I'm a scrivener—right up until a few days before the examination. This time I haven't worked in a year. It's been all study."

"How did you manage that?"

"I found myself a patron. I was sleeping in a temple, and next to the temple lived an old man. I started spending time with him—drinking wine, playing cards, things like that—and figured out he was pretty rich. I began telling him about how poor I was and how I wanted to take the Imperial Examination but couldn't afford to. Eventually he offered to support me for a year while I studied and to pay all my expenses. He even bought me two new suits of clothing." The man gestured at his dark-blue robe.

"What are you going to do if you pass?"

"I'm distantly related to a family named Zhen that's high up in the imperial bureaucracy. Once I pass, I plan to start spending so much time at their mansion they'll eventually figure out they can't get rid of me. They say the head of the family, old Lord Zhen, likes to keep men who have passed the Imperial Examination around as secretaries. That's what I'm aiming for—to become one of his secretaries. If I can get that far, I know I'll be able to find an official position."

I knew the Zhen family; they were part of my family's social circle, but I chose not to reveal that fact to the man in the next cell. I couldn't help remembering that some of the secretaries my father had kept around over the years had stolen from him and ruined his career when he was grain commissioner in Jiangxi.

"What are you going to do if you don't pass?"

A scowl came over his face. "I don't think about that. I am *going* to pass. I *have* to pass."

I was worried the man would ask me questions. I didn't want to disclose my family background, and I certainly didn't want to discuss my future plans. Fortunately, he showed no interest in me whatsoever. He was interested only in himself.

The sun began to set, a sooty darkness crept over the examination compound. According to the plan I had formulated weeks before back at the mansion, this was my time to meditate. I closed the curtain in front of my cell and sat down facing sideways, with my desk plank to the left of my head, the curtain to my right.

I felt hemmed in, the plank and curtain both too close. The packed dirt floor beneath me also felt wrong. Even the straw-covered floor at the Temple of the Prison God had felt better.

In the past, I had usually been able to calm myself by focusing on my breathing. That night, however, the more I breathed, the more anxious I became. I tried to focus, but my disobedient mind wandered.

Why had I been so confident, so absurdly confident, that I would pass the examination, and pass it the first time?

Because I had no idea who the competition was, that's

why. The men I had been observing for the past twenty-four hours were older than I, more experienced, veterans of numerous previous examinations, wise to all the tricks of the examination process. I was a neophyte, still wet behind the ears.

My brief conversation with the man in the next cell next gnawed at me. He seemed so confident, so determined, so masculine. More than that, he had real motivation for passing the examination. His life depended on it. If he passed, he could look forward to a lifetime of wealth and power. If he failed, he would be back to living in temples, begging, leading the sad life of an impecunious scholar.

Compare his motivation to mine. I was taking the examination simply as a favor to my family. It was men like him—poor, hungry, ferociously determined to succeed—who would pass. Dilettantes like me, with no real motivation except a vague desire to please others, would fail.

As these worries played havoc with my mind, I began to itch all over my body, first slightly, then more annoyingly. Did my cell have fleas? Trying to scratch, I banged my head against my desk plank. Meanwhile, my back still hurt: I hadn't recovered from all those hours carrying a heavy rucksack. The half-lotus I was using for meditation seemed to be making the pain worse.

I decided meditation was not working, and I should not force the issue. Instead, I should arrange my bedding and go to sleep.

I reached up to the high plank at the back of my cell and brought down my bedding. The embroidered silk satin my family had insisted I bring had been embarrassing when the soldiers had ridiculed it. Now, holding and feeling it, letting its opulent texture caress my hands and cheek, I found its feminine softness a much-needed antidote to the examination compound's masculine harshness.

To go to bed, I had to lie down on the floor on my back, then scoot backwards, first underneath my desk plank, then underneath my bench plank. Once I was fully inserted into the available space, the top of my head was pressed against the back brick wall of my cell, my face was only a whisper below the splintered elm of my bench plank, and my feet stuck out into Harvest Alley. As a finishing touch, the cell was so narrow I could barely move my arms.

Truly, my cell was the size of a coffin. Except that in a coffin, my feet would not have been sticking out.

I needed to sleep. I had not slept the night before—the prolonged entry process had occupied the entire night—and had managed only a couple of hours of disturbed napping during the day. If I was to have any chance at all of doing well the next day, I needed a good night's sleep.

Every muscle in my body cried for rest. My mind was so exhausted it had lost the ability to keep thoughts separate; everything was a swirl. Yet sleep eluded me.

Why had I agreed to do this? Why hadn't I simply said no? By now it was too late. All the gates leading out of the examination compound were locked. I couldn't leave, even if I tried.

A passage from Zhuangzi ran through my mind: "Someone offered Zhuangzi a court post. Zhuangzi answered the messenger: 'Sir, have you ever seen a sacrificial ox? It is decked in fine garments and fed on fresh grass and beans. However, when it is led into the Great Temple for the sacrifice, even though it might earnestly wish to become a simple calf again, it's now impossible!"

My back kept hurting. No matter how I arranged myself in my narrow cell, I seemed to be pressing down on the sorest part. The itching also returned, striking randomly and unpredictably at odd parts of my body.

I could not shut out the squalid examination compound. The noise was constant; the stench, ever-present. My ears rang with the wails of other candidates. When I moved my foot, it hit my slop jar.

As I lay in my cramped bed, battling to go to sleep but never succeeding, gloomy thoughts pervaded my mind. I was now worrying, not about the examination and my competitors, but rather about the other side of my life, the Buddhist side.

I had a well-thought-out plan to escape my family and become a wandering spiritual seeker. But did I have the courage to go through with it?

Little in my previous eighteen years had called for courage. Still, there had been two occasions on which I had had an opportunity, even a moral obligation, to show it.

The first ...

Someone in a nearby cell began vomiting. The poor man's retching went on for several minutes, echoing along the brick walls of the dark alley.

The first test of my courage was when my mother awoke to see the flirtatious servant girl Goldie and me passing a peppermint candy between our mouths. The second was when Amber was dying of consumption and Mother came to Happy Red Court, coldly dismissed her, and ordered her to leave our mansion immediately.

On both occasions, I had responded with cowardice, not courage. I had hidden behind Goldie, then slipped out of Mother's room on my hands and knees. I had watched silently as Mother's henchwomen dragged dying Amber out of Happy Red Court.

Twice in my life I had been challenged to show courage. Twice in my life, I had failed. Was I now a better person?

I lay sleepless, gripped in the vise of my cell. I thought the night would never end, but of course, it did.

Well before dawn, the sky still black, groups of minor officials went up and down the alleys distributing answer sheets and draft paper. All of us taking the examination had purchased our answer sheets and draft paper days earlier, at government stores set up for the purpose. We weren't allowed to take our purchases into the examination compound ourselves, however; we could only take in a receipt. Now, the officials were collecting our receipts and handing over our purchases.

As soon as I received my sheets and paper, I lit a candle and examined them. The answer sheets were thicker and glossier, the draft paper thinner and duller. Otherwise, they were identical: imprinted with a red grid twenty-two cells across and twenty-five cells down. Answers had to be written one character to a cell. Each sheet could thus accommodate precisely five hundred fifty characters.

Despite the glossy paper, the answer sheets I would turn in would not be what the imperial examiners would read. To prevent bribery and favoritism, an enormous staff of professional copyists would reproduce every answer of every candidate onto new answer sheets, using red ink. As part of the same process, candidates' names would be turned into numbers. That way, an examiner reading an answer would not know the name of the candidate or even be able to recognize his handwriting.

Each morning for the next three days, examination officials would distribute a sheet with the day's questions. On the first day, there were always four questions: three calling for essays based on quotations from the *Four Books*, the fourth requiring the composition of a poem to a designated rhyme.

I sat on my plank bench, placed my arms on my plank desk, and worried. Would I recognize the quotations from the *Four Books*? Would I be able to use the answers I had so carefully prepared back at the mansion? Would one of the poems I had composed and memorized fit the specifications of the poetry question? This was my first time, the first time I had ever taken a competitive examination. How would I fare?

As faint light appeared in the sky, I heard shouts in the distance. Officials were going down the alleys handing out question sheets. The triennial Imperial Examination had begun.

I squeezed my jade pendant. If you have any magical powers left, *please* bring them out now.

The shouting drew closer. My throat tightened, my heart raced. In contrast to the slowness with which everything else over the past day and a half had taken place, the officials were racing down the alleys, handing out question sheets without bureaucratic formalities. An official dashed by my cell and thrust a question sheet at me. I took it, drew my candle close, inhaled deeply, and looked down.

22

> Essay topic: "If the people have enough,
> how could their ruler not have enough?"

I felt as if I'd swallowed a magical elixir. The quotation was more than familiar to me. It was from the *Analects*, Book Twelve, Section Nine.

Back in my study in the Jia mansion, I had many times practiced writing an essay based on this quotation, and over time I'd developed one I was proud of. Now, I didn't need to think; I just needed to remember and reproduce the essay I had already meticulously honed and polished.

On my inkstone I ground ink and mixed it with water. Taking out draft paper, I began to write.

The essay topic came from a conversation between Duke Ai of the State of Lu and You Ruo, a disciple of Confucius. Confucius himself is not part of the conversation; he simply reports it.

In the conversation, Duke Ai bemoans that the crops in his state have failed and the taxes he imposes on his subjects, which are set at the rate of two-tenths, are not bringing in enough revenue to support his government. What is to be done? he asks You Ruo.

You Ruo suggests: Why not tax your subjects at the rate of *one*-tenth?

What? the duke responds. If I'm not getting enough money

with two-tenths, how could I possibly get enough money with one-tenth?

You Ruo replies—and this is the sentence that, two thousand two hundred years later, was confronting me in the Imperial Examination—"If the people have enough, how could their ruler not have enough?"

The answer I had prepared provided everything the imperial examiners were looking for. It was written "in the voice of the sage"; in other words, as if Confucius himself had written it. It complied with all the myriad rules of the eight-legged essay literary form. It abounded in extravagant rhetoric and literary brilliance.

Early on, I needed to demonstrate I knew where the essay-topic quotation came from. I couldn't do this in either of the first two legs of my eight-legged essay; they were supposed to be simply paraphrases of the quotation. The third leg, the preliminary exposition, gave me opportunity. Speaking in the voice of Confucius, I named You Ruo and praised him for the "wisdom and profundity" of his answer.

The fourth leg, the initial argument, was where the rhetorical fireworks could begin. This leg was supposed to consist of three pairs of parallel phrases. The two phrases in each pair had to have the same structure but use different words.

Here's what, working in my study back at the Jia mansion, I had devised as my three pairs:

> *Pair 1:*
>
> If indeed the farming lands were tithed with a commitment to be thrifty in expenditure and mindful of the welfare of the people;
>
> and if indeed the one-tenth tax on agriculture were levied with care to avoid exploitation of the people and enrichment of the ruler;
>
> *Pair 2:*
>
> then, the exertions of the people would not be burdened with excessive taxation;

and the savings of the people would not be exhausted by undue demands.

Pair 3:

The savings of even common households would be ample, alleviating concerns over the care of the elderly and the raising of the young;

and the harvests of wheat and millet would be abundant, warding off anxieties about food for the living and honors for the dead.

Not bad, I thought, as I wrote away in my tiny cell.

An eight-legged essay was supposed to become more flamboyant as it went along, its literary grandiosity properly culminating in the seventh leg, the final argument. (The eighth leg, the conclusion, was supposed to be simply a two-sentence summary.) The final argument I had prepared for this essay topic consisted of two four-phrase paragraphs parallel to each other in their entirely, with a pair of parallel phrases in each paragraph. Sounds complicated? It was. Here's how it worked:

Paragraph 1:

Phrase 1 of pair: The sacrificial animals and ritual cereals are plentiful for use in religious offerings,

Phrase 2 of pair: and the jade carvings and silk bolts are abundant for use as diplomatic gifts.

Even if these were insufficient, the people would supply them in full.

How could there ever be a shortage?

Paragraph 2:

Phrase 1 of pair: Meat and drink are well stocked for the entertainment of state guests,

Phrase 2 of pair: and horses and arms are
well supplied for the defense of the state.

Even if these were inadequate, the people
would take care of the needs.

How could there ever be an insufficiency?

Five thousand two hundred men were writing eight-legged essays on the You Ruo quotation that day. Was mine one of the best ninety-eight? I was cautiously optimistic.

The next question went just as well. It read:

Essay topic: "There are three things a gentleman fears."

This was an either-or question. Either you knew where the quotation came from and what the next sentence was. Or you didn't. Fortunately, I did. The quotation was once again from the *Analects,* and the next sentence was: "He fears the will of heaven, he fears great men, and he fears the words of sages."

The third and last of the three essay questions posed that day was once again one for which I was well prepared. The quotation was from *Mencius*: "When good government prevails in the Empire, ceremonies, music, and punitive military expeditions proceed from the Son of Heaven." I had an answer already prepared and simply wrote it out.

Since I was regurgitating rather than creating, I was at times able to let my mind wander. When that happened, one thought kept recurring: This is all completely meaningless.

The eight-legged essays I was copying out bore no relationship to reality. Indeed, they were not even *supposed* to bear any relationship to contemporary reality. If an answer referred to any event that took place or any person who lived after the death of Mencius, two thousand years before, the answer would be heavily penalized. In truth, examination answers were about nothing more than manipulating words. It was all rhetoric, literary tricks, fancy wording, words uttered not because they meant anything but because they balanced other words that also didn't mean anything.

To anyone seeking spiritual or philosophical sustenance, the Confucian claptrap flowing out of my brush offered nothing. I could speak from experience. Confucianism offered me nothing when I experienced the deaths of two girls I loved. It offered me nothing when I was beaten half to death by my father. It offered me nothing when I was sick in mind and body. It offered me nothing when I was unjustly imprisoned by unchallengeable authority.

True, I was good at writing eight-legged essays. I had worked hard and mastered the craft. Just because I was good at it, however, didn't mean I believed in it.

In the end, though, my opinions didn't matter. I was not taking this examination to please myself; I was taking it to please my family. To please Grandmother, who had made my childhood and earlier years a continuous joy. To please my father, a man I had been unable to please in any other way. To give something to Baochai, to whom I had given little else.

Sitting in my cramped cell, perched over my plank writing desk, my wrist and arm starting to tire from holding my brush, my concentration constantly interrupted by the need to grind and mix new ink, I kept saying to myself: Don't dwell on the fact it's all meaningless. Just keep writing out the answers accurately. Two more days and it will all be over.

The fourth and final question that day was the poetry question. It read:

> Poem theme: The sorrow caused by separation due to war.
>
> Poem form: Qi-lu.

This question called for a precisely cut jewel of a poem. A qi-lu poem was short—only fifty-six characters—but the formal requirements were fierce. A qi-lu poem had to have eight lines of seven characters each. The first, second, fourth, sixth, and eighth lines all had to rhyme. The two middle couplets had to be parallel in both structure and meaning.

It would have been hard—probably impossible—to create a decent qi-lu poem from scratch in only two or three hours, particularly under the cramped, tense circumstances of a cell in the examination compound. Fortunately, I didn't have to. The same question had appeared on numerous prior examinations, and back at the Jia family mansion I had used my ample time to compose a first-class answer. Now all I needed to do was transfer my poem from memory to paper.

I wrote out a clean copy of my poem on an answer sheet. Then I headed to the broad avenue to hand in all my answers at the counters set up there. With that, the first of my three days of taking the Imperial Examination was over.

Once I had turned in my answers, I made a second trip to the broad avenue to refill my water jar. The examination compound was becoming a pigsty. Many candidates had never emptied out their slop jars, and some had done so carelessly, spilling contents along the way. I stepped gingerly around puddles of human waste.

The candidates themselves looked just as bad. Most were disheveled: their hair unkempt, their faces unshaven, their clothing dirty and rumpled. Many had deep black shadows beneath their eyes. The omnipresent soldiers, on the other hand, looked fresh and supremely confident.

As soon as I got back to my cell with my fresh water supply, I pulled some food bags down from the high shelf at the back of my cell and began to eat. I was ravenously hungry; during the day I had been so focused on the examination I had eaten nothing. Fortunately, my family had packed a wide variety of doughy treats for me: dumplings with pork and chives, dumplings with lamb, buns with chicken, buns with bean paste, chestnut buns, pancakes with pork and sea cucumber, pancakes with beef, green-onion pancakes. To top off my meal, I opened my lacquer box and feasted on candied ginger root and dates. My only regret was that I had to eat everything while sitting sidewise on the dirt floor of my cell, squeezed in by narrow walls, surrounded by the stench of the examination compound.

I wanted to adhere as much as possible to the original

plan I had formulated back at the Jia mansion, which included a period of meditation every evening before going to bed. Thus, despite my lack of success the night before, once I finished my dinner I again sat down to meditate.

I steadied my breathing: slow inhalation, pause, slow exhalation, pause. Soon I began to feel calm and relaxed.

The first day of the examination had lifted the glum spirits that had dragged me down the previous night. I didn't want to boast, but I was confident I had done well. The question had always been: how I would perform taking a competitive examination? I now had at least a partial answer: very well. With my better spirits, mediation became both possible and pleasurable. My back still hurt, and now my writing hand also hurt, but I was able to put the pain aside. Gradually, I slipped into insight meditation.

My meditation led me back to the solemn event that had taken place two days before in the Jia mansion's main reception hall, when my family and I had said goodbye to each other. My family had thought we were saying goodbye only for the duration of the examination. For me, with my secret plan, much more had been at stake. Even though the event had taken place two days before, so much had happened in the interim I had not had time to sort out my feelings.

I was happy with the way my farewells to Grandmother and my parents had gone. We had all conducted ourselves with dignity and respect. My father had even found things to praise about me.

I had been surprised at how emotional Grandmother had become in expressing her hope I would pass the examination. I had always underestimated the importance she placed on that. Thinking about it now, I was glad I was taking the examination and had spent so much time and effort in preparation.

As for my farewell to Baochai, that had not been as successful. To tell the truth, after our marriage—our forced, duplicitous, loveless marriage—Baochai and I never had a satisfying conversation. My botched farewell was of a piece with every other attempt.

I continued to meditate for about an hour, mostly repeating

in my mind some of my favorite Buddhist sutras. After that, I unrolled my bedding and scooted back underneath my planks into my sleeping position. Soon I fell into a deep sleep. The next morning, I awoke refreshed.

The second day of the examination consisted of five questions on the *Five Classics.* As before, each question read simply "Essay topic" and then a short, unidentified quotation.

I had eight-legged essays prepared for four of the five questions. The fifth I knew to be from the *Book of Poetry,* and I was fairly sure I knew which poem it was from. As a result, I was able to improvise an eight-legged essay. It wasn't my best of the day, but it was respectable.

Something strange happened that afternoon. I was writing away on my plank desk, with my curtain pulled back and the sun streaming in through the cell's south-facing front. Suddenly, the sun disappeared. I looked up and saw ... the scabby-headed Buddhist monk and lame Taoist priest. The monk's wide body occupied most of the cell's opening, the priest was trying to squeeze in on the right. The priest had his shorter leg forward, and as a result was tilting into my cell.

The monk's furrowed brow and open mouth conveyed dismay. "Baoyu, your fortunes seem to have declined."

"That's right," the priest said. "When we first met you, you lived in a grand palace. We had to wait outside the gate, and—my, my—what a majestic gate it was. Three big openings, all covered in red and gold, with a whole row of servants standing underneath." The priest's look of rapture turned to mock concern. "Now you're living in what looks like a rat hole."

The two burst out laughing.

I was so surprised to see them I was speechless. What were they doing here? How had they gotten past all the guards and checkpoints?

"We can't stay," the monk said. "We have to be off. But it won't be long 'til we see each other again."

"That's right," the priest added. "Soon. Very soon."

The monk's bulky frame disappeared from the opening. The priest tilted back onto his longer leg, turned, and followed the monk.

Questions flooded my mind: Did they know about my plan to become a wandering monk? Was I supposed to meet them somewhere? If so, where? Did they have some sort of plan for me?

I needed to talk to them longer. I started to chase after them, but to do this I had to lower myself onto the packed dirt floor, scoot underneath my desk, then stand up. By the time I got to the front opening of my cell, the monk and the priest had disappeared. I could see all the way to both the beginning and end of my alley—with the examination in progress, no one was outside—but there was no trace of the mysterious pair.

Was that a dream? I asked myself. No, it couldn't have been: it was the middle of the day, I was undeniably awake.

What was it then?

I couldn't answer that question. I had a sense, though, it was a good omen.

The third and final day of the examination consisted of five policy questions. These questions addressed, or at least purported to address, issues of contemporary public policy.

The policy questions were always much longer than the questions on the first two days, and the premise was that the Emperor himself was addressing you. Each question began with a stock phrase: "Tell me your ideas that I might hear and personally evaluate your ambition to serve the people and myself."

You as the answerer were supposed to assume the voice of a newly appointed government minister. Each answer was supposed to begin: "The minister has heard. The minister responds." Both times the word "minister" appeared, it was supposed to be written in small case and slightly off to the right, to emphasize the lowly position of anyone responding to the Emperor. Each answer was supposed to end with the phrases:

"Because I have just been promoted from commoner status, I have carelessly broken conventions and presumptuously offended the invincible power of the Emperor. My fear is such that I am on the verge of fainting dead away. I have respectfully responded to the Emperor's policy question."

To be honest, nobody took the policy questions seriously. It was widely believed they had little influence on your overall score, and hence on whether you passed. In addition, because the policy questions were politically touchy—always lurking in the background was the possibility of offending the Emperor—they tended to be ridiculously simple. The joke was you could generally answer a policy question simply by repeating the question, leaving out the interrogative particle.

I had not spent much time preparing for the policy questions but had composed some generic answers on topics that routinely appeared triennium after triennium: How can officials be encouraged to do their jobs well? How can the selection of the talented for government service be improved? How can the common people be protected against the predations of the rich?

With one exception, I was able to match my pre-prepared answers to the questions handed out. The exception was a question referring to the Emperor's recent conquest of the Western Regions. I answered this question by rehearsing platitudes about how the Emperor would make many wise decisions and therefore the addition of the new territories would result in greater prosperity and happiness for everyone.

My answers were, in a sense, hypocritical: I didn't believe much of what I was writing. I didn't feel guilty, though. I was taking the examination for my family, and my answers reflected what they believed.

The third day of the examination was the last, and as soon as you turned in your answer sheets you could pack up and leave the examination compound. Because the policy questions were lightly regarded, and because the examination compound by now was a fetid swamp, most candidates left early.

I filled my answer sheets in rapid time, but because few candidates were leaving when I finished, remained in my cell and waited. Finally, when candidates were beginning to stream out in large numbers, I joined the crowds. I deliberately left behind my rucksack, silk satin bedding, lacquer box, writing materials, and other remaining supplies.

As I was leaving, I turned around to take one last look—at the broad avenue, the tall watchtower filled with soldiers, the rows upon rows of tiny cells. Soon a happy thought suffused my mind: I will never, ever, see any of these sights again.

23

I passed through the Dragon Gate for the second time, this time with the fierce yellow dragons to my back. The area between the Dragon Gate and the Great Gate was where, four nights before, I had been searched and processed. That night, lit only by lanterns, filled with hostile soldiers, it had seemed threatening. Today, in the early afternoon sun, with no soldiers around, it seemed simply a clutter of dilapidated sheds.

I came to the inner side of the Great Gate. My muscles tensed, my heart pounded in my chest. This was where everything would be decided. This was where I would find out whether I was a person of courage and moral integrity ... or a coward. This was where, if I was ever going to lead the life I wanted to lead, that life had to begin.

On the other side, waiting for me, was a squadron of Jia family servants.

The number of candidates approaching the Great Gate waxed and waned from moment to moment. I waited until a particularly large cluster appeared. Then, clenching my fists and gritting my teeth, I stepped forward and maneuvered until I was in the center of the group. The candidates around me—drained, exhausted, dazed from four days inside the examination compound—didn't notice.

We entered the tunnel of the Great Gate. Darkness enveloped us. We walked slowly, hesitantly.

The tunnel opened to the bright sunlight of the outside

world. I stayed in the center of my group, while my eyes searched the panorama in front of me. Crowds jammed the huge, dusty open area: people waiting for candidates to appear, people greeting them when they did, candidates filtering through to other destinations.

Immediately I saw what I was expecting: ten servants from the Jia household, all mounted, towering over the melee below. The ten were straight ahead, about fifty paces away.

I hunched down—my above-average height was a disadvantage—and veered right. In that direction lay the Gate of Respect for Culture, the nearest gate out of the Manchu city.

I slithered along the front wall of the examination compound, taking care to keep myself mixed in with other people. I bent my knees to make myself appear shorter; I hunched my shoulders around my face and lowered my head. I did not look back: better the suspense of not knowing than the mistake of giving myself away.

I finally reached the far end of the open area, where a dense maze of hutongs took over. I plunged in.

About five paces into the nearest hutong:

"Second Master! Second Master!"

I stopped midstep, paralyzed. Should I try to outrun whoever it was? Should I try to hide? Should I plead with the person to go away?

"Second Master! Second Master!"

The voice was now closer, and I recognized it: Tealeaf, my chief page.

Of course. Tealeaf. He was always so devoted, so loyal, such a good friend. If anyone was going to find me, it would be him.

By now the options of outrunning or hiding were no longer available. Tealeaf had caught up with me. "Second Master, what are you doing? You're going the wrong way. Please come with me back to the mansion. Everyone's there waiting for you. Why are you here?"

I was stunned. All my planning, all my courage, my smooth escape from Grandmother's ten henchmen—and now this. "Tealeaf, …" I couldn't finish the sentence.

Tealeaf stood opposite me, his face pleading. Finally I said, "I'm sorry, Tealeaf, but I can't go back with you. I have to go my own way. If I go back to the mansion, I'll be miserable for the rest of my life. Please try to understand.

"In fact, can you do this for me? Can you go back to the mansion, tell them you looked and looked and looked but couldn't find me? Don't tell them anything about seeing me here. If you care for me, that's what you'll do. Can you do that for me, Tealeaf, please?"

Tealeaf reached out his arms. "No, Second Master. Everyone's there, waiting for you. We all want to celebrate your finishing the examination. You can't leave us, the mansion wouldn't be the same without you. We all love you, Second Master. Please." He began to cry.

A wave of shame swept over me. What kind of monster was I? How could I coldly toss aside a friendship as close and long-lasting as Tealeaf's? Did I have a spark of human warmth left in me?

My resolve began to crumble. Was I making a horrible mistake? Was Tealeaf right? Should I head back to the mansion with him?

Then, a series of memories intruded: The anguish I felt following the deaths of Daiyu and Amber. The horror of realizing I had been tricked into marrying Baochai, not Daiyu. The excruciating pain of my beating. The nightmare of my long, debilitating illness. The misery of my time in the Temple of the Prison God.

I thought about the peace I found in meditation. The truths I found in the teachings of the Buddha. The mysterious words of the scabby-headed monk and lame priest.

My will reasserted itself. I had thought about my plan for months, even years. What I had said to Tealeaf was right: If I went back to the mansion, I would be miserable for the rest of my life. If I was to be me, I could not be who others wanted me to be. Even Tealeaf.

"I'm sorry," I said. "I can't go back. You just have to accept that."

Tealeaf looked down, closed his eyes, and shook his head, a portrait of dejection.

I took advantage of his inattention to sprint away. I ran as fast as I could, twisting my way through the confusing maze of hutongs. I turned left, right, then left again and right again, trying to leave as untraceable a trail as possible. I ran until my breath gave out, then ran some more.

I never saw Tealeaf again.

My exchange with Tealeaf was the last time I ever saw a member of the Jia household. My last contact with my childhood and youth.

Except ...

Except for one chance encounter.

                                24

TWO YEARS LATER. My twentieth year.

A place south of Beijing, along the Grand Canal.

I was walking along the towpath that paralleled the canal.
I was on a pilgrimage to Mount Tai and planning to cross a
bridge over the canal a few minutes' walk away. I wore the felt
crimson robe of a Buddhist monk. My head was shaved, and
my feet, by now heavily calloused, were bare.

Traveling with me were the scabby-headed Buddhist
monk and lame Taoist priest. They had appeared before me as
I was racing through the hutongs, fleeing from Tealeaf. Somehow, I had not been surprised, and we had been together ever
since.

My jade still hung from my neck on its silk cord of five
colors. Buddhism normally forbade any wearing of jewelry by
monks. But my scabby-headed friend had convinced me that,
since my jade had brought the three of us together and hence
allowed me to escape the snare of worldly attachments, my
situation warranted an exception.

The weather that day was raw, the leaden sky threatened
a storm. A strong wind blew, and a few flakes of snow had
already fallen. Only one boat was still being towed, the others
had all found shelter. The Grand Canal smelled, as it always
did, of dead fish, rotting vegetation, and spicy cooking.

We came to an area where a side canal veered off the
Grand Canal, and at the juncture was a small harbor. Six or
eight boats huddled in the harbor, their decks so close one

could easily walk from one to another. The boats creaked and groaned as they fought the fierce wind. Behind the harbor, on land, two inns competed for the traveler's business, with tables both outside and in. Given the weather, all the tables were empty.

Most of the boats moored in the small harbor were cargo vessels, but one was a passenger boat, and a luxurious one at that. The boat's cabin featured a band of painted designs below its roofline, lattice windows below that. Despite the wind and snow, one of the lattice windows was open, and inside, a man was sitting at a desk, writing.

The man looked like my father.

I drew closer to the boat. Standing at the edge of the embankment, I could see the man clearly. He *was* my father!

Should I flee and avoid any contact, as I had fled from Tealeaf? Should I offer myself to Father and see if he would accept me as I was?

In truth, I didn't make a conscious decision. As if propelled by an invisible, outside force, I stepped onto the deck of my father's boat.

The snow had picked up. I had to walk carefully, for the deck was wet and slippery, and my bare feet were numb. My shaven scalp was bitterly cold and wet with melted snow.

I stopped in front of the open window and stared at my father. He was absorbed in his writing and did not look up. He looked much the same as he had the last time I had seen him—in the main reception hall of the Jia mansion, bidding me farewell as I headed off to the Imperial Examination.

Father looked up. He stared at me, mouth agape.

I placed my hands in anjali mudra—together in prayer over the heart. In Buddhism, a respectful greeting or offer of reverence.

My father got up from his desk and came out to the deck through a nearby door. We faced each other through a gauze of falling snow.

At first, Father looked bewildered. Suddenly, he gasped, his eyes bulged, and he craned his head forward. "Baoyu, is that you?"

I said nothing. My throat was so tight I could not have said anything even if I had wanted to. I maintained my anjali mudra.

"Baoyu, why are you dressed like that? What's the matter with you?"

The scabby-headed Buddhist monk and lame Taoist priest came up, grabbed me, and started pulling me away. "Your worldly obligations have been fulfilled," the monk said. "No reason to waste any more time."

The monk and priest turned me around until I was facing the embankment, and the three of us began walking away. As I was making my way across the slippery deck, with my back to my father, he said:

"Baoyu, you placed seventh in the Imperial Examination. Out of five thousand two hundred candidates, you placed seventh."

I stopped walking and, supported on either side by the monk and priest, fell limp. I had passed. All my hard work had paid off. I had, to use Baochai's words, repaid my obligations to my family, my ancestors, the Emperor.

However, this accomplishment had taken place in a world that no longer meant anything to me. It had nothing to do with the person I had become.

The monk and priest pushed me forward, and the three of us began walking again. We stepped off the boat deck, onto the embankment, and started back up the towpath.

"Baoyu," my father called out again, his voice now faint in the distance.

"Baochai had a boy. A baby boy."

Again I slumped over, and this time tears came. I had given my family, if not everything they wanted, at least the two things they wanted most. My companion, the Buddhist monk, was right. I had fulfilled my worldly obligations.

I turned around to take one last look at my father. But it was too late. Snow filled the air. All I could see was white.

Author's Note

This novel was inspired by an eighteenth-century Chinese novel entitled, in Chinese, *Hong Lou Meng* (pronounced "hong low mung").

Hong Lou Meng is a Chinese cultural icon, often said to be the finest work of imaginative literature in Chinese history. It has been translated into English numerous times and under several different titles: most commonly, *Dream of the Red Chamber,* but also *Dream of Red Mansions* and *Story of the Stone.*

Hong Lou Meng is a work of staggering length and complexity. In English translation, the complete novel runs 1,800 to 2,500 pages. It is said to have thirty major and 400 minor characters. Obviously, my novel follows only a few of the multitudinous plot threads that run through the work.

But how did I, a white American male, born and raised in the Midwest, come to write a historical novel set in eighteenth-century China?

The answer starts with the fact that, for many decades, I've been partnered with a Chinese-American man, Calvin Lau. (We were legally married in 2013.) In the 1990s, he embarked on a personal journey to read what are considered the six classic Chinese novels. These are:

The Romance of the Three Kingdoms
The Water Margin
Journey to the West
Jin Ping Mei (The Golden Lotus)
The Scholars
Hong Lou Meng (Dream of the Red Chamber)

Initially, I wasn't interested in joining him, but after several months of hearing him talk about how much he was enjoying his project, I decided to read the six too.

I found all the novels interesting but was absolutely smitten with *Hong Lou Meng*. I found many of the characters fascinating, especially the novel's boy protagonist—sensitive, thoughtful, complex Baoyu. *Hong Lou Meng* also offers a rare insider's view of daily life in an aristocratic household in eighteen-century China.

But, in addition to its jumble of characters and plot threads, *Hong Lou Meng* has a complicated textual history. It exists in several different versions, and even its authorship is uncertain. Its principal author was a man named Cao Xueqin. Another man, Gao E, also played a role in the writing of the novel, but exactly what that role was has been a subject of debate for centuries. Indeed, there exists in China a recognized scholarly discipline devoted to *Hong Lou Meng,* its textual history, and theories about its authorship. The discipline is called *hongxue*, meaning *red studies* or *redology*.

The two best and most recent English translations of *Hong Lou Meng* are:

Cao Xueqin and Gao E, translated by Yang Xianyi and Gladys Yang, *A Dream of Red Mansions* (6 volumes, English and Chinese texts), Foreign Languages Press and Hunan People's Publishing House, 1999.

Cao Xueqin and Gao E, translated by David Hawkes and John Minford, *The Story of the Stone* (5 volumes, English text only), Penguin Books, 1973-86.

I ended up reading several different translations of *Hong Lou Meng* (published, confusingly, under several different English titles). All the time I kept thinking: this novel tells compelling, moving stories, but they certainly are badly told.

Meanwhile, I had been writing fiction for more than ten years, was a member of an excellent writing group, and had already published one novel. While I didn't consider myself a great novelist, I was familiar with the techniques of contemporary fiction writing and knew how to use them.

I realized I could isolate the single most important of the many plot threads running through *Hong Lou Meng*—the one tracing the childhood and youth of Baoyu—and, using the craft skills I had acquired, write a novel that would appeal to the contemporary reader. I could deepen the major episodes, eliminate the extraneous characters, and tell Baoyu's fascinating and moving story in a way that would do it justice.

Hong Lou Meng has twice—first in 1987, then in 2010—been turned into a Chinese television miniseries. The 1987 version became a 12-disk DVD set; the 2010 version, an 8-disk set. The two miniseries offer fascinating (and differing) visual realizations of the Jia family, their mansion, and their story.

The 1987 miniseries left an additional legacy. To film the series the producers created on the outskirts of Beijing a thirty-two-acre imagined re-creation of the Jia mansion's garden, complete with a Happy Red Court, Bamboo Lodge, and all the other cottages. Once the filming of the television series was over, this garden was turned into a theme park open to the public, and it remains such today, known in English-language guides as the "Grand View Garden."

Hong Lou Meng has engendered a vast body of literary criticism. I found particularly illuminating the relevant section in C. T. Hsia, *The Classic Chinese Novel: A Critical Introduction,* Cornell East Asia Series Reprint, 1996. Susan Chan Egan and Pai Hsien-Yung, *A Companion to The Story of the Stone,* Columbia University Press, 2021, provides an invaluable chapter-by-chapter plot summary plus concise comments on each chapter.

Turning from the Chinese original to what might be termed fan fiction, another English-language novel inspired, like mine, by *Hong Lou Meng* is Pauline A. Chen's marvelous *The Red Chamber*, Alfred A. Knopf, 2012. Chen's approach is very different from mine. Whereas I focus on a single male character—Baoyu—she focuses on three female characters—Daiyu, Baochai, and one who does not even appear in my novel, Xifeng. Our two novels hardly overlap at all, a tribute to *Hong Lou Meng*'s richness in plot and inspiration.

Hong Lou Meng is also the basis of an English-language opera entitled *Dream of the Red Chamber,* with music by Bright Sheng and libretto by David Henry Hwang and Bright Sheng. It premiered at San Francisco Opera in 2016.

While my novel was inspired by *Hong Lou Meng*, large

parts are my own invention, with no analogue in the Chinese original. These parts include all those relating the eighteenth-century Chinese educational curriculum, the Imperial Examination, the Imperial Examination Compound, and Baoyu's preparation for and taking of the examination.

For these sections I drew upon Ichisada Miyazaki, translated by Conrad Schirokauer, *China's Examination Hell,* Yale University Press, 1981; Iona D. Man-Cheong, *The Class of 1761*, Stanford University Press, 2004; and L. C. Arlington and William Lewisohn, *In Search of Old Peking*, Oxford University Press, 1991. Baoyu's answer to the first question in his examination was adapted from C. I. Tu, "The Chinese Examination Essay: Some Literary Considerations," in *Monumenta Serica* 31 (1974-75), pp. 393-406.

The description of the function of a grain commissioner is based on Harold C. Hinton, "The Grain Tribute System of the Ch'ing Dynasty," in *The Far Eastern Quarterly,* Vol. 11, No. 3 (May 1952), pp. 339-354.

With all this insight, I set to work, and that's how this white boy from the American Midwest ended up writing a historical novel set in eighteenth-century China.

Acknowledgments

I owe an enormous debt to my editor, Robin Henry, for helping me turn this novel into a much better work, and to my publisher, Colin Mustful, for having faith in me. I also need to thank Drs. Jianing Liu and Xiangfeng Wang for educating me about Chinese culture and history and guiding me to sources in Beijing. Finally, thanks to my early readers—Paul Cohen, Jane Cullinan, Melissa Hurley, and Jack Sanders—who provided helpful criticism and encouragement.

Originally from Kansas City, Missouri, Charles Bush earned degrees from Harvard College and the University of California, Berkeley, both in history. But faced with a dismal job market for professional historians, he switched directions, attended the University of Chicago Law School, and became a lawyer.

In the early 2000s Bush phased out his law practice to focus on writing fiction. He mined his legal career for his first two novels: *What Went Wrong with Oscar Toll?* and *Houseboat Wars*. With his latest, *The Boy with the Jade*, he returns to his first love—history.

Bush lives in San Francisco with his husband in an 1877 Victorian they've restored.

About HTF Publishing

Founded in 2023 as an imprint of History Through Fiction, HTF Publishing is hybrid publisher of compelling, high-quality historical novels. Following in the tradition of History Through Fiction, HTF Publishing seeks to provide readers with engaging historical narratives that are rooted in detailed and accurate historical research. As a hybrid press, we want to work with authors who are serious about their craft and aspire to share imaginative, important, and well-researched, historical narratives with the world.

If you enjoyed this novel, please consider leaving a review. It's the best way to support us and our authors. Plus, you'll be helping other readers discover this great story.

Thank you!

www.HistoryThroughFiction.com